VAMPIRE HUNTER

**Three exhilarating vampire tales
full of dark desire!**

VAMPIRE HUNTER

KAIT BALLENGER
PATTI O'SHEA
ANNA HACKETT

MILLS & BOON

First published in Great Britain 2013
by Mills & Boon, an imprint of Harlequin (UK) Limited,
Eton House, 18-24 Paradise Road, Richmond, Surrey TW9 1SR

VAMPIRE HUNTER © Harlequin Enterprises II B.V./S.à.r.l. 2013

Shadow Hunter © Kaitlyn Ballenger 2013
Shadow's Caress © Patti O'Shea 2011
Hunter's Surrender © Anna Hackett 2010

ISBN: 978 0 263 90417 8
ebook ISBN: 978 1 472 00681 3

089-1013

Harlequin (UK) policy is to use papers that are natural, renewable and recyclable products and made from wood grown in sustainable forests. The logging and manufacturing processes conform to the legal environmental regulations of the country of origin.

Printed and bound
by CPI Group (UK) Ltd, Croydon, CR0 4YY

SHADOW HUNTER

KAIT BALLENGER

Kait Ballenger is a full-time paranormal romance author, wife, professional belly dancer and graduate student living in Central Florida. *Twilight Hunter* is the first full-length novel in her Execution Underground paranormal romance series, following *Shadow Hunter*, a prequel novella. When Kait's not preoccupied with paranormal creepy-crawlies, she can be found slaving over endless amounts of schoolwork or with her nose buried in a book. She lives happily with her husband, their doggie-daughter, Sookie, and two mischievous cats, Elliot and Olivia—all three of whom are named after fictional characters. Kait believes anything is possible with hard work and dedication. One day, she intends to be a bestselling author and have people name their pets after her characters, too.

For my husband, Jon. No hero will ever compare.
I'll love you always.

Chapter One

Damon Brock clutched the neck of the guard and twisted. The crack of broken bone pierced the silence in the alleyway as the spine snapped beneath his fingers. The wind whistled in a large gush of freezing air, so cold that Damon's breath swirled in front of his face. The guard's pulse beat several feeble times against his hands before fading.

Not a single scream. Damon released the guard, and the body crumpled to the cold winter ground. He nudged the corpse with the steel toe of his boot.

No movement. Only deadweight. A quick kill.

Not even 9:00 p.m. and already he'd taken out one blood-sucker. Rochester seemed promising.

He stepped over the corpse and slipped through the back entrance of Club Fantasy. A silver dagger under the sleeve of his leather trench coat, a Desert Eagle .44 caliber semi-automatic tucked into the back of his jeans, one silver throwing knife in each boot and a smooth, lacquered wooden stake inside his coat—you could never be too prepared when it came to vampires. The leeches were nearly impossible to kill. While bullets and silver would give them pause, only a severed spine, decapitation or a stake through the heart destroyed the undead.

Like a neon sign in a red-light district, the establishment's name flashed over the door: Club Fantasy.

He shook his head. Club Fantasy? More like club hell. If only the patrons knew the monster vampire who owned it. The man sitting at the top of Damon's hit list.

He pushed through a second door and into the main level of the club. If the night went well, he would gladly up the body count to at least four.

The thick smell of liquor, cigarettes and sweat from one too many dancing bodies assaulted his nose as he scanned the crowd. Bright red lighting flashed over the floor, and the bass of the heavy dance music pounded in his ears. The most difficult thing about hunting vamps: they were damn near indistinguishable from humans. After nightfall, the pulses of the undead beat with the same intensity as any human civilian, but their craving for blood, their inhuman strength and their drive to drain life from unsuspecting victims lingered. If only humanity knew what they were up against.

Damon strode across the dance floor, navigating between writhing bodies before he slid onto the black leather bench of one of the club's booths. His hands ran across the smooth, newly lacquered black tabletop. Despite the underlying seediness, the atmosphere of Club Fantasy came out on top compared to most of Rochester's low-scale raves. With western New York prices and Manhattan quality, Club Fantasy had young twenty-somethings flocking to it like drunken sheep led to a bloodlust-fueled slaughter. High quality aside, Club Fantasy was twice as dangerous as any New York City club. At least, the City offered ample backup.

He'd admitted one disadvantage to himself: navigating the supernatural scene of a city with no hunting division would be damn hard. But he was up to the challenge. He'd tracked his target to Mark's hometown, Rochester, and he wouldn't stop until he avenged his friend. He'd requested assignment to Rochester for that purpose—even if it meant a chance of running into *her.* He let out a long sigh. He couldn't think about that now.

His gaze jumped from face to face, searching for his target: blond hair, blue eyes, medium build, a strong, slightly crooked nose and a small but noticeable scar beneath his left eye. He dreamed of that face every night.

An ancient piece of Roman shit, Caius Argyros Dermokaites ruled over the Rochester vamp nests with an iron fist, more because he was old as dirt, rather than because of some great attribute of his own. The older the vampire, the more deadly he—or she—became, and Caius was the highest on Damon's hit list.

Damon was going to kill him. He would make sure of it this time.

His eyes locked on to the vampire. Though the swaying limbs of the dancing patrons skewed his view, he could see Caius sitting on the other side of the club. Anger bubbled up inside his chest, and pure rage filled every inch of his body. It took all he had not to pull his Desert Eagle and shoot Caius point-blank before driving a stake straight through his heart.

His hands clenched into fists. It was his fault. His fault that Caius sat there laughing while Mark's ashes had gone unburied. His fault the only woman he'd ever opened his heart to wished him dead. He'd failed Mark—his closest friend—and he had failed *her,* too.

A grin crossed Caius's face as he wrapped his arm around the skimpy-leather-and-fake-silver-chain-clad woman next to him. He was surrounded by women. Not surprising. Few things were larger than a male vampire's ego, and Caius overcompensated like a pair of tricked-out rims on an already overpriced car. Damon observed the vampire's interactions. If there was one thing he'd learned during his field training, it was how to be a quick judge of character. Vanity was no doubt Caius's number one weakness, and striking that vein would make him bleed.

A sexed-up raspy voice purred right next to Damon's ear. "You gonna order a drink, hot stuff, or just stare into the crowd all night?" A cheap pair of too-tight latex pants blocked his view.

The bottle-blonde waitress smacked her lips together as she chewed on a piece of gum. She leaned down and rested her elbows on the table in front of him, treating him to a prime-time view of her fake chest. Her breasts squeezed into a top smaller than some women's panties. Her breath reeked of over-chewed bubble gum and the sharp smell of cheap gin.

She licked her lips. "You look like a vodka-on-the-rocks kind of man to me—strong, bold, served on ice but easily warmed."

Damon barely glanced at the woman. He leaned back in his seat, aligning his vision with Caius again. "I don't drink."

The waitress sighed and peeled herself off the table. "Well, if you're not gonna order anything, you can't take up an entire booth."

A slender redhead ran her fingers through Caius's hair and pushed closer to his body. The women surrounding Caius literally threw themselves at him, practically begging to be drained, but Caius's stare was fixed on something out of Damon's line of sight. If he could just see where...

The waitress huffed. "Uh, hello? Did you hear me?"

Moving about the club for different views was a better option than staying put, Damon decided, and stood, then brushed past the now pissed-off waitress. Nothing was going to distract him. A drive to fulfill his quest pulsed through him. With six human women missing from Caius's inner circle and a growing number of gruesome, fatal street attacks, neglect was not an option.

When he'd joined the Execution Underground, he'd sworn an oath to protect innocent humans from the dangerous creatures lurking out of their unsuspecting sight.

An international elite group of men, the Execution Underground trained hunters to annihilate everything from vampires to werewolves, demons, shifters and more.

Though trained extensively in combat and packing loads of hard-earned muscle, no plain man could fight the supernatural alone. Upon swearing in, each hunter received a serum injection, and while the resulting longer lifespan, increased strength to battle the supernatural and extra healing capabilities were perks, putting their lives on the line every day was one hell of a sacrifice. Even with the serum, they still couldn't match the supernaturals' strength completely. That was where the training came in, to ensure they weren't easily annihilated. They swore to protect their fellow humans no matter the personal cost, swore to keep the supernatural world hidden from view and away from the vulnerable. They promised to give everything, even their lives, if needed.

Mark had given his life for the safety of others, and Damon wouldn't dishonor his memory. He'd meant every word of that promise he'd made.

Damon followed the line of Caius's gaze and strode to the bar. He found a seat in the far corner, right where he could see Caius. He followed the ancient vampire's eyes and found their target.

A woman. No surprise.

Her back was turned toward Damon, revealing nothing but a thick mane of dark brown waves cascading over her shoulders. The bartender handed her two glasses of red wine. Slowly, she sashayed to Caius's side, his gaze never leaving her body. Her gender didn't matter. He intended to hurt Caius and his minions in any way he could, but even to avenge his fellow hunter, Damon refused to endanger the innocent human patrons around him. Mark wouldn't have wanted it any other way. He would need to lure Caius away from the crowd.

Damon's outrage simmered at the thought of all the innocent lives lost.

The instinctive fight-or-flight response forced most people away from supernatural predators. But used, beaten, downtrodden and abused humans swarmed the undead like flies on a half-eaten corpse, and they were the most susceptible to supernatural manipulation. Somebody needed to protect them. Somebody needed to give a damn about their lives when no one else ever had.

Damon's cell phone vibrated inside his jacket pocket. Headquarters.

But he couldn't return the call out in the open. He slipped away from the bar and headed toward one of the private club rooms. He ducked through the curtained door and into the empty space. Scanning the room, his eyes adjusted to the darkness, revealing nothing more than the outlines of assorted couches, throw pillows and other ordinary furniture. He was alone.

He pulled the phone from his pocket and flipped it open, quickly glancing at the message.

The all-capitalized text glared across the screen. New information from his contact at headquarters. UPDATE. CALL BACK.

Damon's jaw clenched. Damn. An update meant another dead body. Another death piled on to his conscience. If he hadn't failed Mark that night three months ago...

He cursed under his breath and quickly hit Redial.

Chris answered on the second ring. "You're not going to like what I have to tell you."

Damon rested his free hand on his head and ran his fingers through what little hair remained after his buzz cut. "Get on with it."

Chris let out a long sigh. "You're not going to like any of this. You want the shitty news or the straight-up awful news first?"

Damon shook his head and paced the room. "Out with it."

Chris sighed again. "Well, first matter of business— there's another dead body."

Damon dug the fingernails of his left hand into his palm. His fist itched to punch through the plaster wall. Someone might as well have stabbed him in the back and twisted the knife. Knowing the news before he called didn't make it any easier.

"Damon, you still there, man?"

Damon unclenched his fist and tried to focus. He would not let his emotions distract him. Not again. "Yeah, I'm here." He shook his head. The Rochester P.D. would jump all over this. Already they deemed the murders the work of a serial killer with vampiric delusions. Another victim with fang marks would fuel the fire.

What kind of bloodsucker didn't seal up the damn fang

holes after he sank his teeth in? Even the dumbest vamps knew to keep themselves hidden from the public eye. Was one small lick to close the wound too much to ask?

"Victim is a Caucasian female. Only sixteen. Found four blocks away from Manhattan Square Park. A connection with the police force called it in to us. Body's in the morgue of the Golisano Children's Hospital at the University of Rochester Medical Center. As of now, she's listed as Jane Doe. No ID on her and, well…from the crime scene photos we've been sent, it won't be easy to identify her. You better get over there soon."

Damon leaned against the nearest wall and rested his head on his forearm. "What's the other news?"

A moment of silence passed on the other end of the line before Chris cleared his throat. "There's, uh…there's been a new development in Mark's case."

Damon snapped upright, his whole body rigid. All his senses peaked, and adrenaline raced through his bloodstream. "What do you mean 'a new development'? He's dead, Chris. His body burned in the fire. I saw him lying on the ground, bled out and dead, before the building exploded, and we know exactly who killed him. What kind of 'new development' can there be?" Desperation and anxiety hit him hard, and he knew his voice wavered. His hands were shaking.

"I'm so sorry, Damon."

All the wind rushed from Damon's lungs and bile rose in the back of his throat as he realized what Chris was saying. "No. No. He can't…no…." He lost the ability to speak. His stomach churned.

"Another hunter spotted him in New York City a few days ago. The information just made it into the system. He's not dead, Damon. He turned."

The phone fell from Damon's hand. His heart pounded in his ears, and red clouded his vision. A sharp pain flamed in his chest as if someone had driven a blade straight through his heart. Mark had turned. He wasn't dead. No…

A loud angry battle cry ripped from Damon's throat, and tears ran down his face. He gave in and punched his fist into the wall. A large chunk of plaster crumbled to the floor, but no one heard over the loud thumping of the music.

Mark was worse than dead. He was a bloodsucking leech, and the fault fell on Damon's shoulders. Images of him and his best friend, his comrade, flashed through his mind.

"There's nothing worse than becoming a vamp." Mark sharpened the end of his silver blade as he sat next to Damon.

The training room smelled of male sweat, blood and heavy artillery. After a full day of training, all the muscles in Damon's body ached. He nodded. "Nothing worse."

"At the very least, I'm glad my family didn't turn. In that respect, I'm glad they're dead." Mark glanced down at the blade in his hand. "Promise me that if I ever get turned, you'll stake me straight in the chest."

Damon shook his head. "That'll never happen."

Mark thumped him hard on the back. "I mean it, D. Promise me."

Damon let out a long huff. He clapped Mark on the back in return. "I promise."

Damon threw another punch at the wall, then started pounding the plaster with his fists and praying the images in his head would disappear. Mark's body lying on the pavement with puncture wounds in his neck. The blood. Oh, God, the blood and the stillness of his body as he lay across the concrete. Dust clouded the air, and Damon's knuckles bled as he released every ounce of rage coursing through his bones.

If he'd been a weaker man, he would have eaten his gun right then.

Chapter Two

Rage surged inside Tiffany Solow as she handed the ancient vampire his Bordeaux. She wished she could smash the delicate glass on the table and plunge the leftover shards into his neck. Waiting hand and foot on Caius Argyros Dermokaites sent waves of anger and hate through every inch of her body. As if rubbing shoulders with the creatures she hated most wasn't enough, Caius was the worthless bloodsucking piece of crap who'd murdered her brother and the definition of arrogance. She would kill him. It was only a matter of time, and when she did, she would enjoy every single second of it.

"Thank you, my precious," he purred.

My precious? Gross. I hope you choke on it, you undead piece of crap.

Tiffany forced a smile on her face and slid into the booth beside him. Caius snaked his arm around her. The rank smell of his skin mixed with the aged Bordeaux and a faint hint of blood. The stench hit her nose full force, and she fought to keep from gagging. Thank God she was an amazing actress. If she didn't have such a rock-solid poker face, infiltrating Caius's inner circle would have been damn near impossible.

But every time he made her skin crawl was well worth it if it gave her the chance of murdering the son of a bitch. There was no such thing as a decent bloodsucker. They'd proved that the day she'd first become a hunter—the day her family had been stolen from her.

Caius would be tough to kill. Everything in her craved to stab him right then, get it over with. But if she even made a quick move at him, he would crush her before she blinked. She had to catch him with his back turned. His trust was key to his death. And she'd baited him perfectly into wanting her as a Host.

Serving their purpose for a short time, Hosts fed the vampires and sated their blood thirst, but once the anemia set in, the vamps had no more use for their weakened prey. Humans with knowledge of vampires were too high a risk to keep around. Hosts always ended up dead or undead. And despite the Hosts' presence, vampires weren't only leeches, they were greedy; feeding regularly on Hosts didn't stop them from massacring innocent civilians for sport; it only delayed the actions on occasion.

Tiffany had found ways to warn multiple women and men during the time she'd spent with Caius, but it was no use. They were too entranced, nearly hypnotized, by the charm of the bloodsuckers to listen to reason. Tiffany had to admit, that charm was hard to ignore. But every time she thought of the deaths of her parents and brother, not to mention the loss of a deep friendship, her disgust snapped into place and she remembered exactly why she lived to drive stakes through vampires' hearts. She thanked her lucky stars that Caius was still trying his persuasive skills on her, practically begging her to be his.

He could tell she was healthy and strong. To keep her iron high and appealing, she ate enough red meat and spinach to last her a whole lifetime—the thought of one more piece of spanakopita or rare steak made her stomach churn. Hell, every spare cent she possessed went toward that. Steak wasn't exactly in the usual budget for a flat-broke college senior with four years of med school and then several more years of residency ahead of her. But it worked in her favor. Caius knew from her scent that she would provide a long Host relationship with all the expected sexual benefits, ensuring that she was too tempting for him to kill her in one quick meal. Caius wanted her for the long term.

Little did he know his efforts would have been more effective on a piece of broccoli. She almost snorted. Was she hungry or what?

He interrupted her thought. "Darling, do you see that private room over there?" Caius gestured toward the far side of the bar.

Tiffany nodded. "Yes."

Caius sipped his Bordeaux, his eyes fixated on the closed curtain of the private room. "I believe we have a new visitor. Vampire, it appears. He has the movements of a predator." He set down his wineglass a little more force-fully than necessary. "I won't have an unannounced alpha traipsing around my club. Please go fetch Calvin and see that he's taken care of."

"My pleasure." She smiled and stood to find the body-guard. As soon as she turned her back on Caius, her smile faded into a frown.

Eat my stake, you nasty leech.

She was really feeling the pure bitchiness tonight. But then again, spending more than five minutes with Caius would turn any sane person into a complete basket case. He would pay for everything he'd done. She would gladly drive a stake into his heart and watch him explode to pieces like the blood bag he was. Vampires were so damn messy to kill, but she didn't care. She wanted nothing more than to make him bleed.

As quickly as possible, she navigated through the crowd toward the back of the club. She exited the first door and stepped into the small area leading back to the offices. She glanced up and down the hall. No Calvin.

An immediate chill ran down her spine. The hairs of her neck and arms stood on end, and goose bumps prick-led over her skin. Something was not right. She needed to get out of there, and fast. Pushing through the final exit, a rush of cold winter air hit her hard in the face. She stepped out into the alleyway and fell straight on her ass.

What the hell?

Her eyes widened as she took in the sight of what she'd

tripped over: Calvin's dead body. His neck was twisted at a strange angle as he lay lifeless on the pavement. Not a single drop of blood or any evidence of a fight.

Damn. It took a lot of *cojones* to snap the neck of a vampire. Whoever had done this was vicious.

She hopped to her feet and brushed herself off. No skin off her back if Calvin was dead. One less bloodsucker made for a better world. Though Caius would go ballistic at the news, and she didn't want to deal with one hell of a pissed-off vampire, unless…

Her eyes widened again. She knew how to lessen Caius's anger: deliver the new alpha vampire.

She rushed through the back door and reentered the club. If she could move fast enough and deliver the head of the anonymous vamp to Caius, she would be that much closer to gaining his trust. One step closer to destroying the scumbag who'd murdered her family.

Pushing her way through the club patrons, she headed toward the private room. She weaved in and out of the crowd to avoid Caius's gaze. Once she reached the curtained entrance, she pulled her Smith & Wesson from her jacket. Always loaded with silver bullets, her rounds sure wouldn't kill a vampire, but they *would* inflict a serious wound, enough to make the leech pause.

She quickly slipped inside. With her eyes already adjusted to the darkness from being outside, she searched through the dimness, gun aimed.

No one.

She stepped farther into the empty room.

The end of a gun barrel pushed against her skull. The small click of the hammer sent adrenaline pumping through her body. Her heart thumped hard against her chest.

Positioned at the end of a vampire's gun.

Royally screwed didn't even begin to cover it.

Damon held the Desert Eagle without a single ounce of fear in his body. If there was one thing he was excellent at, it was staying detached in intense situations. He wasn't used to dealing with vampiresses, but there was a first time for everything.

He held the gun steady, resting right against her skull. "Drop your weapon."

With slow tentative movements, she spread her arm to her sides, so he could see the firearm. She released the magazine clip, and it fell onto the floor before she dropped the gun.

He increased the pressure on the base of her skull. "Names. All the high-ups in the Rochester nests."

In a risky decision, she spun away from his gun, grabbing hold of his hand and digging her long fingernails into his metacarpals. A very smooth martial arts move. He let her go and released the gun, not from the pain, but from the reassurance of his silver dagger. Giving her a false sense of accomplishment could work in his favor. With quick agility, she threw a roundhouse kick. He blocked the blow from his face, but the force of her attack gave him pause.

She was strong and an impressive fighter, but she was no match for him. He grabbed hold of her leg and twisted.

She lost her balance, toppling toward the ground, but he caught her midfall, holding her.

With precision, he pulled his dagger from his sleeve and forced it against her throat. Not enough to make her bleed, just so she could feel its presence. He had to know for certain if she was a vampire. He couldn't bring himself to harm a woman without being sure.

She stopped struggling. Smart.

He backed her into the corner nearest the light switch. If he got lucky and she was angry or afraid enough, her irises would reveal the answer to him. "Turn around."

She did as she was told. He pushed her body against the wall with his own, the dagger still at her throat. With his free hand, he flipped the switch.

Then wished he hadn't.

Damon's breath rushed from his lungs, and his heart skipped several beats. Adrenaline kicked into his system like a tidal wave. Every inch of his skin electrified. He was a live wire, all senses enhanced and awake from their deadened state. His arousal was instantaneous as the sweet smell of her perfume hit his nose. She smelled like baked cinnamon apples, autumn spices, vanilla and sweet, sweet sex.

He'd never been one to stop and take in the beauty of the world, but he was certain that her face was more gorgeous than anything he'd ever laid eyes on. Her thick dark brown hair fell just past her shoulders, and from that he recognized her as the woman from the bar. His eyes trailed over that gorgeous hair, which stopped just above a pair of ample breasts that pushed against him. Her slender frame felt amazing against his body.

But what completely entranced him was her stare. A pair of large honey-colored eyes rimmed with dark layers of full lashes gazed up at him. A slight hint of fear showed behind her irises, mixed with the drive to fight, and he immediately hated himself for being the one to put that fear there. He cursed silently. What was wrong with him? He never regretted terrifying bloodsuckers, and she wasn't even afraid enough to give him the answer he sought. He cursed himself again. God, she was gorgeous. Vampiresses were impressive beauties, but no woman he'd ever seen, human or vampire, compared to her.

No. He snapped his attention into focus.

He wouldn't be distracted. He clenched his jaw and crushed his own desire. How could he be thinking of sex? Mark was a vampire, and it was his fault. His own neglect had killed his closest friend—more than once. It was his fault Caius had stolen Mark's life. If he'd only staked Mark as an extra precaution before the building exploded, Mark wouldn't…

He pushed all his feelings deep inside himself, where there was no escape. His focus wouldn't be broken, not again. He had three tasks he needed to accomplish: kill Caius to avenge Mark's death, end the gruesome killings plaguing Rochester's streets…and murder his best friend.

He would not let her faze him. His brain fought to concentrate, but his body was saying otherwise. Not once had he ever had this problem. Well, not since *she* refused to answer his letters.

He wished he could end it right then, draw the blade across her throat and free himself from the agony of wanting her. He scowled, disgusted with himself. Wanting a vampire? The thought made his stomach churn. But bloodsucker or not, he'd never laid a hand on a woman, and he hoped he wouldn't have to change that now. Unless an innocent life was in danger, he doubted he could bring himself to do it, and his life was far from innocent.

Still, something in his gut protested that he needed to know for sure what she was, and there was one sure way.

He shook his head. The sight of her Mark of Caine would shock him back to normal. To the version of himself that had little interest in women when there was a job at stake—and there always was, especially now.

"Turn," he said. When she didn't move, he increased the pressure on her neck. "Turn around."

With a glare of pure hate in her eyes, she turned away from him.

Before she could escape, he locked his arms around her, pressing her back against his body. He held the knife to the front of her throat and forced her to bend over. If the mark was there, he wouldn't hesitate to use the necessary force to get answers from her. Then, female or not, he would do what he had to do.

As his gaze trailed the length of her spine, he caught himself admiring the curve of her ass. Her round behind rubbed against him. Holy smokes… Had he ever wanted a woman so badly? He couldn't remember the last time he'd been interested in sex.

No distractions. He was weak, selfish. Stupid.

Need raced through his veins while he lifted the hem of her black tank top. He hooked two fingers beneath the edge of her leather pants, then slid them down an inch. The two cute dimples just above her ass were enough to leave him wanting for days, but her skin was smooth and unmarred.

No mark. A female vampire's Mark of Caine always appeared on her lower back. He blinked several times. He found himself at a loss for words. "Where's your…?"

"My what? My vamp stamp? News flash, buddy, I don't have one."

That she even knew what a "vamp stamp" was gave him pause. He released her shirt and allowed her to stand up straight, but he maintained the knife at her neck. An odd sense of relief washed over him, and he immediately chastised himself. Whether she was human or not, he had a job to do. "Who are you, and why are you wielding a gun in a dark room in a known vampire club?"

She shook her head. "Tell me who you are, and then maybe I'll consider sharing."

He pressed the sharp blade against her skin, reminding her of its presence. He didn't have the patience for this. "I'm the one with the knife," he said.

She stood completely still, nothing but the rise and fall of her chest giving away her agitation. "Touché."

He forced her toward the wall again. She turned around before he even told her to do so. She was trying to show her lack of fear by taking the lead, not waiting for directions. Not surprising, with her overly trigger-happy attitude, but her confidence was her weakness. Her gaze met his in a show of defiance, but he wouldn't let himself be fooled into picking a fight. He was easily twice, if not three, times her size. Though she well trained in fighting, she would never be a match for him.

He held her stare until finally she looked away.

"Tell me your name," he demanded.

She closed her eyes, glanced at the floor and let out a deep breath. Her eyes flickered up to meet his gaze again. "Sandra—"

He pushed her harder against the wall. "Real name."

She gaped at him as if he'd slapped her. "How do you know that's not my real name?"

"Everyone has a poker tell." One of the things he'd learned in his time at the E.U. headquarters was to interpret body language. It came in particularly handy when trying to distinguish vamps from humans, though detecting lies was always advantageous. She glanced down and to the left when she lied—a classic sign for many people and overly predictable. But he wasn't about to tell her that.

"What's your *real* name?" he asked again.

Her jaw clenched. Her anger at her current position was apparent in her eyes, but her voice was a sexy feminine alto when she finally said, "Tiffany Solow."

The air rushed from Damon's lungs as if a high-speed bullet had hit him straight in the abdomen. His head spun, and it took every ounce of self-control he had not to shake with anger. He couldn't believe the night had actually gotten worse, although he knew he deserved the massive beating the universe had just dished out to him.

Tiffany Solow…Mark's baby sister. His own Achilles' heel.

Rochester was a huge city. Though it was her hometown, when he transferred there in order to hunt Caius, he'd hoped like hell he would never run into her. What the hell were the chances? And what was she doing hunting vampires?

The memories flashed through his head in a nonstop pulse. His training officer's voice rang in his ears. *Brock, see a therapist or find someone to tie yourself to. Pronto!*

With no family to support him, Damon had been deemed at risk of "low morale" by the Execution Underground. They'd thought the pressure of hunting might turn him into some crazed psycho if he didn't have someone to talk to. They covered their asses by insisting on "therapeutic ties."

Rather than see the resident shrink, he'd opted for Choice B: to forge a bond, anonymously, with someone outside the E.U. He'd preferred to write a few BS letters to a stranger than have the E.U. psychiatrist record his every thought. The Execution Underground already rode his ass about everything. He didn't need them inside his head, too. And being his usual giving self, Mark had volunteered to help his best comrade and had contacted his baby sister.

Headquarters was all about "family contacts." In other words, they ensured that their hunters had something to live for besides the hunt alone. It was a numbers game to them. An overwhelmed hunter who committed suicide forced the E.U. to shell out money to train a replacement, not to mention compensation for the family. They were saving their pocket change.

Tiffany was in the same age group as many of the female victims the hunters set out to avenge, so the E.U. found her an appropriate contact. Because she'd known already that vampires existed, because she'd lost her parents to a vampire attack and had a hunter for a brother, there had been no security breaches involved in writing to her. According to the E.U., it also benefited her to know there were other men out there, aside from her brother, keeping her safe at night. Damage control, really.

Headquarters called it personalization and bond forging. He called it a load of crap. Like he'd needed any more incentive to do what he'd been trained to do. He would never forget the first letter he wrote to her.

> Tiffany,
> They say I need to write someone, so here it is.
> Yours truly,
> B

She'd replied with an eight-page letter telling him all about her. Little did he know when he'd signed that first damn letter "yours truly," he really *would* be hers. In a matter of weeks she'd clutched his heart in her hands.

The last picture Mark had shown him of Tiffany, she'd been only seventeen, long before Mark's death…before everything fell to shit...before she grew to hate Damon. Now she was twenty-two. He met her gaze and took in the breathtaking woman standing before him.

Mark had loved her more than anything in the world. She had been the only family he had left, and he would have wanted her cared for, protected. Not in the line of fire of the same vampire who had killed him. Damon lowered his eyes. How could he look her in the face when he held the blame for her brother's death? And if she knew Mark had turned...

No. She would never know. Damon had sworn to Mark that if he were ever turned, he would drive the stake through Mark's heart himself. A small part of him would die as he did it, but his promise stood firm. But she couldn't know any of that, which meant he needed to get her out of Club Fantasy, away from Caius. An overwhelming need to protect her surged through him, accompanied by the desire to claim her as his own.

No.

Without a doubt, he could not seduce her. Not only for the sake of his job, but because he owed that much to the memory of his fellow hunter and best friend. Taking Mark's sister into his bed? He might as well spit on his grave. Her eyes showed she didn't know who he was. She'd never met him in person, never seen his face. There was no way she would recognize him, and it needed to stay that way. Not even his name would give him away. He was thankful revealing his full identity had been against the rules during their correspondence. He would protect her anonymously and nothing more.

He inhaled a deep breath to cool his head. He tried not to think of how sweet her voice would sound saying his name as he drove himself into her. *No.* He wouldn't get attached to anyone again, then he couldn't fail anyone, then protocol couldn't get in the way of relationships. Hunting, protection. Nothing more. "What are you doing here?"

She scoffed. "Shouldn't I be asking *you* that? I'm here every night. You're the new vamp on the block."

He growled, low in his throat like an animal. Anger boiled inside him at the accusation. "I am *not* one of those worthless leeches."

She froze. Her eyes widened. "You're too strong to be human." She scanned his body, her eyes stopping on the muscles of his arms, chest and abs. "Prove it, then."

Tiffany stared at the stranger before her, her eyes locked on to his icy gaze. A shiver ran down her spine, but heat pooled between her legs. That alone made him dangerous.

"Go on. Prove you're human." Her pulse began to race from excitement instead of fear as she challenged him. Her gut screamed not to fight him, that he was no threat to her, but the knife at her throat and the ferocity in his eyes said otherwise.

"Just trust me on this," he said.

Not a chance. "Well, unfortunately for you, I don't trust people easily." With as much force as she could muster, she stomped on his instep.

He didn't cry out, but the move surprised him enough that the knife shifted slightly away from her throat. She seized the advantage and grabbed hold of his arm, pushed his sleeve up and dug her fingernails into his skin. She wasn't against fighting dirty. Not if it saved her sorry ass.

Her assailant didn't even curse at the pain, only grunted in response as her sharp acrylics dug into the flesh of his arm. Blood pooled around the edges of her nails before she released him. She lunged forward, knocking into his midsection like a linebacker. Damn, that had been a stupid idea. The man was built, and running into his abdomen was like hitting her head on a solid concrete wall. That would really hurt in the morning.

He tucked his knife up his sleeve instead of using the weapon against her. What was that about? He grabbed at her as she stumbled back, but she was short enough that she managed to duck out of his reach. He towered over her and was probably twice her weight with all the sexy muscle he was packing.

Regaining her footing, she threw a spinning roundhouse kick. He blocked it with ease as if he often fought third-degree black belts without blinking an eye. He was fierce, no denying it. She continued going at him, throwing non-stop kicks and punches, but he blocked every one, and she was running out of options. Wait! Her gun. Her gun was lying on the floor.

She rushed to reach the weapon. Seconds later, he loomed over her, trying to grab her. Why wasn't he fighting back? She was sure that if he really wanted to, he could kick the living shit out of her.

She snatched the gun from the floor, but she had no time to aim. She threw a sidekick, but he caught it, then swept her other foot out from under her. She toppled to the floor, landing with an audible *oof* as the wind rushed from her lungs.

Before he could make his next move, she spun around and kicked his ankles. Pain shot through the edge of her big toe, despite her high-heeled boots; even his legs were pure muscle.

Without thinking, she lunged into his legs, wrapping her body around his knees. He started to fall, but he caught himself and landed prepared to kick out, except that…oh, snap…she was attached to his leg!

She scrambled backward, but he was too fast. Within seconds he was on top of her, straddling her hips and holding her hands against the ground.

He let out a long deep growl and leaned in near her face. "Next time, I won't hold back from hurting you."

The ice-cold look in his eyes showed he meant it, and she vowed to herself that there would be no next time. The man was pure unadulterated muscle and no matter how good a fighter she was, she knew when to call it quits.

As she stared up into his eyes, she wished she hadn't charged him, because damn it, her head hurt and her brain was sending all sorts of crazy mixed signals into parts of her body that had never been lit up before. Though he was on top of her and she was clearly in a vulnerable position, he wasn't threatening her, just pinning her down and, oh, man, what on earth was wrong with her, because she didn't mind one bit.

Her gaze traveled over his rock-hard body. His chest heaved in and out from the adrenaline. Through his shirt she could see a nicely defined pair of pecs, and she knew from the pain in her head that washboard abs hid beneath.

Even his forearms, which she'd dug her fingernails into, were well defined. She could tell from the fluid way he moved that he wasn't some steroidal bodybuilder. No, his muscles were honed from serious training. The thought of his nearly naked body covered in a sheen of sweat as he worked out flooded her mind.

Whooaaaa, Nelly. Back up for two seconds. She *never* fantasized about men. Ever.

A small pang hit her heart, equal parts pain and anger. Her thoughts traveled to B, the nameless hunter who'd stolen her heart, only to break it to pieces with his betrayal. She could admit a teenage girl had her needs, and she'd fantasized about meeting B in the flesh so many times that real men need not apply. She'd been solo since she was fifteen, when her brother had left home to hunt monsters, and without B in the picture, she intended to keep it that way. She didn't need any distractions. Her one goal in life was to avenge her family, not snuggle up all lovey-dovey with some sweet guy, get married and have loads of chubby-faced cherubic babies. Not that Mr. Tall, Dark and Scary would ever fit that scenario, anyway. From the looks of things, he was a grade-A badass.

What was wrong with her? She needed to get back to Caius. If she disappeared for long enough, someone would come searching for her. Wasting time ogling a hot man wasn't in the cards for tonight—for any night. Not while Caius lived and breathed. Besides which, she chastised herself, she didn't know anything about this man. He'd held a knife to her throat, for God's sake.

But when she met his cold ice-blue eyes she thought she could drown in their intensity. She wanted to run her hands over his black buzz-cut hair as he pushed inside her. The thought alone sent a wave of heat rushing between her legs and a jolt of electricity shooting down her spine.

A long silence passed between them as he watched her, those haunting blue eyes boring into her.

"I guess I'm not really in a position to bargain now, am I?" She tried to make it sound lighthearted in hopes that maybe he would release her.

He glared at her. His stare alone was enough to make her want to talk.

Clearly he wasn't a vampire or he would have sunk his fangs into her throat by now. All her instincts said he didn't intend to harm her, and no vampire would ever take a no-harm approach against someone who'd attacked him.

She cleared her throat. "One of us has to go first, and from your stiff upper lip, I can tell it's not going to be you." She sighed. "If I start talking, will you at least let me go?"

He didn't reply. But the intensity of his gaze compelled her to confess.

She sighed again. "My name is Tiffany Solow, and I'm a vampire hunter."

His brow furrowed, as if the words *vampire hunter* confused him. "A female hunter?"

She frowned. Nothing annoyed her more than men who thought women were incapable. She was certainly capable of taking care of herself and of killing supernaturally strong vampires to boot.

"Yeah, buddy. You have a problem with a little girl power?" She wasn't weak. But this guy had the strength of a vampire and the training of an extremely professional hunter, not someone self-taught.

Could he be from…?

No. What were the chances of *that?*

His eyes widened before they narrowed again. "You're alone? No one trained you?"

She nodded. "No one but my brother taught me, so, yeah, I'm solo. You know, Solow—like my last name."

Usually that got at least a little bit of a chuckle out of people, but Mr. Tall, Dark and Scary didn't so much as crack a grin.

He released her hands, still pinning her to the ground with the weight of his body. She tried not to think of the way his hips pushed against hers and the obvious thickness she felt beneath his belt buckle.

He shook his head. "You're no hunter."

She frowned. "Oh, yeah? And what qualifies you to make that judgment? I could say the same thing of you, after all."

He shot her a look that said *Don't make me laugh.* "Why are you here? Are you a Host?" A look of disgust crossed his face.

"Hell, no! I would never let those leeches feed off me. Don't insult me."

The side of his mouth twitched slightly at that. The closest he'd come thus far to a smile. Apparently he appreciated a hate for the undead.

"Caius wants me as a Host, but he's not going to get me. Other than that, the reason I'm here is none of your damn business."

He didn't respond, only scanned the length of her body. Watching his irises as he drank her in was like watching fire flicker and blaze beneath crystals of ice. Breathtaking.

He wrenched his eyes away from her figure and met her gaze. "You're right. It isn't."

She sucked in a deep breath and balled up the courage in her chest. She needed to push him, to challenge him, even though he had the advantage. "Why are you hunting on my turf?"

He ignored her question. His spine straightened, and she could practically see him training his senses on something like a lethal animal.

"What is this room usually used for?" he asked.

"What?"

He lowered his voice. "What is this room used for?"

She gaped. What the hell was he getting at? "Uh…I don't know. I think people come in here to have sex and drink from their Hosts in private. But why—"

"Shhh."

"Why are you hushing me? What the—"

He shoved his hand over her mouth to silence her, but with her hands now free she quickly wrenched it off. "No way are you shutting me up, buddy. I'm—"

Before she could comprehend what was going on, they were nose to nose. With gentle but strong movements, he cupped his hand behind her head and his soft lips met hers. All her thoughts came to a screeching halt as the force of his kiss overwhelmed her. His tongue moved against hers in a slow sensual rhythm as his warm body pressed against hers.

The sweet scent of his skin filled her nose like expensive aftershave and amazing, mind-blowing sex. Another wave of heat rushed to her core, and she felt herself buck against him. She didn't even know his name, but her body was screaming in need for him. She'd never wanted anything, anyone, so badly in her life. Every inch of her skin was electrified as wave after wave of arousal rushed through her.

With soft smooth movements he lifted her so her torso was cradled in his arms while her hips were still pinned beneath his. The hard length of him pressed between her hips, and she felt herself slicken. No man had ever had such a powerful effect on her.

Somewhere in the distance, she was vaguely aware of the sound of an opening curtain.

"Oh, shit. Sorry," an unknown voice said. "Didn't know the room was taken."

Within an instant, his lips were gone.

She gasped for air. The world spun, though he still held her in his arms. Cold air hit her lips, and her heart thumped hard as she longed for the warmth of his kiss to return. He lingered over her, his face barely inches away.

Slowly he released her and stood, walking to the other side of the room. Her head cleared. A distraction. He'd kissed her as a distraction. She'd said people had sex in the room, and someone had come in, so he'd deliberately given the impression that they were having sex. She exhaled a long breath to collect herself. Without his weight on her body, she felt strange and uneasy. Though she knew she shouldn't, she wished the moment hadn't ended.

Once she caught her breath she didn't quite know what to say. Finally she managed to whisper the only words she could manage. "What's your name?"

"Damon Brock." His voice was cold and distant, no different from before.

Tiffany sat on the floor, completely stunned. Just like that, she'd had her first kiss ever, and from a tall handsome stranger.

Chapter Three

Damon didn't know what the hell had happened or why the fuck he'd chosen to kiss her....

He glanced down at Tiffany as she sat on the crimson carpeting, and his heart jumped. Her gorgeous hair was slightly ruffled from where his hand had cradled her head, and her bottom lip was flushed a brighter shade of pink where he'd gently suckled it. Shit, he had never intended the night to go this way.

When he'd heard the approaching footsteps and covering her mouth wouldn't shut her up, well...he'd done the first thing that had come to mind. And damn if that hadn't been a huge freaking mistake. If he'd wanted her before, now he wanted her tenfold. His body was begging for him to take her, to press her up against the wall and make love to her until she screamed. His thoughts raced. What the hell was wrong with him? He'd never lost his head like this before. This was Mark's baby sister!

He fought the temptation to curse under his breath. He needed to knock some sense into himself. But he wouldn't lose his cool. Before he'd sworn himself to the Execution Underground, if there was one thing his father had taught him about being a hunter it was not to lose his cool. And he'd never had a hard time with that until tonight.

He hadn't even been with Tiffany more than half an hour and she was already unraveling him, but he sure as hell wouldn't let that get in the way of his job. He couldn't.

He closed his eyes and rubbed his fingers in slow circles over his temples. There were six missing women out there, all probably dead, and who knew how many murdered and drained of their blood on the streets. It was *his* job to protect the future victims. The weight fell on his shoulders alone. He wouldn't neglect his job, his sworn oath, for any woman, even Tiffany.

Not sure of what he was doing, he picked up his Desert Eagle and holstered the piece behind his back again.

Tiffany grabbed her Smith & Wesson from the floor, reloaded the magazine clip and stood.

He glanced at her, and his heart jumped into his throat. He had to get out of here, but he sure as hell couldn't leave her behind.

She opened her mouth to speak. "I—"

He shook his head and cut her off. "You shouldn't be dealing with these vampires. I won't allow you to place yourself in danger like this."

Her jaw dropped. She crossed her arms and fixed him with a hard stare. "Who do you think you are? Last time I checked, I didn't wake up in the morning with the goal of pleasing random strangers. I'll do whatever I damn well please."

He should have expected her reaction. He just wasn't used to dealing with women.

Damon fought the urge to throw her over his shoulder; he didn't care if she kicked and screamed the whole way, nothing would stop him from protecting her. He exhaled a long breath. "This city isn't safe for you. Six women are missing, and more have been murdered. I won't have another death on my conscience because I let you waltz back into that club and play with murderers."

Tiffany strode across the room to stand straight in front of him. The top of her head barely reached his pecs, but she glared at him as if she were seven foot two. She jabbed a finger into his chest. "Look, buddy, I've handled myself perfectly well for twenty-two years without any help from you, so I don't care who you are, I'm not taking orders from you unless I damn well choose." She jabbed at him with her finger again. "I'm a vampire hunter, not some tutu-wearing princess who needs to be rescued."

Pushing past him, she stomped off toward the dance floor.

Just as stubborn as her older brother. Mark had always refused help when he'd needed it most.

Damon followed her. His eyes locked on to her figure as she nudged her way through the sweat-covered bodies on the dance floor. The pulsing red lights cast shadows on her hair, tinting it gorgeous shades of red and purple. Even from behind she was gorgeous. He pushed through the crowd until he reached her.

Before she knew he was there, he grabbed her around the waist and pulled her against his body. Using his leather jacket as a cover, he placed the Desert Eagle against her spine, leaned down and growled into her ear, "Walk toward the back door quietly and we won't have a problem."

"This is how you try to protect me?" she seethed.

Damon nudged her with his gun, and she walked forward. He battled the urge to suck on the delicate skin of her earlobe, to kiss his way down the length of her neck and collarbone. The smell of her skin was intoxicating. "I'd rather take you to the E.R. for a bullet wound than scrape your insides off the pavement because some demented vampire attacked you. At least with the gun you'd have a chance of survival."

He forced her to march ahead of them until they reached the back of the club. He pushed open the door and corralled her into the dimly lit street alley. A burst of cold air hit his face, giving him the wake-up call he needed.

"Are you going to take the gun off me now?"

Without a word, Damon patted down the sides of her jacket and confiscated her Smith & Wesson. His hand slid over the stake inside her coat pocket.

"What the hell do you think you're doing? I thought you wanted to protect me." The pitch of her voice dropped as her impatience rose.

He tucked the gun into his inside coat pocket. "I'll let you keep the stake for protection, but I can't have you wielding a gun at me." He patted down her jacket again. "Any other weapons I should know about, or can I trust you?"

She didn't answer. Her jaw clenched, and he could tell from her body language that she was seriously ticked off. Her expression made it very clear that she didn't like being stripped of her weapons.

Damon lowered his gun.

She spun to face him. "You know—"

Before she could finish speaking he slung her over his shoulder as if she weighed no more than a feather from a very pissed-off eagle and jogged toward his gunmetal colored BMW Z4.

She kicked her feet and slammed her fists into his back, but he barely noticed. She yelled profanities at him the entire way to the car, but he didn't care. He just needed to get her out of there. With the way Caius had been fixated on her, it wouldn't be long before he questioned where she was, and he wasn't going to be too happy about his dead bodyguard, either.

When they reached the Z4, Damon quickly hit the unlock button on his remote, wrenched open the door and dropped Tiffany, still kicking and screaming, into the passenger seat. He slammed the door. She shoved herself against it and beat against the window as he slid into the driver's seat. Thank God for automatic locks and bulletproof glass. Standard issue from headquarters.

Within seconds he was shifting into Drive and stomping on the pedal. They zipped out of the alley at sixty miles per hour.

"What's wrong with you?" Tiffany yelled. "Stripping me of my weapon and then throwing me over your shoulder like a sack of potatoes? What are you? A caveman?"

He tried to tune her out, but it was no use. Damn him, he'd just sucked face with Mark's little sister. But if he admitted it to himself, how many times had his thoughts wandered in that direction as he'd read Tiffany's letters? Not while she'd been a teenager, but later, once she entered college, when the handful of years separating them hadn't been as big a deal. Yeah, he'd wondered, all right.

"Hello!" She banged her fist on the dashboard. "This is the twenty-first century. This is called abduction, and in case you didn't know, it's illegal in every state!"

Damon growled, so low and throaty he surprised even himself. "Don't."

The tone of that one word shut her up.

He let out another grumble. "I'm trying to keep you safe, whether you like it or not. Sit back and put your seat belt on."

Slowly she relaxed into her seat and clipped the seat belt into place. Damon sped toward the Golisano Hospital at full speed. The city lights and few people roaming the streets blurred as they sped by. There was no way of knowing the next best move without seeing the victim. Crime scene photos never did the actual carnage justice, and now that he was on the scene he needed to see the details firsthand.

After several minutes of silence, Tiffany finally broke. "Why are you doing this? Why do you care about me?" She fixed him with a hard stare. "Why do you care if I die?"

Damon bit his tongue and concentrated on keeping his expression flat, distant. He couldn't let her know who he was. If he did, she would hate him and never trust him to keep her safe. But he couldn't avoid her questions for long.

"It's my job," he said.

She shook her head, clearly not buying that for a single minute. "What about the other humans in there? Isn't it your job to keep them safe, too?"

He gritted his teeth. She'd hit him right where it hurt, but he would never let her know that. "I can't save everyone."

She crossed her arms over her chest. "So you save the one person in the entire building who needs the least amount of saving?" He didn't respond. She huffed. "That makes total sense."

He shot her an icy stare. "That sort of attitude is exactly why you need saving. You're not invincible."

She scoffed. "Neither are you." She yanked up the sleeve of his leather coat. "See, I jabbed you right…" Her voice trailed off as she ran her fingers over his skin.

Electricity shot through his limbs. One small caress and she could bring him to his knees. He clenched his teeth. Everything in him fought against that knowledge. He couldn't grant her power over him.

She stared at his forearm. The wounds had already

begun to heal. The only remaining signs were several pink crescent-shaped scars, which at this rate would soon disappear.

Her eyes widened. "What *are* you?"

Tiffany stared at Damon's arm. Her fingernails had dug deep into his skin not even half an hour earlier, and already the healed wounds were nothing but faint pink lines and some residual dried blood. She ran her fingers over the skin once more. Desire pulsed through her every time her skin connected with his. Her nipples hardened into taut peaks as she brushed the muscles of his forearms. She wanted to touch him all over. Run her hands up his thick biceps and onto his chest, down to places where she'd never touched a man before. The thought of their kiss lingered in her mind. She didn't care that he'd only done it out of necessity. Her lips burned with the need to touch his again.

She drew in a sharp breath. She needed to calm herself. She barely knew this man. How could she want him, need him, so desperately? "What are you?" she repeated.

He didn't look at her, just continued to stare at the road. "A vampire slayer, a hunter."

"My brother, Mark, was a vampire slayer before he died." She held back a small smile. "He's the one who taught me how to kill vampires."

Damon's whole body stiffened like a rigid board. His hands squeezed the steering wheel tighter. The ice behind his eyes blazed a captivating blue.

Tiffany wished those eyes were hovering over her as his

muscled body slammed into hers. She cleared her throat and blinked several times. She needed to get the image of him naked out of her head, no matter how delicious she was sure he would be. She knew nothing about him. She snapped her wits back into place.

"Look, I get that most hunters have this overwhelming sense of duty to protect the innocent. My brother was the same way, always spouting at me about what to do if a vampire ever attacked me and feeding me horror stories so I wouldn't stay out too late at night. But I don't need protecting. I may be a woman, but you seem to forget that I hunt vampires, too."

Damon stared straight ahead at the road, his face unmoving and cold. "Not in my sanctioned territory, you don't."

Hot as he might be, the man had some serious control issues, and she would only take so much bossing around. "And who gave you the authority to claim this territory?"

He didn't respond.

Realization washed over Tiffany like a tidal wave. She stopped her jaw from falling open. She deserved a good whap upside the head. How could she be such a moron? The thought crossed her mind briefly before, but it had seemed so unlikely.

"You're a member of the Execution Underground," she said. "Just like my brother."

And B...

His hands tightened on the wheel. She didn't need his confirmation to know she was right.

"You probably knew him."

While she didn't know many specifics about the clandestine organization, she did know that they trained men to be elite hunters of the supernatural and dispatched them across the globe to protect humanity. The Execution Underground had recruited her brother once they'd gotten wind of their parents' brutal deaths. During the attack, he'd managed to save her from the monster, though he was totally untrained. The Execution Underground had been interested in him from that point on. They'd whisked him away to a private facility to train, while she'd stayed with their aunt Cecelia.

Whenever Mark had visited, he'd never shared much about the Execution Underground with her. She'd always gotten the impression that she wasn't meant to know, and at the time she didn't have the courage to ask.

To this day, she still didn't know which vampire led the attack that killed her family, but she was determined to find out. Mark worked every day after their deaths to find their killer and to destroy the monsters that had stolen their parents' lives, but Caius had taken his life before he could avenge their family. Now she wouldn't rest until both Caius and the murderous vampire who destroyed their parents exploded like the overstuffed blood bags they were. She would never forget the moment when she discovered who Caius was. All the Execution Underground disclosed to her was the location of the nest Mark had raided. Their letter said he died "valiantly fighting the leaders of the nest." It didn't take much snooping around the vamp world to find out who that leader had been. Once she'd put two and two together, hunting Caius had consumed almost all her waking thoughts.

Without a word, Damon pulled the car to a stop outside Golisano Hospital.

She raised a brow. "What are we doing here?"

He turned to face her. "Would you cooperate more if I said I'm working a case and you could help me as long as you listen to my instructions?"

"I'd be more inclined than when you're ordering me around for no reason."

He fixed her with a hard stare before he exited the car. Once he pressed the unlock button, she scrambled after him, eager for more information. She'd never been part of an official case before. She'd only worked to avenge her family's deaths, and always alone. Sure, she'd killed other vamps in the process, helping one innocent soul or another, but she had never worked a case.

Apparently there was a first time for everything.

Chapter Four

Dead was an awful smell to get used to. The scent of formaldehyde hit Damon's nose as he and Tiffany walked into the morgue. After a few calls to the E.U. in order to clear things with security, they were able to enter the room with ease. The reflective silver surfaces and sharp sterilized instruments laid out on tray tables made the room as cold as the chilled air around them. She coughed and covered her face with her sleeve. Though Damon was new to working on his own, he'd shadowed some of the world's most elite vampire slayers for the past several years. The smell of dead bodies no longer churned his stomach.

But the thought of all the children in the silver drawers lining the walls *did*.

There was nothing worse than working on a case involving children. The fact that Jane Doe was on the older

side of childhood didn't make it any easier. So much for
sweet sixteen.

He walked to the small coroner's desk in the corner and
riffled through the files. There was bound to be more than
one Jane Doe in the morgue, but only one with the type of
extensive damage they were looking for.

Tiffany cleared her throat, still wiping desperately at
her nose as if she were trying to erase the smell. "Do you
know who we're looking for?"

He continued searching through the stacks of papers
without answering. She had to be somewhere near the top.
He noticed a freshly printed page sticking out of a manila
folder. He pulled at the edge. The header of the report identified Jane Doe by her extensive mutilation. This was not
going to be pleasant.

"Damon," she said again.

He turned toward her with the paper in hand. "Yeah,
I know."

Reading over the IDs, he matched the number on the
report to the corresponding label on a drawer. He placed
his hand on the cold metal handle as Tiffany walked to
his side.

He nodded toward the drawer. "Don't watch this."

She shook her head. "I'm fine. I don't have a weak stomach."

"There are some things nobody should have to see."

She crossed her arms over her chest and planted her
feet firmly.

He let out a long sigh. "Suit yourself." He pulled open the drawer and fought not to gag.

Immediately Tiffany ran to the small wastebasket near the coroner's desk and hurled. Damon didn't blame her one bit. He stared down at the unidentifiable body as anger built inside him. Even if they'd found an ID, it would have been next to impossible to identify this girl, and no parent deserved to see their child like this. A large, gaping hole took the place of her face. The lips, eyes and mouth were gone, like some gruesome figure in a haunted house or a B horror film.

As if the facial mutilation wasn't enough, several sets of fang-size holes marred her neck and collarbone. From the heavy purpled bruising, they were evidence of the M.O.D.—method of death: exsanguinations. Damon had stopped hoping for the existence of a higher power long ago, but, damn, he prayed the mutilation had occurred after she'd already been drained. The thought of her suffering from the injuries to her face as a vampire slowly bled her out was more than even he could handle. Every inch of his being longed to kill the sick bastard who'd done this. The worthless piece of shit deserved to die a slow, painful and torturous death. And he intended to make sure that happened.

He carefully examined the holes on her neck. There was no mistaking it. Her wounds were definitely fang marks, the exact shape and width of the average vampire's canine teeth. Walking to the coroner's cabinet, he searched until he found three cotton swabs and the containers used for sending away samples for DNA analysis. He traced one around the edge of her fang bites, another near the edges of her facial wounds and the third over a small speck of dried blood on her cheek. He capped all three samples and glanced down at the body.

A feeling of disgust hit him. Desecrating the poor girl's corpse was the last thing he wanted to do at that moment, but he couldn't risk her turning into a vampire within one month's time. He needed to take preemptive measures to ensure she wouldn't turn, the measures he should have taken with Mark. Pulling his stake from inside his coat, he placed it over her heart. He closed his eyes, inhaled a deep breath and thrust the stake downward.

He opened his eyes again. Dry bloodless flesh, but otherwise there was no reaction. He let out a long sigh of relief. It was bad enough she'd been murdered by a vampire, but thank God she hadn't turned in the process. Bile rose in his throat as he thought of Mark being one of those bloodsuckers. Of Mark killing humans to fuel his own immortality. Because once turned, there was no fighting the change, and for the first year a vampire's blood thirst raged so hard that all the self-control in the world wouldn't aid him.

Removing the stake from her heart, he pulled his cleaning rag from his pocket, wiped off the lacquered wood and placed the stake inside his jacket again, then closed the drawer, sealing the corpse inside, and walked to Tiffany's side.

Tiffany lifted her head from the trash bin. Shoving her

hair away from her face, she inclined her head toward the drawer. "Is it closed now?"

Damon nodded. "Yeah, let's go."

She shot out of the morgue and toward the car as if someone had lit a fire under her ass. Judging by her pale white face, she was more than a little spooked. She didn't speak again until she slid into the passenger seat.

"I thought you had a strong stomach," he said as he slid behind the wheel.

She shook her head. "I thought so, too."

Damon wasn't surprised. Regular people thought being immune to motion sickness constituted a strong stomach. Dealing with the dead was different. She would need to toughen up for med school, if that was still her goal. She'd been prepping for her studies when they'd last communicated, several months ago. He opened his mouth to comment, but caught himself.

Do not go there, Damon.

He shifted the car into Drive and paused to plan out his next move. Getting the samples into the headquarters database via his personal analysis equipment before the evidence could be comprised needed to be his first priority.

Within a few seconds they were back on the street, and he sped away from the hospital.

She slumped against the headrest and closed her eyes. "Where are we going now?"

He held back a string of profanities. Sending off the samples meant taking her to his place. What the hell would Mark say if he knew he was taking Tiffany home with him?

His hands tightened on the steering wheel. The image of her lying across the black Egyptian cotton sheets of his bed sent his sexual imagination into overdrive.

No. Nothing would result from her being in his home, near his bed. He owed Mark that respect. "To my apartment."

She let out a long sigh. "What for?"

Damon shifted into gear. "To analyze the samples."

When they reached the Temple Building on Franklin Street, Tiffany's eyes widened.

"Holy guacamole! You live in the Temple Lofts?" Her eyes scanned the tall brick building. "Very nice."

He didn't respond.

She gave a slight laugh. "That's definitely not where I expected you to live. I mean, obviously, driving this Beamer, I'd be stupid to think you didn't have some dough, but dang. My little hellhole of a college apartment is nothing compared to this."

Damon slid out of the car and slammed the door. Tiffany followed suit.

He led the way to the entrance as she trailed behind him. Several minutes later they were on the third floor. He unlocked his door and flipped on the lights.

Tiffany followed him into the two-story loft apartment. Her face lit up. She glanced at the twenty-five-foot-high ceiling, clearly admiring the open staircase and the high quality furniture. Mostly black, white and tan. He'd gone for muted but classy, not to mention that he prided himself on keeping his apartment virtually spotless.

"Wow. Very impressive." She walked to the skyline window and studied the lights of the city.

Damon closed the door behind him and locked the deadbolt. "What were you expecting?"

She spun to face him. "Huh?"

"You said this wasn't what you expected from me. What *did* you expect?" He stripped his jacket off and laid it on the kitchen island.

She shrugged. "I don't know. I guess something a little bit…rougher around the edges."

He removed the Desert Eagle from the back of his pants and placed it on the counter.

The large silver gun thunked as it hit the countertop. Rough around the edges? Try jagged on every corner.

He watched as Tiffany ran her hand over the banister of the wooden staircase.

"If you're a member of the Execution Underground, what are you doing in Rochester?"

Damon froze for a moment, but then forced himself to relax. He kept his back to her and managed to speak evenly. If she knew he was responsible for her brother's death, she'd never trust him. Sure, there were other reasons for hunting Caius, but he knew how sharp Tiffany was. He would need a damn good excuse to make her think he had absolutely no connection to her brother, much less any knowledge of his death. Keeping his mouth shut was the best option.

He walked to the refrigerator and pretended to search

for something to drink. "Who said I was a member of anything?" He grabbed a bottle of water and closed the fridge.
After chugging down the water in a few quick swigs, he
turned to her again.

She rolled her eyes. "Look, my brother was one of you,
okay? I understand how you guys are with keeping your secrets, never admitting your true occupation to anyone, blah,
blah, blah, but there's nothing to hide here." She shrugged
as if secret international networks of lethal hunters chasing the supernatural were no big deal. "I already know
the Execution Underground exists, so why the tight lip?"

He recapped the now-empty plastic bottle and placed
it on his countertop. "Organization or not, I don't make a
habit of sharing my personal life—with anyone."

She gestured to the large open space around them.
"Uh…I'm in your apartment. How's that for *personal?*"

He smashed the empty water bottle with his palm. Man,
she drove him up a wall with the nonstop questions. But
what wouldn't he give to throw her over his shoulder and
carry her up to his bedroom. Maybe in another life.

Another life where he wasn't a worthless excuse for a
hunting partner, where his mistakes didn't cause innocent
people to get killed and where the deaths of more than one
person didn't rest on his shoulders. Mark could have gone
after Caius without the need for a transfer, closing in much
sooner than Damon could. And any extra time meant bodies piling higher.

"There's no division of the Execution Underground

in Rochester. I know that because otherwise my brother would have worked here. So why are you here?"

He took the samples from his coat pocket and walked toward the tech room. It had been meant as nothing more than a bedroom, but it hadn't even taken him two days to hardwire everything in place. His own personal contact with headquarters.

"Stay here."

She shot him a scathing look before she marched to the other side of the room and flopped on to the white leather couch.

Certain she was firmly planted in place, he slipped down the short hall to the tech room. He punched in several series of codes to unlock the door and stepped inside. The wall was lined with monitors of all shapes and sizes. The highest-end technology headquarters could supply him with was all contained within this one room. It was a tech nerd's wet dream.

Damon dropped into the desk chair and typed several numbers on the keyboard. The monitor rang like a telephone until a small beep confirmed that Chris had answered the other line. Seconds later his face appeared on one of the monitors.

Chris's expression was one of concern. "Hey, Damon. How you holding up?"

Damon held up the three samples. "I need these processed as fast as possible. If I load them into the DNA analysis machine, can you connect with my database and look them over?"

"Yeah, sure. Though...want to trade jobs? I'd rather be an assassin."

Damon fought back a small smirk as he rolled his chair to the opposite wall and carefully loaded the specimens into the scanner, which processed the data instantly, locking the genetic code into Damon's control system. Only the technological abilities of the Pentagon and the CIA rivaled those of the Execution Underground, and even they sometimes fell short.

"The samples are from the latest victim. One blood culture, one saliva analysis and one unknown." He fixed Chris with a hard look. "Looked like the killer *ate* the body. Ate it. If I didn't know any better, I'd say the bloodsucker ate it."

Chris raised an eyebrow. "Like a zombie?"

"Sure, whatever you want to call it. But vampire, zombie or who knows what, I don't care what it is. I just want to know who and where it is so I can stake it straight through the heart."

Chris focused on one of his monitors and typed at full speed. "The blood looks normal, nothing unusual about it. But the saliva and the unknown, I'm going to have to get back to you on those. There's something off about them."

"Off like how?"

"Like there's a different genetic marker that's screwing up the whole code. They don't look anything like normal." Chris pounded away at his keys. "Are all these from the victim on the far side of Franklin Street?"

Damon gripped the arms of his chair like a vice. "What do you mean, the far side of Franklin Street?"

Chris stopped typing and looked at Damon through the screen. "The most recent killing ten minutes ago on the far side of Franklin Street. A P.D. informant tipped us off. He said he'd call you. He saw it on patrol, and he's been holding off on calling the cops. I thought you said this was the most recent one? I—"

"I have to go." Damon stood and jabbed at the keys, beginning to shut down his system. "Chris, I didn't know about the newest killing and F.Y.I., I live on Franklin Street."

Tiffany pressed her ear against the door. She strained to hear even the smallest sound, but the door was apparently soundproofed. She sighed. She missed her brother every second of every day, and, as pathetic as she knew it was, she needed to know if Damon was in the Execution Underground, regardless of whether he'd fought alongside her brother or not. Anything that would help her hold on to Mark's memory was worth fighting for. And she had lost B, too....

Part of her hated him for the role he'd played in Mark's death. The other part missed him like hell. She could have used a friend these past three months.

The steel-reinforced door was yanked out from under her ear, and she toppled into Damon's chest. "What the hell?"

Holy guacamole!

Looking past him, she spotted what he was hiding: a control room that wouldn't have been out of place at NASA.

Damon slammed the door shut behind him, helped her regain her balance and then hurried past her in a full-on jog. She heard his steel-toed boots clomp up the staircase. What in the world was going on?

She raced after him.

When she reached the top of the stairs, she watched as he threw open the doors of a walk-in closet lined with weapons.

Whoa. Mr. Tall, Dark and Scary sure packed a whole lot of heat.

He shoved various weapons into the military loops on his belt before he slammed the closet doors shut and thundered down the stairs again as if she weren't even there.

She followed. "What's going on?"

He grabbed his jacket and gun from the counter, slipping the jacket on and tucking the gun into place before she could blink.

He wrenched open his front door. "If you're coming, then haul ass. If not, stay here and keep this door locked no matter what."

He nearly closed the door on her as she rushed after him.

She stayed at his heels as he ran out to the street. She grabbed his shoulder. "What's going on?"

"Dead body nearby. The vamp probably ghosted it by now, but to be safe, hold your stake at the ready and follow my lead."

A shot of adrenaline raced through her, and her brain switched to hunting mode.

They jogged to the nearest alleyway, but stopped before moving forward. Tiffany's eyes widened as she caught sight of the uniformed police officer on the ground. He slumped against the wall behind him. A trickle of blood ran from the crest of his hair. The man groaned.

Damon knelt beside him. "You the informant?"

The cop nodded. Man, the poor guy had taken a beating. "Were you bitten?"

The officer coughed, blood spewing from his mouth. He spit out a tooth, and then shook his head.

Damon placed a hand on his shoulder. "Good. Are you alright?"

The cop gulped as if trying not to spit more blood, before he managed to say, "Yeah. Hurry. Called patrol, thought I'd lose consciousness. Fifteen minutes till they're here." His last several words came out in a slurred mess. Slowly, he lifted his hand and pointed toward the alleyway. "Go."

Damon gave his shoulder a light, reassuring squeeze. "Thank you."

Standing, Damon slipped into the alleyway and blended into the shadows at its mouth. Tiffany remained close at his heels. Moving at a slow steady pace, she snaked around the corner right behind Damon. She followed each careful step he took with equal care.

Halfway through she bumped into his shoulders as he came to a sudden halt.

In the middle of the alley, half-hidden by shadows, lay

a limp and bloodied body. A pool of dark blood, black against the barely lit pavement, formed in the shape of a halo around...*his* head?

Tiffany covered her mouth. Her head spun, and she steadied herself on the brick wall of the building that formed one side of the alley. Most vampires preyed on the weak, on those they thought were the easiest targets— not because they couldn't handle it, but because they liked an easy snack. The only exception was the most ancient bloodsuckers, whose strength was legendary. They barely had to lift a finger. Nausea hit her stomach. The last time she'd seen a young, strong, capable man killed by a vampire was when she and Mark found their father lifeless on their living room floor as their mother clawed uselessly at the monster's arms. He'd sucked the life from her throat, deaf to Mark's and Tiffany's screams. Though she hadn't yet found him, she would never forget his face.

"He's not drained completely," Damon said, his words barely above a whisper.

Tiffany shuddered. There was something not right about this.

Vamps didn't leave leftovers, yet a puddle of blood surrounded the man's head. A newborn vamp wasn't capable of that kind of self-control, but an ancient vamp would lick his dinner plate clean and leave. Near invincible or not, vampires chowed down, drank every last drop of their victim, then they beat feet. They weren't about to make themselves known to the human population. They were greedy arrogant bastards, but they weren't stupid. Modern man packed an arsenal of weapons, and an all-out attack from the human race would lead to their demise. Tiffany often wondered if the world would be better off knowing what monsters crawled out after dark. But humanity couldn't cope with the existence of anything "other," anything different. They couldn't handle the truth. They would panic.

Numb, Tiffany stepped out of the shadows and slowly walked over to stand near the corpse, a young guy of around thirty-five who looked as if he'd been healthy and fit before the vamp got him. Now the man's arm was detached from his body, gnawed to shreds. Exactly the way the young girl's face had been. His eyes were wide-open, staring toward the night sky, the stars drowned by the lights of the city. Bending down, she carefully brushed her hand over his eyelids, closing them for the final time. She stood.

"Tiffany!" Damon roared.

Before she could comprehend what was going on, he tackled her full force and knocked her to the ground. A loud hiss pierced the darkness, and her mind snapped to attention. A fierce, red-eyed vampire stepped forward from the shadows, its fangs already extended and blood ringing its mouth.

Damon crouched in front of her, blocking her from the vampire's attack. As the creature lunged, Damon ripped the Desert Eagle from his waistband and fired a round into the bloodsucker's gut. With such a high-caliber bullet, the vamp's midsection blew to pieces. Blood and guts splattered over the alleyway, but that wasn't enough to kill it. Only a severed spine, decapitation or a stake straight through the heart would destroy a bloodsucker for good. The vampire screeched and staggered. It held its internal organs in as the damaged flesh knitted over, healing the bullet wound. It lifted its head. Glowing red eyes pierced through the darkness.

"You will die, hunter." It crouched in front of the body, guarding the corpse as a lion guards its prey.

Suddenly it ran at Damon, barely visible thanks to its intense speed. It clawed at Damon's throat, but he kicked his steel-toed boot straight into its still-healing wound. A feral growl escaped the monster's throat. Damon fought the vampire blow for blow, matching its supernatural strength with a power she'd never seen in a human being before.

For several seconds she stared, completely frozen. She watched their killing dance as the vampire's blood spilled in all directions, yet each time it lunged, Damon emerged unscathed.

Holy hell. She couldn't sit there. She had to help. She ripped her own stake from her belt and rushed into the fight.

She lunged at the vampire from behind and stabbed the meaty flesh of his shoulder. Not enough to kill, but enough to injure. In an angry fury, the vampire spun and grabbed at her. She dropped to her knees and sucker punched the bloodsucker straight in the groin.

Take that, sucker.

Human or vampire, getting hit in the crotch hurt like hell.

The creature doubled over in pain, falling on top of her.

They rolled across the pavement, each trying to gain the upper hand. Though she was stronger than the average man, the vampire's supernatural strength overpowered hers. With all its weight it pinned her to the ground. If it sank its fangs into her neck she would be done for. Like a snake, it hissed and threw back its head to attack. A growl, deep and full of anger, sounded in her ears.

It wasn't the vampire.

Chapter Five

Suddenly the weight of the vampire's body disappeared. Tiffany's chest heaved from adrenaline and fear. She stared upward and saw the vampire's feet dangling above her as the creature struggled helplessly. Damon clenched the monster by the throat. His whole body shook with uncontrollable rage as he crushed the bloodsucker's esophagus.

"Stake it before I tear its head from its neck," he growled.

She scrambled to her feet and with both hands drove the lacquered wood of her stake into the vampire's heart. One last batlike screech ripped through the night before the monster exploded like a bursting sack. Blood splattered over her face and torso, and she thanked God she'd remembered to close her mouth.

Damon lowered his hands and unclenched his fists, and the last remnants of the creature's flesh fell to the ground.

With her one semi-clean hand Tiffany wiped the vile liquid from her face. "I hate when they do that."

Damon fixed his stare on her. The raw power that surged from him hit her full force. He was fierce, terrifying and beautiful all at once.

"You are *not* leaving my sight," he said. "Understood?"

She nodded, at a total loss for words.

Drenched in vampire blood, he walked over to the dead man and hoisted him into his arms.

He resettled the weight of the dead man's body over his shoulder before nodding for her to follow him. They needed to get out of there before the cops showed up, and fast. As they snaked down the back of the alley, the distant sound of sirens, followed by the red-and-blue lights casting into the alleyway, lit a fire under their feet. They moved faster. Tiffany sighed. Thank goodness help for the wounded officer had arrived.

They kept to the shadows all the way to the Temple Building before slipping up the fire escape. Two people soaking wet with blood, holding a mutilated corpse, was not a sight for civilian eyes. Damon hit a keypad beside the fire escape window and they climbed into the loft. Wow. Keypad on the fire escape? How paranoid *was* he?

Once they were safely inside the apartment, they positioned the body on the kitchen island. She stripped off her leather jacket, and Damon followed suit. He held out his arm, and she laid her coat across it. He placed both coats in his laundry room before returning to the kitchen. They both used the sink and washed the caked-on blood from their faces and hands.

Tiffany stared at the body as she used a dishrag to dry her face. "What the hell was wrong with that vampire?" They were the first words either of them had spoken since the alley.

Damon shook his head. "I don't know. I've never seen a vampire guard a dead body, or leave so much leftover blood in its victim like that. And I've *definitely* never seen a baby vamp capable of stopping in the middle of a feeding to take a breather, and strong as it was, from the sloppy movements of that thing that was a baby vamp as sure as I live and breath."

She attempted to wipe some of the blood off her shirt and failed miserably. "It was like it was an animal with a piece of food. Vampires are chickenshits. Every peon vamp feeding off the street runs like hell if their victim is already dead and someone approaches. And you're right, what kind of bloodsucker leaves blood like that? I've learned at least that much from hunting."

Damon shot her a look. "You shouldn't be hunting vampires alone."

She glared at him. "Oh, yeah, why's that? I've been hunting vampires for years."

"You're not trained. If I hadn't been there, that bloodsucker would have drained you."

She turned away from him. Her jaw clenched, and frustration built up inside her.

"How many times have you come that close to death?" he asked.

She stared at the floor.

"How many times, Tiffany?"

"Lots, okay?" She spun to face him. "You're just like my brother, acting as if I can't handle myself. Just because I'm a woman doesn't mean I'm incapable of fighting. Why do you act like I can't hold my own?"

Something sparked behind Damon's eyes, something she couldn't interpret. "Because you can't."

"I am not weak. I'm not a victim." Her hands balled into fists.

Damon walked toward her, his boots clomping against the hardwood floor. He towered over her, staring down into her eyes. If she'd been a weaker woman, she might have been intimidated, but she refused to back down.

His tone remained calm and even despite the clear frustration behind his words. "Vampires are stronger and faster than even the most powerful human. Being a woman has nothing to do with it. Being untrained on top of being a normal human is what makes you incapable of fighting, not your gender. The vampire in that alleyway was nothing compared to a vampire who has lived even twenty years, let alone thousands. The bloodsucker we fought tonight couldn't have been a vampire for more than a few days, and still he would have bested you…"

She looked away from him.

He let out a long sigh and held her chin gently in his hands, forcing her to face him. Even when he was covered in blood and dirt, his touch sent electrifying waves through her, and as mad as she was, she wished she could kiss him again. She cursed herself. She didn't know this man. She still wasn't even sure why he was so intent on protecting her.

"Tiffany, look at me."

She did as he asked, studying the contours of his face. He seemed so familiar, but she couldn't place where she'd seen him before. Though she knew he wasn't, it was as if he was an old friend she hadn't seen in years. His presence was both tantalizing and comforting.

"Stop flirting with death. I can tell by looking at you that that's why you're doing this. Only someone with a suicide wish would try to fight something they know they can't win."

A lump blocked her throat, and she fought hard to keep her eyes from watering. She blinked to hold back the tears and prayed he wouldn't notice. Damon cupped her cheek, his touch gentle for a man so gruff and strong. She swallowed the lump in her throat and turned away from him.

No one had ever said something so blunt to her. No one had ever seen straight through her before, been so right about her motivations—not even her brother. No one…

…except B.

Even though she'd never met him. She'd been asked to correspond with B to give him something to hold on to in tough times, but in those letters, he'd been *her* savior. Now, with no more letters cluttering her mailbox, B seemed like a distant dream.

* * *

Damon watched Tiffany step away from him. His fingers buzzed with electricity, where their skin had connected. He bit his lower lip. He hadn't meant to put her on the slab and expose her like that. The last thing he wanted was to make her uncomfortable. The look in her eyes said he'd seen right through her.

She cleared her throat, acting as if he hadn't nearly made her cry, which seemed very *her*. From what he'd gathered, she wasn't the type of person to show weakness.

"Tell me why you brought him back here." She gestured toward the dead man.

"To examine him." Time to focus. He ducked into the downstairs bathroom and returned with his scalpel. It had saved him a time or two, letting him avoid unnecessary trips to the emergency room. Nothing like explaining why you had a bullet wound in your shoulder to open up the kind of investigation he didn't need.

She raised an eyebrow at him. "Do I even want to ask why you keep a scalpel in your bathroom?"

"Useful if you get something lodged in you. Glass, bullets, whatever."

"That happens to you a lot?"

"Comes with the job." He ran the scalpel from the dead man's sternum to his navel before he glanced at Tiffany.

All the color drained from her face, leaving her skin with a slight greenish tinge. She gulped.

He nodded over his shoulder, trying to hide a smile. "Bathroom, if you need it."

She frowned. "Don't get haughty. It's different seeing it for real, that's all."

He tugged back the skin.

"Ugh." She gagged. "Do you have to do it so…forcefully?"

"Yes."

She turned away and walked to the other side of the apartment. His eyes locked on to the sway of her hips, but he forced himself to look away. She would need to get used to dealing with gore if she was going to stick around for long. Damon paused.

Shit. She would *not* be sticking around for long. Only long enough for him to ensure that she wasn't chasing vamps anymore, that she was safe.

He'd already done enough to Tiffany. If she stuck around, things would only end with him ruining her life even more.

He glanced in her direction. She was staring out the window at the city lights. Her lips had tasted like warm brown sugar when they'd kissed. His gaze lowered to her sweet behind, and the thought of cupping her ass in his hands before he trailed kisses over the porcelain skin of her neck sent a shiver down his spine.

Damn. He ripped his eyes away from her. He would not think about her no matter how deliciously round her ass was or how perfectly ample her breasts were.

Dead body. Dead body. Dead body.

He looked at the corpse lying on his counter. That was enough to act as a cold bucket of water for anyone. Pushing

Tiffany from his mind, he stared down at the dead man's insides. What was it about the latest victims that caused vampires to act like zombies, going for flesh and not just blood? Why were they eating these people? And the way the new vampire in the alley had guarded this man's body screamed of a predator protecting its prey.

No. Leeches were leeches.

Once a human was drained, they moved on. Wham, bam, thank you, human. Aside from Hosts, leeches didn't stick around and play with their food. As much as he hated the relationship, at least Hosts served a purpose. Better a couple pints low than dead, though most Hosts drove themselves to that, anyway. But in all his years of hunting them, he'd never seen a single vampire interested in anything but blood—until now.

From the look of the man's insides, there was nothing unusual about his blood or his organs. Damon pulled latex gloves from one of the kitchen drawers and slipped them over his hands. He reached inside the open cavity of the man's midsection and moved around several organs, searching for anything even remotely unusual that would cause a vampire to behave uncharacteristically.

Nothing. No tumors or anything out of the ordinary.

Damon removed his hands from the chest cavity. He pulled at the edge of his glove, ready to be done with his examination, then paused. Something in his gut told him it was worth checking *inside* the man's organs, as well.

He reached deep into the man's body and began to palpate the organs. He bit his lip as his hands squished against the soft tissue. How the hell did morticians and coroners manage to do this for a living? Then again, how did he manage to kill for his?

When he finally reached the man's kidneys he used the scalpel to extract one. The organ was already cold. Carefully, he slid the scalpel through the spongy tissue.

A loud hiss filled the room. Something vile poured from the kidney, and heat like liquid fire washed over his hand. He ripped the glove off just in time for the greenish liquid to eat through the latex like acid. A putrid smell hit his nose, and bile burned at the back of his throat. Drawn by the noise and the stink, Tiffany came running over from the window.

The damn mess was like a sixth grade science fair project gone wrong, one of those spewing volcanoes every kid built at least once. He hardly noticed Tiffany running off and rummaging in the fridge. A second later, white powder clouded the air as she dumped an entire box of baking soda on top of the acid.

"What the hell *was* that?" she demanded.

Coughing from the soda cloud, he tossed his gloves in the kitchen garbage can, chuckling. "Overkill on the baking soda much?"

She frowned. "For all you know that could have exploded and I saved your sorry ass. Now, what the hell happened?"

He dusted baking soda from his clothing, not that it did much good with all the blood already there. "There's something wrong with the kidney fluids."

"Ya think?" She stared at the rest of the green acid oozing from the dead man's kidney.

A smile crossed his face. He had to give her credit. Even though he knew she was probably fighting not to toss her cookies, she was standing there like a champ.

He appreciated a strong woman.

She wrinkled her nose. "That's just disgusting. What *is* that? Maybe you should check the other organs, too."

Putting on a new pair of gloves, he held the man's heart carefully, preparing to jab it with the scalpel. Just as he got ready to slice, the corpse lurched.

Shit!

Damon jumped back as the now newly turned vampire sat upright, hissing and reaching for Damon's neck. How the hell had the thing changed so quickly? Before he could respond, Tiffany plunged her stake deep into the monster's exposed heart. One high-pitched screech pierced his ears before the vampire exploded like the blood sack it was.

Blood splashed onto his face and throughout his kitchen.

He looked at Tiffany, who smiled despite all the blood she was covered in. "I told you I could hold my own."

Damon narrowed his stare. "Sometimes." He pointed to the stairs. "You can use the shower upstairs. Toss your clothes over the balcony and I'll throw them in the washer."

"You don't need to ask me twice."

Stake still in hand, she trudged up the stairs. A minute later a large pile of bloody clothes flew over the balcony rail and landed on his hardwood floor with a splat. He quickly threw them in the washer, trying not to think about how deliciously naked she was, about the hot shower water running over the curves of her body. He pushed the thoughts aside.

Down, boy. Focus.

With any luck, he would at least be able to get most of the blood out of their clothes. He glanced down at his own threads. He was covered in blood and dirt, but there was no point in changing before he finished cleaning up.

He reached under his kitchen sink and removed a mop and bucket, a sponge and a gallon of bleach. It was times like these when he wished he wasn't too paranoid to employ a maid.

Not that your average housecleaner could handle a kitchen resembling a horror movie.

Chapter Six

An hour later he'd thoroughly scrubbed down the kitchen, returning it to a near sparkling clean. He would give it another going over later. Right now he needed a shower. Using the downstairs bathroom, he scrubbed all the blood, guts and debris from his body. When he finished, he wrapped his hips in a towel, threw his own clothes in the washer and padded up the stairs to his bedroom.

Water from the shower pummeled the tiled floor, sounding like heavy rain. He didn't blame Tiffany for the extra-long shower. When you washed the blood off, no matter how clean you got, sometimes you still felt dirty.

He finished drying off and threw the white towel into the laundry bin. He slipped on a pair of old loose-fitting jeans, zipped and buttoned the fly, then reached into the top of his closet for a black shirt. Tiffany cleared her throat from behind him.

Still shirtless, he turned around. The breath caught in his throat, and every inch of him stiffened. His erection was immediate. She was standing in the middle of his bedroom, still slightly damp from the shower, one of his towels wrapped around her. It took all the strength in him not to rip the towel from her body and take her on top of his bed. Thinking about what was underneath that towel would be the death of him.

He watched as Tiffany scanned the length of his body and a look of hunger filled her eyes. She inhaled a deep breath, and he admired the rise and fall of her chest. Her every movement exuded raw sexuality. If she looked at him that way much longer...

Her gaze dropped to the floor. "I *knew* you were with the Execution Underground."

He nearly swore. Damn. She'd seen the E.U. brand on his shoulders, a variation of the symbol Mark and every other hunter had. It marked them as humans with something more—their incredible strength, their speed, their fighting abilities. Each member was branded with his own unique symbol upon graduating the Execution Underground training.

A sad smile crept across her lips. "I like your design more than the one my brother, Mark, had." She continued to stare at the floor. "The first time he came home after he got his, he flaunted it as if it were a badge of honor. The purple heart of tattoolike brandings."

Damon froze at the sound of his best friend's name. He let out a long breath through his nose. She couldn't know he was responsible for her brother's death—and worse. His jaw clenched. She couldn't know that he was going to have to kill Mark all over again.

She shifted from one foot to the other nervously. He admired the sway of her hips and immediately cursed himself. She was Mark's baby sister. It didn't matter if she was twenty-two, or that she was her own independent woman, that he'd known her for years—he owed it to her brother's memory to stay away, to keep his hands off. Not to mention that he needed to stay objective, detached from his mission if he was going to complete it successfully. And how could he be detached while sexing up the sister of the man he was avenging?

The sound of a car horn down in the street brought him back to reality. He would have to gouge out his eyes and break his eardrums to avoid wanting her. Her looks, the sound of her voice, her scent... She drew him in like a siren.

She broke the silence. "Sorry, I didn't mean to make it awkward, like I was being creepy and sneaking a peek at your emblem. I know your vow to the Execution Underground is kind of a personal thing, so it's none of my business. Anyway, uh...do you have a blow-dryer?"

If he hadn't been too busy raking his eyes over the gorgeous hourglass figure beneath the towel, he would have chuckled. He ran his fingers over his buzz cut. "I don't have much hair to dry."

She met his eyes quickly, then lowered her own gaze to the floor again. "Do you have any more towels, then?"

He pointed to the bathroom. "Under the sink."

She hunched her shoulders, curling in on herself as if she were embarrassed to stand before him, barely covered. "I didn't see any."

Exercising every bit of self-control possible, he walked past her to the bathroom. He reached under the sink, feeling for the stray towels. Finally he found one tucked far in the back corner. He pulled it out, stood and turned, ready to take it to her, only to find her standing directly behind him. Her large amber eyes examined his torso again, lingering on the line of highly defined muscles leading from his chest to his hips.

He couldn't resist. "Like what you see?" he said playfully.

The deep red blush that bloomed across her face sent his heart racing into overdrive, and he knew that if she dropped her gaze she would see his excitement.

"Sorry," she said, starting to turn away.

He held the towel out toward her. "Don't be."

She reached for the towel, and her soft, delicate fingers brushed against his hand. She met his eyes and stared up at him, her expression innocent and perfect. She bit her lower lip. He thought of the perfect taste of her mouth on his own. Being honest with himself, he had to admit that she'd tasted delicious when he'd kissed her, just like he'd always dreamed she would.

Another blush crossed her cheeks. She glanced toward the floor before she met his gaze again. Her desire was palpable. He hated himself for it, but he couldn't hold back any longer.

* * *

The fiery look in Damon's normally icy-blue eyes sent Tiffany's heart thumping hard against her chest. He stepped toward her. She didn't care if she didn't know him. He was handsome, strong, intelligent—and dangerous. Dangerous to the monsters they hunted. Dangerous to her. Her mind, her heart. And worse, he was hell-bent on protecting her. For a woman who'd been on her own for so long, been alone for so long, here, finally, was a man who knew her secrets. Understood her on a level no one else ever had. No one except B.

And, boy, did that spark a fire inside her.

He reached out and toyed with the edge of her towel. She wanted him, and from the look in his eyes, he wanted her, too.

She balled up her courage and dropped the towel to the floor.

Within seconds he was pressing her against the tiling of the shower as his lips met hers. The delicious masculine taste of him flooded her mouth as he kissed her deeply. No one else had ever kissed her, but there was no doubt that Damon's abilities were mind-blowing. His tongue danced with hers in sensual, soft movements.

Gently, he suckled on her lower lip. She moaned and bucked her hips against him. Heat rushed to her center. Every inch of her body longed for a man's touch, for Damon's touch. She ran her hands over his shoulders and onto his strong muscled chest. Her fingers crossed the hard ridges of his abs before her hand slipped into his jeans.

A growl rumbled in his throat as she stroked the length of him, feeling the power that came from touching him, knowing she was pleasuring him. His lips trailed from her mouth, and he nestled his head beside her neck so he could kiss the sensitive skin of her collarbone. Shivers rolled down her spine.

His hands slipped behind her back and cupped her ass, then lifted her with ease so her hips were up against him. He pulled back from her neck, taking in the view of her naked form. Supporting her with one arm, he trailed his hand along her skin and down to the juncture of her thighs. A wave of excitement rushed over her. No one had ever touched her there before. Should she tell him?

His warm hand nestled between her legs, and he rubbed his fingers in slow circles over her most sensitive flesh. She moaned, and a fresh wave of heat flooded her. His fingers were covered with her sweetness. She was so wet. Should she be embarrassed? He met her eyes and slipped his fingers into his mouth, licking off her nectar. A deep moan escaped his lips. She nearly moaned herself, to know he liked that....

He lowered his hand between her legs again and massaged her. Fire coursed through her body, warming her in a way she hadn't known was possible. The last of the water drops from her shower dripped onto her skin. The coolness sizzled against her in an amazing sensation.

He placed his cheek against hers, his mouth trailing sweet kisses up to her ear. The heat of his breath sent waves of electricity rolling through her body.

He gently nipped at her earlobe. "You taste so sweet."

Still supporting her with one arm, he captured her hand in his and led her fingers down to the button of his jeans. She knew what he wanted. She inhaled a deep breath. She wanted him more than anything imaginable. She was ready for this. Leaning forward, she undid his jeans and his pants fell to his ankles, revealing the hard strong length of him.

She fought back a gasp. He was enormous, and the thought of him plunging deep inside her sent both chills and fear racing through her body. Kissing her deeply again, he placed himself just outside the entrance to her body. Adrenaline and excitement overwhelmed her as the pressure increased.

She pulled back from his kiss. "Damon, wait," she whispered.

He stopped immediately and met her eyes.

"I…I…" she stammered. As tough as she was, she was no tigress in the bedroom—not yet.

"It's all right, Tiffany, we can stop. I don't want to pressure you if you don't want—"

"No," she interrupted. "I want to." Her eyes trailed over the length of his body again. Her desire for him surged and built the courage inside her. She inhaled a deep breath, then let it out in a rush. "I'm a virgin."

Damon's eyes widened.

She bit back a groan. Did he not want her now that he knew she was so inexperienced? She could tell from his raw sexuality and strong confidence that he'd known his fair share of women. A large lump rose in her throat, and her eyes welled with tears.

With his thumb he wiped away the tears from her eyes. Then he stroked his knuckles over her jawline, and a slight purr sounded from his throat. His sweet smile told her that he was sincere. "I'll be gentle with you."

Before she could respond, he scooped her into his arms and carried her into his bedroom. He laid her out on the bed. The soft mattress engulfed her in a sea of black sheets. His eyes drank her in. She marveled at the sight of him kneeling over her.

He ran his fingers over her thighs, and she shivered. "So, you've never been with anyone before?"

She shook her head.

For a brief moment, she worried what he thought of her. Twenty-two wasn't too old to still be a virgin, was it? But all her nerves subsided and were replaced with excitement when she saw the ravenous hunger in his eyes.

"I promise you, I'll be gentle, and I'll make certain it won't hurt." He slid off her and knelt near her feet. He pushed her legs open, and his lips trailed kisses and soft caresses up the insides of her thighs. Her heart quickened.

Before she could prepare herself, he ran the length of his tongue over her lower lips. He massaged and sucked the sensitive flesh.

Tiffany threw her head back and moaned. Electricity radiated from her center, sending waves of pleasure throughout her body. She bucked against him. Her spine arched as heat pulsed through her core.

He teased her with his mouth until she reached the brink of ecstasy, faster than she'd ever expected. With one more hard pull from his lips, sweet release hit her hard and fast. She clasped her hands around his head, riding his face as he tasted her.

She gasped for air when he released her. He smiled from between her legs and licked his lips. The look in his eyes was enough to make any woman want him between her bedsheets.

White hot need crashed over her. She wanted more. She moaned. Oh, she wanted so much more.

"Damon, can you do that a—"

A grin crossed his face, and he chuckled. "You don't need to ask me twice."

Damon latched his mouth onto her and savored the moment. He could drown in the taste of her, the scent of her. She was divine. He hardened with need as he pleasured her with his mouth. He wanted to be inside her, losing himself in the softness of her.

No, not want…need. He *needed* to be inside her.

But his desire to make her first time magical and painless was more important than his own desire. He intended to make her come until she was so soft, so wet, that the width and length of him would be a welcome relief to her overwhelming desire.

She moaned. The sound of her pleasure intoxicated him.

How many women had he turned down over the years because they weren't his Tiffany? It didn't matter that he only vaguely knew what she looked like, that he'd never heard the sound of her voice, never felt her touch until now. Despite all that, he knew her, and not one of those women ever measured up to the one woman who cradled his heart in her hands. Hell, she didn't even know what she did to him. The ache in his chest built. The ache that brutally reminded him that she was so much more than a one-night stand.

He ran his hands over the sweet creamy skin of her thighs. No matter where or how he touched her, energy raced through every ounce of him. He increased the pull of his mouth as her muscles tightened in pleasure. She was so close to climax again, and he could taste it.

She cried out. Her orgasm gripped her hard, and she bucked her hips against his face from the sweet feeling of release. But he couldn't let her go yet; he needed to work her until she was begging for him inside her, needing every inch of him.

Without stopping, he continued to suck her sweetness into his mouth. He angled his chin slightly upward, making enough room so he could position two fingers outside her entrance. Her wetness coated him as he rubbed her slick flesh.

Slowly, with gently increasing pressure, he slid his fingers inside her. She moaned in pleasure. He curled his fingertips up to the top wall of her core to tickle against her G-spot. He fought back a grin as he continued sucking her. The deep throaty cry that escaped her lips as he fingered her didn't sound like the cry of a meek virgin.

"Damon…Damon…"

The sound of her whispering his name sent power and adrenaline through him. Another release crashed over her, and he felt the bed beneath him rock with the force of her straining and pushing against his mouth.

"I want you," she panted.

He released her and licked his lips. He grinned. "What was that you said?" he teased.

"I…mmmhhh…I…" She attempted to catch her breath. She kept her eyes closed. All the muscles in her body visibly relaxed from enjoyment. "I can't say it."

He chuckled. "Yes, you can." He crawled up the bed, lingering over her body, only inches separating them.

She opened her eyes and met his gaze.

He leaned down and kissed her deeply, digging a hand into the damp tresses of her gorgeous hair. He pulled away, but only far enough to speak. His lips brushed against hers as he said, "I'll do anything you want. Never be too shy to ask."

She lifted her hand to his face and ran her fingertips across his cheek.

"Anything," he repeated.

A blush colored her cheeks, but fire filled her amber eyes. "I want you inside me."

He growled, nipping at the soft skin of her neck before he took her breast into his mouth. His tongue circled over one sweet hard nipple, then the other. He took care to pay equal attention to both her delicious breasts. She sighed, relaxing against him.

When he released her nipple from his mouth, he positioned himself outside her entrance. Her eyes widened, and a mixture of emotions crossed her face.

"Don't be nervous." He smiled down at her. "I'll take good care of you."

He eased himself inside her, and she whimpered with pleasure. Damon moaned. She was so tight. So unbelievably tight. He'd never wanted anything more than he wanted this. He wanted to drive himself deep inside her, pounding hard into her until she pulsed against him. Being inside her, being so close to taking her hard and aggressively, was like sweet torture. The thought of her screaming his name nearly drove him over the edge.

With slow movements he rocked into her as gently as he could, careful not to penetrate too deeply. But she caught him off guard. Her walls clenched around him, and she was already teetering on the brink of climax.

Damn. His whole body shook as he fought to hold himself back.

White-hot moisture flooded her tight opening. She threw back her head and moaned, eagerly meeting his every thrust as she peaked.

He gripped the headboard with one hand to brace himself. In all his time hunting and training, nothing he'd faced could compare to the difficulty of holding back from ravishing her.

Keep your cool. This is about her.

He whispered against her ear. "How are you feeling?"

"Like I'm in heaven." She let out another moan and

pushed against him. "Like I want every inch of you deep inside me. Like I want you hard and deep."

He clenched his teeth. Everything in him wanted the same. "If you keep teasing me, I might not be able to hold myself back, and I don't want to hurt you." He kissed her forehead.

With a devious grin, she ground her hips into him.

Damn and double damn!

He nearly lost it right then and there. Couldn't she see how hard he was trying to exercise restraint?

He stroked his fingers over her cheek and pushed into her. "You're playing with fire. I don't think you know what you're getting yourself into."

She bit her lower lip in a "come and take me" look and ground into him again.

"Tiffany...!" All the muscles in his body strained, and he gasped for air.

Before he could stop her, she kissed him hard and ran her hands over the muscles of his chest. When she pulled away, she smiled and shot him a seductively playful look. "I *do* know what I'm getting myself into, and I want you deep inside me. Hard and fast."

If she really wanted it, he would give it to her. He lightly bit her ear. She whimpered, and goose bumps prickled across her skin. "Anything you ask."

Within seconds, Tiffany found herself flipped and lying on her stomach, and she marveled at Damon's strength and power. He gripped her by the hips and pulled her up toward him. Her ass ground against his hips as he positioned himself outside her slick hot entrance he had withdrawn from only seconds before.

He thrust into her, harder than she expected. She cried out. The pressure as he filled her was amazing. She'd been scared of her first time. She'd been scared of the pain, the bleeding and the embarrassment of lying naked beneath someone's eyes. But Damon had destroyed all those fears with the intense hunger behind his eyes.

He wanted her, but he was man enough to take his time with her, preparing her for his possession. As she'd expected, there had been a flash of pain, but she'd been prepared for it. What she hadn't anticipated was so much pleasure.

"How deep do you want me, Tiffany?"

She shivered. The sound of him saying her name sent every nerve in her body into spasms of arousal.

"However deep you want me."

The pressure of his fingers on her hips tightened, exciting her.

He ran a hand down the length of her spine. "Don't tempt me. I might not be able to hold back."

She inhaled a deep breath. She wanted to hear his pleasure. Wanted him to cry out her name. She was ready. She turned her head to look at him, narrowed her eyes and challenged him. "Try me."

The fire in Damon's eyes blazed, gorgeous and intimidating in its intensity. He let out a dark chuckle. The grin that crossed his face was devious, and sexy as hell. "You asked for it."

He thrust into her so deeply that her whole body lurched forward. She cried out and moaned, bracing her hands against the headboard as he pounded into her. His strength was incredible. Her core stretched wide to take the full length of him. Wave after wave of white-hot need pulsed through her.

"Damon!" she screamed. Her legs shook, and she fought not to collapse beneath him. Her core slickened with wetness and heat. Holy smokes. The man was a sex god—she was sure of it.

Damon palmed her breasts as he continued to thrust deep inside her. Her walls pulsed against him, clenching. The pressure inside her built until she teetered on the brink of ecstasy, the pleasure so intense it was almost too much.

Damon rolled her right nipple between his fingers. The tips of both breasts tightened into taut peaks, tingling beneath his touch. "Tell me what you want," he demanded.

"You," she said. "I want you." The words came out as a breathless whisper.

"Louder."

She raised her voice. "I want you."

Pulling harder, he thrust into her with every ounce of his strength. Her whole body shook as he brought her to the brink.

"Louder," he growled.

"I want you!"

She screamed and Damon let out a harsh groan. With

another massive thrust, she clenched against him as wave after wave of ecstasy crushed her. He pumped into her. There was nothing but Damon. His touch, his scent, the feeling of him buried deep within her. She wanted to drown in him and never resurface. She fell onto the bed, unable to hold herself up against the weight of him any longer. He collapsed next to her and pulled her into his arms. She snuggled into his chest and he kissed her forehead, before stroking his fingers through her hair.

She'd never known such sweet bliss.

Her body relaxed into his and within moments she was drifting into sleep.

Chapter Seven

Damon lay on his bed wide-awake as Tiffany slept peacefully with her head nestled against his chest. She was the most beautiful thing he'd ever laid eyes on.

And his best friend's baby sister.... God help him.

What had he done? He'd told himself he wasn't going to get emotionally involved in this mission, but sleeping with a woman under your protection was one hell of a way to keep work separate from pleasure. He'd told himself he wouldn't touch Mark's baby sister. Well, he'd done a lot more than touch her.

He let out a long sigh. What was wrong with him?

He glanced down again at the beautiful woman lying against him. He knew what was wrong with him. She was everything he wanted in a woman. She was strong, fierce, intelligent, passionate and beautiful. Any man would be lucky to have her, yet here she was in bed with him—a killer. He made his living off destroying things. Granted, he fought monsters and sometimes that saved lives, but it didn't change the fact that being successful at his job meant being ruthless, cold and bloodthirsty. When emotions entered the mix, that was when missteps crept in and innocents died. That was when good men like Mark died.

What kind of a lowlife was he that he'd gone to bed with Mark's sister? Mark had trusted him to write to her with no idea of the consequences. No matter which way he looked at it, there was no justification for what he'd done. Even as they'd made love he'd tried to convince himself that Mark would have wanted Tiffany to be protected. That he would have wanted her to find a man who could defend her and care for her to stand at her side. Maybe at one point that man *could* have been him. But after all he'd done, everything that had happened, it certainly wasn't him now.

He stroked the soft tresses of her hair and watched the rise and fall of her chest.

Stunning.

He shook his head. What was she doing with someone like him?

A lump lodged in his throat as he thought of the last words in the final letter she'd sent him. They were burned permanently into his mind and his heart.

I don't know how you can miss a person you've never met, but somehow, I miss you every day.
With love,
Tiffany xoxox

He knew that after Mark's death the Execution Underground had given her as many details as they could, to help her achieve closure, which meant she knew he could've saved Mark, but he failed. There was no way she didn't know. She'd never answered a single one of his letters after that.

Careful not to wake her, he slipped out from beneath her and rested her head on one of his pillows. He made quick work of throwing on some clothes before he headed downstairs. They'd slept most of the day away, and now, with sundown not far away, his work day was about to start.

He thought of the time he'd spent with Tiffany last night. Already he'd been neglecting his job, making love to her instead of closing in on Caius or searching for the vampire who was killing innocent women. There were so many things wrong with this situation. Images of partially devoured corpses, the awakening bloodsucker's kidney exploding with green acid and the way the vamp in the alley had guarded the body, flooded his mind.

He punched in the security code for his tech room, and the heavily reinforced door unlocked. He shoved it open, stepped into the room, flopped into his chair and dialed Chris's number. The monitor beeped on, and Chris stepped in front of the camera.

"Hey, man—"

Damon interrupted him. "Green acid came out of his kidney."

Chris's eyes widened. "What? Whose—"

"After you told me about the killing I went and located

the body. The guy was in his thirties, fit, already drunk from, and chewed up like the girl was, only his arm this time. Then a vamp jumped from the shadows and started guarding the body like it was a three-course meal."

Chris shook his head. "This is fucked up, Damon."

Damon nodded. "It gets worse—and stranger, too. There was an abnormal amount of blood left at the scene, wasted, which a newly turned vampire wouldn't even be capable of leaving. They'd be way too hungry. The vamp that attacked us was newly turned, which means it wasn't the one who took the guy out. Baby bloodsuckers don't have that much strength."

Chris ran a hand through his short blond hair. "What do we do next?"

Damon held up a hand. "There's more. After the vamp was dead, I brought the victim's corpse back here to examine. His kidney had green acid in it, too. It nearly burned my damn hand off."

Chris started pounding at his keyboard. "That's not normal, Damon. That's bad, really bad."

"That's not all."

Immediately Chris stopped typing and looked at Damon.

"The dead guy turned into a vamp an hour later. Had to stab him in the heart. He exploded like a blood bag."

Chris's mouth fell open. "Only an hour later? That's barely a fraction of the normal transformation period. You've got to be kidding me."

Damon leaned forward. "Wish I was."

Chris buried his face in his hands. "And to add fuel to the fire, I got in five new reports for your area last night."

Five? Rage filled Damon's chest, and his hands clenched into fists. "What?"

Chris raised his head. "It's not what you think. Not vamp news."

Damon sat in silence, waiting for Chris to elaborate.

Chris let out a long sigh and swore. "I hate to tell you this, but Rochester is swamped with supernatural predators. There are reported werewolf sightings, possibly a full-on pack, there are demons lodged so deep the people they've possessed are pretty much done for, there are several small witch covens, loads of non-werewolf shifters— oh, and that's not even including all the poltergeists and ghosts reported in the old abandoned asylum."

They both sat in silence, uncertain what to say. Words couldn't express what deep shit Damon was in. Welcome to Rochester.

Chris cleared his throat and broke the silence. "You know you can't handle all that on your own."

Damon clenched his teeth and slammed his fist onto the desk. He wasn't ready to lead another division, not given the way he'd failed Mark. But the laundry list of supernatural waste Chris had just dished out was far more than any hunter could handle on his own. The Execution Underground trained all their members to deal with a variety of supernatural creatures, but then headquarters assigned each hunter a species and conditioned them into elite specialists. Damon excelled across the board and was one of the few who'd been granted their choice of specialization. But none of that would do him any good in hunting other beasts full-time. There were too many. Per his choice, hunting vampires was his only true purpose.

He clenched his fists, and fought down his frustration and anger. "Send me a list of prospective hunters for every type of monster we have in the city. I'll look through them, pick a team and put in a request to headquarters."

He wanted to bash his fist into a wall. He'd thought coming to Rochester would let him work alone, since there were no other hunters in the area and until now there hadn't been all that much paranormal activity. But not even New York City was drowning in as many supernatural preda- tors as Rochester suddenly was. He'd landed in the exact situation he'd been trying to avoid: being the lead hunter of an entire division.

"You got it," Chris said. "But let's focus on one thing at a time. I ran those samples, but I was only able to determine one thing. Something caused a mutation in the vampire's saliva, which probably means the vampires themselves have morphed into something new. The weird thing is that the mutation has a lot of similarities to a human virus."

If Damon had been a more lighthearted man, he might have laughed. "The vampires are sick?"

"Yes. I think somehow they're passing around some sort of virus, and that's causing the strange behaviors you described. But based on the change in their DNA, I think it's only being passed on to newly turned vamps. Maybe it has to happen at the moment when a new vamp is made, and that's why the old ones can't get it. I have no idea what the original source could be, though. Does any of this fit what you're thinking?"

Damon ran his hand over his hair. "Not sure. If the vampires have a virus, the weird behaviors make sense. But what about the dead guy turning so quickly? It only took an hour for him to turn and regular vampire gestation is at least a month, sometimes longer, when buried in the ground. He shouldn't have changed that quickly."

Chris started typing again. "The virus could be causing a genetic mutation in their makeup and speeding up the transformation process."

Damon rested his head in his hands. "So we have sick vampires running around who are mutating into zombie-like monsters. But that doesn't explain why a newborn vampire would leave blood. Once a baby vamp bites, it doesn't detach until the person's drained, and this guy wasn't."

Chris gave a single nod.

Damon finished his thought. "But a stronger vamp could do that."

Chris stared at him. "You're thinking an older vamp is killing these people and then feeding the leftovers to the baby zombie vamps?"

If an older vampire was controlling younger ones within the Rochester city limits, there was a clear culprit. Damon and Chris exchanged knowing looks. They didn't need to say it aloud to know they were on the same page.

Caius Argyros Dermokaites.

* * *

Tiffany yawned and stretched as her eyes flickered open. She blinked away the sleep from her vision and rolled over. Sitting up in bed, she glanced around the bedroom. No Damon. She flopped back into the pillows and let out a long sigh.

Holy smokes, the things they'd done…

A sweet ache pulsed through her core. The slight soreness was just enough to remind her of every move they'd made between the sheets. She'd never thought she would have been capable of anything even close. A small smile crept over her face.

She'd never thought her first time would be with a strong handsome hunter, though if she'd been the kind of girl to daydream of the perfect man, Damon or someone like him—someone like B—would have been the star of her fantasies. The members of the Execution Underground were brave warriors, the soldiers of the supernatural world, and Damon embodied everything the E.U. stood for. He was strong, intelligent, skilled, ruthless and passionate. Wow. She'd never been one for the sappy stuff, but the thought of the night they'd spent together gave her butterflies.

She stood and stripped one of the sheets from the bed. Wrapping it around herself, she padded down the stairs. She went into the laundry room and pulled her clothes from the dryer, checking them over. Still mildly stained with blood. No surprise there, but it would have to do. She dropped the sheet and threw on her clothes before heading into the living room in search of Damon. Who wasn't there, or in the kitchen.

Where the heck was he?

She heard a heavy door closing, and moments later he emerged from the downstairs hallway with a scowl twisting his face.

"Did someone spit in your coffee?" she said.

Without a word, he flopped down onto the sofa and buried his head in his hands.

Tiffany raised a brow. "Okay, then. No 'hope you slept well after that crazy time we had.'" She dropped her hands to her sides with a slight humph. Was she an idiot to expect a little sweetness? Given how tender he'd been earlier...

"Is this city really overrun with supernaturals?" he asked, lifting his head from his hands.

She blinked several times. "What?"

He let out a long breath. "According to H.Q., this city is overrun with supernatural predators. Way more than just vampires. Is that right?"

She nodded. "Yeah, pretty much. Mark never taught me anything about hunting supernaturals other than vamps, though, so I stay clear of the others." She walked to the couch and sat down beside him.

He glanced toward her. "How do you know they're here, then?"

She grinned. "Once you know of the existence of supernaturals, it doesn't take a trained hunter to spot one. You know how it is. It might be a flash of a wolf eye here or there, or just a strange feeling when you encounter someone. I've learned never to ignore my instincts."

A moment of silence passed between them. She waited for him to speak. When he didn't, she finally cleared her throat and asked, "Why does it matter?"

"I need to assemble a division of hunters."

Her eyes widened. "So you mean there's going to be a whole load of you guys here in Rochester now?"

He nodded. "Five others." He got up off the couch and walked across the room. His demeanor matched his distant tone.

She knew he had a lot on his mind, but after last night she…well…she wasn't really sure what she'd expected, but more than this, anyway. Damon's skills between the sheets made the guys in the romance novels she read look like bumbling idiots. But out of bed, cold and distant was his default setting.

"What's so bad about that? About bringing in other hunters?"

Damon ignored her question. "We've got worse things to worry about. The results of the samples I sent to headquarters arrived. The bloodsuckers have some sort of virus they're passing between them. That's what's making them act like zombies and causing their victims to turn so quickly."

Tiffany whistled low and long. "That is *not* good. How are they passing it around?"

He shook his head. "No idea. But it seems the vamps contract the disease at transition. Chances are it started from one vamp who turned someone and continued from there. I don't know how or why, much less how to stop it, but I have to find out."

"If it keeps spreading, won't the entire vampire population be overrun with these freak zombie leeches?"

Again Damon didn't respond. His stare was fixed and distant, and she could tell he was lost in thought. Suddenly he snapped back to attention. "If we find the source of the virus and destroy it, then we can go after all the spawn. We think the current existing vamps can't contract it, since they're already turned. I think one of the old ones is behind this, though—creating an army of monsters to destroy, maybe to gain more power in the vamp world, and make hunting humans easier, as well—and I think I know who it is."

She knew exactly what he was thinking. "If you expect to go into Caius's nest with guns blazing, you're out of your mind." She stood up and walked toward him. "I have a better suggestion." Lingering directly in front of him, she wrapped her arms around his neck, stood on her tiptoes and pulled his head toward her for a kiss. Their tongues swirled together, and immediately heat rushed between her legs. She pulled back. "*I'll* kill Caius."

"Over my rotting corpse." Damon wrapped his arms around her waist and raised a single brow at her. "Did you really think kissing me would get me to agree to that?"

She shrugged. "It was worth a shot."

Damon let out a long sigh. "Tiffany, look—"

"Let me finish," she said, cutting him off. "Whether

you like it or not, I know a lot more about the dynamics of this city's vampire scene than you do. All the local vamps have their heads so far up Caius's ass they might as well take up permanent residence. They'll do anything he asks of them, and they'll kill to protect him."

"Vampires have no loyalty. Why do you think they're so devoted to him?"

She crossed the room again to sit on the sofa. "Caius is a good leader, I'll give him that. He's good at controlling, even other vamps. He's been here only three months when he fled here from New York City, after he killed my brother. Since Club Fantasy was already his, this was a natural place to relocate, I guess. He'd been an absent club owner before that. In only three months, he's taken a disbanded group of rogue-like vamps and changed them into an organized nest. He must have been some sort of Roman version of Charles Manson in his day. He's a manipulative psychopath. He was only second in command when my brother raided his nest in New York City. With the head honcho dead, Caius is the big fish now, and he takes his position very seriously." She shot Damon a pointed look. "With so many vampires in this city, in order to kill Caius you'd have to get him alone, and in order to do *that* you'd need to gain his trust." She pointed to herself. "I've already done that."

He met her stare. "What are you proposing?"

"I'll get back inside Caius's inner circle. I'll make up some excuse for having run last night, and then I'll let you in to help me fight once I have him alone."

Damon shook his head. "Absolutely not."

She placed her hands on her hips. "Do you have a better idea?"

He grunted in exasperation and fixed her with a hard stare. "Why do you keep trying to tempt death?"

She scoffed. "Would you quit with that? Maybe I just want to avenge my brother, all right? How do you know I can't—"

He interrupted her as he walked to her side. "Even if you were completely capable of handling an ancient vampire on your own—" he narrowed his eyes "—which you're not, I still wouldn't want you anywhere near Caius. I don't know what I'd do if you were hurt or if I was unable to protect you." He placed a hand on her cheek. "Don't try to pull the wool over my eyes. You trying to fight a vampire as ancient as Caius is foolish. We both know why you're willing to risk your life. I can see your pain over your brother, and I can't imagine how painful losing your parents to vampires at such a young age was, but there are few things worth throwing your life away over, and your family wouldn't have wanted you to throw it away over them."

Her heart stopped, and her eyes widened. How did he know about…?

She swatted his hand from her face. He froze as she stepped away. "How did you know that?" she rasped. "How did you know my parents were killed by vampires, too?"

He didn't respond.

No. No. It couldn't be.

Damon Brock. Damon *Brock*. The words fell out of her

mouth before she could stop herself. "Has anyone ever called you B?" No. She didn't want to know. She *couldn't* know. It would ruin everything.

Damon flinched as if she'd struck him.

Before she knew what she was doing, she rushed forward and shoved his chest as hard as she could. He didn't even stagger. "Do they call you B?" she yelled.

Tears poured down her face. This wasn't happening. It couldn't. No. She pummeled his chest, but he didn't move, didn't defend himself. "Did *he* call you B?" she screamed.

The muscles in Damon's throat strained as if he could barely choke out the words. "He called me B because my last name is Brock. That's why I signed the letters that way."

All sound, all movement, all feeling…stopped. Her hands shook at her sides, and her heart thumped against her chest, the sound of her own blood throbbing in her ears. Every inch of her body went numb.

Mark had always referred to his partner as B. She never knew it was the letter for a last name. She always assumed it was his first initial.

"B's an amazing fighter, Tiff. I wish you could meet him. I wouldn't trust anyone else to watch my back." He nudged her in the shoulder. *"Good-lookin' guy, too. Maybe you'll find a hunter like him someday and then I won't have to take care of you anymore."* He grinned.

Tiffany rolled her eyes. "Yeah, right. If he's anything like you I'd kick him to the curb."

Mark met her eyes. "Seriously, Tiff. He's a good man."

Mark's voice rang in her ears—the day he'd asked Tiffany to write to B. His fighting partner. The man he'd looked up to when they no longer had a father. Mark had said B had been like an older brother. His best friend.

Something inside Tiffany snapped. No. No. No. No. No. No. She had *not* slept with the man responsible for her brother's death. She *hadn't* lost her virginity to him. She sobbed, sobbed as she hadn't sobbed since she'd buried the last person she ever loved, the last and only person who had ever loved her, only three months earlier.

"How could you abandon him?" She choked on her own tears, barely able to speak. "Why didn't you save him?"

She stumbled backward, and Damon grabbed hold of her wrists, holding her up so she didn't collapse to the floor. Her whole body shook as she looked up at him.

A single tear ran down his cheek, and the pain on his face was staggering.

"No!" She wrenched away from him. How dare he cry on Mark's behalf? As if he hadn't been capable of saving him? "Don't you dare act like you cared about him! He trusted you and you let him down, and now he's dead because of it."

Damon's hands clenched into fists, and his pain was so palpable she felt it in her bones.

Tears continued to roll down her face, drenching her cheeks. "He looked up to you. He loved you, and you let him die in Caius's arms."

Damon's fist collided with the wall so hard plaster fell to the ground, and she felt the force of the blow in her feet.

He threw another punch. Dust flew through the air as he released his rage. Then his head snapped toward her.

"You think I don't blame myself for his death every day?" His ice-blue eyes blazed with anger, pain, sadness, remorse. He strode to her and grabbed her shoulders, staring hard into her gaze. "You think I wouldn't give anything, wouldn't give my own life, to bring him back? Nothing I could *ever* possibly do would be enough to pay for how I failed him. I don't deserve forgiveness, but you *have* to know that I will bear the pain and regret of how I hurt him—" he paused and brushed her cheek, wiping her tears away "—of how I hurt *you,* for the rest of my life."

She sucked in a hard breath. "Why?"

His eyes widened as if he couldn't comprehend what she was saying.

"Tell me why you left him there to die, why you didn't save him."

As if unable to face her a moment longer, he turned away from her.

"Tell me why the valiant, brave, courageous *B* left his partner for dead. Tell me why the man I thought I knew turned out to be a coward."

Damon hung his head, his back still turned toward her. "Because I am not, and never was, any of those things."

She marched up to him and forced him to face her. "Don't evade me. Tell me why, damn it!"

He shook his head. "You don't want to know the details, Tiffany. You—"

She jabbed a finger into his chest. "Don't tell me what

I do and don't want. You don't know me." She pushed at him again. "Tell me."

He cursed under his breath. "Because I let my feelings for the job cloud my judgment. I let my hatred for vampires fuel me and went by the book instead of saving my friend." He ran his fingers through the short stubble of his hair. His jaw clenched as she forced him to remember the moment, remember what he'd done.

"We'd been planning a raid on the nest for months. They'd killed hundreds, that band. We planned everything out, but it all backfired when one of the new hunters-in-training stepped out too early. The vamps rushed us as soon as they knew we were there. Your brother fought hand to hand with Caius. He was a brave man. Then Caius managed to stab him with his own stake. The bastard left him bleeding and ran. I was in pursuit of Caius's elder, the head of the nest. I was right on his heels."

He put his hand over his mouth as if to hold in the words, then dropped it to his side again. "With all the other vampires battling for their lives against other hunters and Caius gone, I knew none of the bloodsuckers would be hungry enough to go after Mark. His wound didn't look deep, and I was so caught up in the fight, in the adrenaline and anger of the chase, that I left him. I followed protocol to kill the vampires instead of saving my partner. I was seeing red. All I could see, all I could hear, all I could think about, was all the dead people I needed to avenge." He let out a long breath. "By the time I finished off the elder and went back for Mark, he was gone. Dead. I tried to save his body, but the vamps had the nest protected with explosives. The building blew up with Mark's body inside. I barely managed to get out alive."

A fresh round of tears streamed down Tiffany's face.

"I was the leader of that raid, and instead of saving my wounded partner, I was too obsessed with making the kill and following orders." Damon's hands curled into fists. "I will never allow my anger, my emotions to get the better of me during a fight again. Ever. And I swore to myself that I wouldn't get close to anyone again, wouldn't make any personal attachments, so I couldn't fail someone, but I failed at that, too." He met her gaze.

"Well, aren't you the good, obedient soldier." Tiffany walked toward the door. She needed out. She needed fresh air to breathe. She needed to be away from him. She placed her hand on the knob and turned the handle. "I hope you enjoyed the kill."

Without another word, she left the apartment, tears still streaming down her face.

Pain stabbed through Damon's heart as if someone had shoved a knife into it and twisted. If words could kill, the pain and sorrow in Tiffany's voice would have destroyed him.

The old feelings of regret rose to their peak. Never had he wished harder that he could have taken Mark's place. That he'd died and Mark had lived. Damon's father had died late in life in the line of duty at an old age, and his mother had passed not even two months later, the grief of her husband's death, of his absence, too much to bear. Both of them had been gone for years, and he'd never had siblings, leaving no one who would have missed him if he'd died in Mark's place. But Tiffany would feel the loneliness from her brother's death for the rest of her life.

And he'd practically stolen her virginity.

Shit.

The pain that had radiated from her floored him. And she still didn't know the worst of it…that Mark had to die again, but this time by Damon's own hand.

It had been a long time since he'd prayed, but it was worth a shot. He wasn't quite sure where to start, so he just closed his eyes. He didn't need any of the formal Catholic rituals he grew up with—he just needed to talk.

"I know I don't deserve it, but I could use some help right about now." He drew in a long breath and waited, expecting no response and receiving exactly that. He hoped for a feeling, just a small indication that someone was out there. Did the Big Man Upstairs even listen to the prayers of a killer?

Damon opened his eyes and let out a long sigh. He stood alone in his apartment, where only a few hours ago he'd autopsied a dead man right on his kitchen counter. And he thought God would want to listen to him? He laughed at his own ignorance before he looked up toward the heavens. "If You're listening, just…just help me make it up to her, all right?" he said into the silence of the apartment.

Then, without even stopping to put on his jacket, he rushed from the apartment and ran after Tiffany.

The cold air of the falling January night nipped at his skin, but it didn't even register in his mind. He needed to find her. He owed it to Mark, and as worthless as he was, the thought of her hurt sent his blood boiling. Nobody would lay a hand on her unless they wanted his knife shoved into their esophagus. *Nothing* would happen to her while he lived and breathed. She was going to get herself killed if she continued going off to fight vampires, but that would *not* happen on his watch.

He jogged for three blocks, eyes constantly scanning the streets for her. Assuming she had a car parked near Club Fantasy, heading toward the club was his best bet. Twenty minutes later, when he still hadn't caught up to her, he sprinted full speed back to the lofts, grabbed his car keys and jacket, and revved up his Z4. She must have taken a cab back to Club Fantasy, which only meant one thing: she was in a hurry…

…because she was going after Caius and she wanted to get to him before morning.

Chapter Eight

Club Fantasy was nearly as dead as the majority of its patrons when Tiffany strode through the front entrance. It was still too early in the evening for all the vamps to be wide-eyed and awake yet. They could survive sunlight, but they sure didn't like it, and it left one hell of a skin rash.

She made her way through the virtually empty club to where Caius normally perched his overly smug self. He wasn't there yet, and she wondered what he was doing before his club's initial rush came in?

Janette, one of Caius's regular Feeds, strolled by, her hips swaying side to side as her bloodred pumps floated across the carpeting. Tiffany tapped her shoulder. The bleached blonde spun around, her face so pale the contrast with her fire-engine red lips was almost frightening. A fresh pair of fang marks were visible just beneath her golden tresses. She looked more like the walking dead than a human.

Then again, to all intents and purposes she *was* the walking dead.

Not much longer and she would be dead from the malnutrition and combined blood loss of being a Host, or—worse—she'd be drained and be a vamp.

Tiffany met the eyes of the grotesque-looking woman. "Do you know where Caius is?"

Janette scanned her, sizing up how much of a threat Tiffany was to her own position in Caius's bed. She must have thought the answer was "not much," because she said, "He's in his office."

"Thanks," Tiffany muttered. She brushed past the woman and hightailed it toward the main office, then skidded to a stop when she was met by a closed door. Caius either wanted privacy as he banged another helpless Host on top his desk or he was meeting with someone.

She pressed her ear against the door and prayed she didn't hear any hot-and-heavy moaning. She could do without those mental images.

"Yes, I'm very pleased with how it's been spreading." Caius's voice was muffled but made it through the door.

Her eyes widened. *Spreading?*

Caius chuckled. "It's becoming quite widespread in Seattle now. I think we're off to a great start. It's moving faster than I expected."

A moment of silence passed. From the one-sided nature of the conversation, she realized he was on the phone.

"Absolutely not. I'll ensure it continues to spread here. No newly transitioned vampire will escape its reach. The hunters won't know what hit them."

Tiffany gaped as she backed away from the door. That son of a bitch. He *was* helping to spread the virus. Anger hit her like a kick to the gut. The cosmos really had it in for her today. First losing her virginity to the man responsible for her brother's death, and now her brother's killer was creating flesh-eating zombies. Just. Friggin'. Peachy.

She cursed under her breath. She'd been foolish to run off. As much as she wanted to hate Damon for what he'd done to her brother, for not saving Mark when he needed it, for what he'd done to *her,* she needed his help to pull this off. An empty feeling balled in her stomach. For a moment, as she'd lain in Damon's arms last night, she'd actually thought she might not be alone anymore. So much for that.

As quickly as she'd come in the front a few minutes earlier, Tiffany rushed out the back entrance of the club. She jumped and pulled her stake as she almost ran head-first into Damon.

Their eyes locked, and a pained look crossed his face. It took everything she had not to brush past him, telling him he could kiss her overly round white ass. Despite everything he'd done, meeting his fiery ice-blue eyes sent shivers down her spine and heat tingling between her legs. She hated herself for it, but her anger at him almost made her want him more.

"What are you doing here?" she snapped, ignoring the

fact that a minute ago she'd been hoping for his help. "Why are you following me?"

He let out a sigh and stepped even closer to her. She stepped back.

"I'm making sure you don't get yourself killed. Nothing is going to happen to you on my watch," he said

"On your watch?" That was it. The hell with his help. "Look, just because I'm not a member of the Execution Underground and I don't have your strength, that doesn't mean I'm not a good hunter. You've seen me in action, so you know I'm good. Now step back and let me handle this myself."

He reached out to touch her cheek, but she turned away. He sighed. "I don't deserve a single ounce of your forgiveness. I know that. But I won't let you out of my sight. I have to protect you. For Mark's sake."

Her hands clenched into fists. If she didn't think his jaw was as rock-hard as the rest of him, she would have punched him right then and there. "For Mark's sake?" Who the hell was he kidding? If he thought she was going to buy into that, he was a few Froot Loops short of a bowl. "Cut the 'I'm sorry' crap, Damon. Sorry doesn't cut it when you're standing right here and Mark's dead."

He winced, and she crossed her arms over her chest, hoping she'd hit him where it hurt.

He lowered his eyes to the ground. "I told you I wish I'd been in his place. I'd give anything to go back in time and fix what I did, to save him, but I can't. I cared for Mark like he was my own brother. I know you don't see that. All you see is the worthless excuse for a hunter who failed his partner, who might as well have killed your brother himself, but I cared for Mark then, and I still do. Allow me to make it up to him, Tiffany. I've never begged for anything, but please, let me do this one thing."

Without a word, she turned on her heel and marched down the alleyway, leaving him in her dust.

Why would she want to grant him closure? A sharp pang hit her heart. Because, despite all he'd done, a small part of her still cared for him, still wanted him. After their night together, she felt as if she'd known him her whole life, and in some ways she had. She'd heard so many stories about him from her brother, exchanged so many letters with him. The courageous, valiant B.

Damon didn't follow her. His feet stayed firmly planted on the cold, wet ground. "I know you want to kill Caius as much as I do."

She stopped in her tracks.

His voice echoed off the walls of the alley. "And we both know you can't do that without me."

If looks could kill, Tiffany's expression would have massacred an army.

She spun around to face him with her lips pursed tight and her eyes blazing. She stomped toward him, her hands balled into fists as she stared him down—sexy and angry as all hell. Despite the negative emotions swarming him, he fought back a smile. He couldn't help it. This felt like a Texas standoff with an angry kitten. But as innocent as she seemed, she was pissed, and that kitten had sharp claws ready to rip him to shreds.

"Who says I need your help to kill Caius?" she demanded.

"Just let me protect you. For Mark's sake. For your sake." And, if he admitted it to himself, for his own selfish reasons, as well. No other woman could make him so angry and so turned on at the same time.

Shit, what was wrong with him? He could *not* continue to think about her like that. Once he'd found out who she was, she hadn't needed to tell him she didn't want him—he already knew. Nevertheless, he wouldn't let Mark down again. Whether Tiffany wanted to admit it or not, she needed protection.

"We work together to kill Caius, then you leave me in peace." She jabbed a finger into his chest. "No following me. No protecting me. None of it."

He let out a long breath. "You'll stop hunting after that?"

Pausing for a moment, she glanced at the night sky, as if she were weighing all the possibilities. Finally she met his gaze again. "Fine. We kill Caius, and then I retire from hunting vamps. I'll leave Rochester's bloodsuckers to you. But if I keep my end of the deal, you agree to leave me alone and never bother me again."

A large lump lodged in his throat. Though it killed him inside, he nodded.

She was right. Once they murdered Caius, Mark's death would be avenged. She could stop hunting vampires, and her life would no longer be in danger. His own next task—

a task she would never know anything about—would be killing Mark again, exactly as Mark had asked him to. After that there would be no way for him to fulfill Mark's wishes and honor his memory besides continuing to be a good hunter. He would never forgive himself for the past, but there would be nothing more he could do, and Tiffany could move on with her life, put him and the entire supernatural world behind her.

It was for the best.

They locked eyes. An emotion he couldn't interpret crossed her face before she quickly looked away.

"All right, then. Let's get this over with as quickly as possible," she said.

Damon suppressed a wince. Yeah, that hurt.

For the best, he repeated silently to himself.

She gestured for him to follow her. "We can't be hanging out in this alley. Show me where you parked the Z4 while I fill you in."

He walked ahead of her, leading the way. "Fill me in?"

"While you were out stalking women fully capable of taking care of themselves…"

Shit. How could she have so much power to hurt him? How the hell had he gotten himself into this damn mess?

"…I was going after Caius."

Damon stopped walking and shot her a glare. "Why do you keep going after Caius alone?"

She frowned. "Because I know he won't hurt me, at least not for now. There's nothing to worry about."

"What do you mean, he won't hurt you *for now?* What

good are you to him if he's not feeding from you? You said you weren't a Host."

She twirled a swath of her perfectly curled hair. "Not exactly."

His eyes widened. "What do you mean 'not exactly'?" The thought of Caius feeding off Tiffany, piercing his filthy fangs into the sweet creamy flesh of her throat, draining her of her life force, shoved him into a state of unparalleled rage. "You let that disgusting bloodsucker feed from you?"

She shot him a pissed-off glare. "Don't insult me. He's never drunk from me and he never will." She paused, as if she wasn't certain she wanted to share. Sucking in a deep breath, she continued. "He *thinks* he'll get to feed from me, but he won't. He wants me as a long-term Host, not a quick feed."

Damon's hands shook at his sides. It would be so easy to lose his temper and release his rage onto one of the brick walls of the alley, but he would *not* forget his head. He'd buried himself in enough emotions for a lifetime, thanks to Tiffany; allowing any more would be a mistake. She didn't want him. She wasn't his to protect. He was protecting her for Mark's sake. Strictly business.

Forcing his breathing to remain even, he spoke through clenched teeth. "How do you know he won't change his mind and drain you immediately, or take you without your consent?"

She stared at the ground, refusing to look at him. "I make sure my iron is high. I'm too valuable in the long-term for him to drain me immediately. As for the lack of consent, that's a risk I'm willing to take."

He pressed his lips together. "I don't think I need to tell you how st—"

Tiffany glared. "Don't call me stupid! I—"

Without thinking, Damon stalked forward and grabbed her hands, pinning her hard against the brick wall. They were nose to nose. "I'm not calling you stupid, but your behavior *is* reckless. Don't try to deny that fact. Now, I'll let you hunt Caius with me, but that doesn't mean I'll allow you to dangle yourself like a piece of succulent meat in front of a ferocious bloodsucking beast. Do you understand?"

She nodded, and he quickly released her. The nearness to her made his stomach churn. It was pure torture, knowing exactly how amazing she felt beneath him, how soft her lips were against his, how sweet she tasted, what a deep and caring heart she had—and knowing he could never have that, never have *her.*

"Caius is the one spreading the virus," she said, breaking the momentary silence. "I don't know how, but I heard him speaking on the phone before I stormed out of the club. He was talking about the virus spreading, and saying that no new vampire would escape its reach."

Damon stood in silence, calculating all his possible moves. As much as he would like to, he couldn't just rush in and kill Caius. If he killed the bastard, which he would, all Caius's loyal vamp friends would swarm him, and even in the unlikely event that he survived, he would be revealed as a hunter in two seconds flat, not to the vamps alone, but to every supernatural in the city. He needed to get Caius alone, where he could destroy him in private. Then he could figure out how to deal with containing the vamp infection without Caius further aiding its progress.

He opened his mouth to speak, but she beat him to it. "You need to get Caius alone, but you're never going to manage that unless I lead him to a secluded spot and you rush in."

Shaking his head, Damon kneaded the base of his neck to ease the tension. "That won't work. What happens if he attacks you during your meeting? I won't be there to see it, and I won't be there to save you."

Tiffany let out a long breath and placed a hand on her hip. "The Execution Underground can equip you with pretty much any electronic device you need, right?"

He raised an eyebrow. He didn't think he liked where she was going with this.

A small smile curved her lips. "Have them make me a panic button. One I can keep somewhere Caius won't see it. Then, if anything happens, I'll hit it. You'll have the receiver and you can trail us, so you'll be able to rush in if I need you."

Narrowing his eyes, Damon analyzed her expression. She couldn't be cocky about this. But from the look on her face, she was serious and focused. It killed him to agree to put her in harm's way for even a moment, but he would be right there to save her. Nothing would happen to her. Nothing.

"I'll set up a meeting with Caius, and then we'll go from there. If all goes well, I'll hit the button when I get him where we want him, danger or not. I'll make sure it's completely private. Somewhere no other vamps should be."

He gave a single nod. She had to know he didn't like it one bit, but they had no other choice.

Whipping out her cell phone, Tiffany pressed the number two and then hit Send.

Damon buried his face in his hands. What in the world would he ever do with her? He sighed. "Tiffany Solow, only you would place an ancient vampire on speed dial."

Chapter Nine

Nothing like a master vampire to go with your brand-new stiletto heels. Tiffany balanced on one lone shoe, her other braced against the Dumpster outside the club. She patted the panic button one more time to make sure it was securely in place before she handed her weapons over to Damon and rearranged her light shawl.

Without a word, they walked to the entrance of the alleyway. Around the corner was the entrance to Château Blanc, the newest restaurant in town. With her budget, she had never eaten there, but she'd heard the place was primo. Thank God Damon—and the E.U.—had loads of cash to buy her a nice dress for the occasion.

"You look ravishing," he whispered from behind her. The heat of his breath on her neck hardened her nipples to taut peaks. Screw him and the sexual dominion he had over her. "But try not to entice the monster too much, okay?"

She inhaled a deep breath, then glanced over her shoulder one last time, expecting to see Damon encouraging her on, but he'd already disappeared into the night. She swallowed the lump in her throat. She felt naked without her weapons hanging by her sides.

Damon was right. Facing a vampire without weapons was light-years different from having a stake at your side. Even if she wanted to, there was nothing she could fight with now. But Caius had never scared her before, and she wasn't about to allow him to scare her now. And all emotions aside, she knew Damon would protect her.

He would be there when she hit the panic button.

She exhaled the breath she didn't realize she'd been holding. There wasn't any time to waste. A master vampire was waiting for her.

She wrapped her shawl more tightly around her shoulders and entered the restaurant. The soft sounds of melodic piano music carried to her ears amidst the murmurs of the demure dining couples. The dim lighting hit her cocktail dress at the perfect angle, and the midnight-blue material glittered like the clear night sky.

Her stomach growled as the smells of lobster bisque, freshly baked bread and fresh herbs filled her nose. For a college student who subsisted on a diet mainly made up PB&J sandwiches, microwave macaroni and cheese, and chicken-flavored ramen noodles, *divine* didn't even begin to cover the nose-gasm she was having.

A handsome restaurant host in a nicely pressed suit cleared his throat. "Are you meeting someone, miss?"

She eyed the layout of the restaurant.

Well, damn.

The only entrance was the door she'd just come through, not even a single emergency exit visible. There had to be a way out, though. The law required it. She searched and saw the Emergency Exit sign right above the kitchen door. Inconvenient, but not worth abandoning the opportunity. Come hell or high water, Damon would figure out how to slip inside the building undetected if necessary.

And where was Caius? She had just started to look for him when the host cleared his throat again. "Miss?"

She snapped to attention. "I'm sorry. Yes, I'm meeting Mr. Dermokai—"

The name hadn't even escaped her lips before the host's eyes widened, and he swept his arm out in a welcoming gesture. "My apologies, madam. Right this way." He hopped to as if someone had lit a fire under his ass and poured gasoline on it. She glided across the restaurant behind him. At least she hoped she was gliding. Heels were not her thing.

Her heart beat hard as the host led her toward the far corner of the restaurant.

Shit.

Privacy was not what she wanted with Caius—at least, not at the moment. She had agreed to have dinner with him before he escorted her to a private location for feeding.

Caius's ill temper and inflated ego needed stroking, and removing himself from the public eye clashed with that deep-seated need. This was not his usual style. She hoped he hadn't sensed something, wasn't intending to change their plans, and she was unable to contact Damon to even give him a heads-up. She focused on the friction of the button strapped to the top of her thigh. She reminded herself that it was a weapon in its own right. All she had to do was hit it.

The host led her to a secluded room, opened the door and ushered her inside.

"Someone will be right with you," the host said before closing the door behind her.

Tiffany's eyes locked with Caius's, and a wide devious grin spread across his face. He was waiting for her at a table set for two, the only table in a room clearly intended to host multiple diners, even large private parties. A pure white cloth was draped across the table, and the lights from a tiered crystal chandelier reflected off the flawless marble flooring.

She was a not-so-helpless romantic, but even if she'd been with someone she *wanted* to be with—she refused to think about the man whose name immediately came to mind—this was a little over the top. Then again, Caius came from an era of overindulgence.

"Good evening." He stood and gestured her forward. "Won't you join me, Tiffany?"

Her gut clenched. She hated the way her name rolled off his tongue with the slightest trace of an accent from thousands of years ago.

She forced a grin across her face. "Gladly."

Crossing the room, she allowed Caius to pull her chair

out for her. She slid onto the comfortable cushions, far from relaxed as he squeezed her shoulder and leaned in to speak. His hot breath brushed against her ear, and goose bumps covered her whole body. The small hairs on the back of her neck stood on end.

"You look good enough to eat," he purred before he returned to his side of the table.

How sweet: a bloodsucker who enjoyed toying with his food. She wanted to roll her eyes. *As if I try to marinate myself to an edible state each day.* The battle between the words that came from her mouth versus what she really thought commenced.

She batted her eyelashes. "I'm glad you're pleased, but I'm nothing compared to how you look. Dashing and handsome." *More like disgusting and vomit-worthy.* "As always."

Caius soaked in the B.S. of her ego stroking as if it were the heat of a rose-scented hot tub on a freezing cold night. "I'm pleased you recognize that."

A moment of silence passed between them. An unreadable smile crossed Caius's face. "Let's eat. Shall we?"

As if on cue, there was a knock at the door, and on Caius's command a waiter entered with two menus in hand. He approached their table with a smile. "Good evening. My name is Joshua, and I'll be taking care of you this evening. May I interest you in something to drink? Perhaps a bottle from our wine list?" He glanced toward Tiffany. Ladies first.

"I'll just have some wat—"

Caius interjected. "If you could bring two wineglasses and a bottle of Pétrus, it would be greatly appreciated."

The waiter nodded. "I'll return in a moment to take your ord—"

Eyes locked on Tiffany, Caius held up his hand. "I think we're ready to order now."

Joshua paused midstride and returned to the table.

Tiffany blinked. *Control freak much?* "I haven't looked at the menu yet," she said.

Caius reached across the table and placed a hand over hers. "Trust me. You'll love this." Releasing her hand, he unfolded his napkin as he spoke. "We'll have a starter of spinach and sea-urchin ravioli in a white-wine reggiano broth, and chèvre-stuffed smoked dates wrapped in pro-sciutto with aged balsamic saba on a bed of arugula. For our meal we'll have fresh herb-crusted Kobe filet mignon, cooked rare, and Maine crab cakes with a micro-green and lobster remoulade served on a plate of pure pink Hima-layan sea salt, and the apricot crème brûlée for dessert."

Joshua's eyes grew to the size of saucers as he scram-bled to write down every detail of the order. Scribbling on his notepad, he nodded vigorously. "Right away, sir." He rushed out of the room to fill their order.

Tiffany removed her napkin from the table and unfolded it across her lap. "You really know how to order your food. Very specific."

Caius ran his fingers through his golden-blond hair. If she hadn't known he was a vampire and a major douchebag to boot, maybe she could have found him handsome—at least before she'd met a certain dark-haired vampire hunter.

"I make it a habit to eat nothing but the finest foods." He grinned. "You only live once."

Tiffany swallowed hard and fought not to clench her hands into fists, ready to protect herself. Was that statement intended to be as threatening as she thought? She returned his smile. "I suppose that's true."

Joshua returned with a bottle of wine, opened it tableside and gave Caius a sip to taste, then poured the red liquid into two sparkling glasses. "Your appetizers will be out shortly." He removed the extra plates from the table before exiting.

Tiffany sipped her glass of Bordeaux. The wine slid down her throat, already warming her cheeks. "Very nice. It has quite a complex flavor to it."

Caius smiled and sipped from his own glass. "Let's get to the point, shall we? We both know what we're here to discuss."

She nearly spat the wine back into the glass. Shit. This was happening much more quickly than she'd expected.

He inhaled deeply. "I can tell by your scent that you'll be a perfect Host. My main Feed." He ran his tongue over his teeth, and she prayed his fangs stayed in place. Leaning back in his seat, he fixed his ice-cold stare on her. "You'll reap all the benefits, of course. I hear the human sensation as we feed is phenomenal."

She nearly choked on her own tongue, then reminded

herself that no fangs would mar her throat. Never. As for phenomenal… Yeah, right. Maybe if you were into pain.

She ran her hand over her thigh, reminding herself of the panic button. And she would wager that the flatware lying before her was at least part silver—an extra protection. Once it penetrated the skin, silver was like acid to a vampire's insides. Her hand itched to hold her stake. When it was strapped to her side, she felt power surging through her in the face of vampires.

Now, she wasn't as certain.

Joshua and a second waiter paraded into the room, balancing their starter plates on trays. Fast service. One of many bonuses of shelling out ridiculous amounts of money for a meal.

They set down the plates in front of Tiffany and Caius. Joshua flashed a respectful smile. "We hope everything is to your liking." Then he and his shadow exited.

Tiffany eyed the plate before her. Artistic foodie explosion or delicious high-class meal? She wasn't quite sure which, but the overcompensating extravagance was certain.

Caius leaned forward in his seat and fixed his stare on her. "Where did I leave off?" He paused, then, grinning, pushed his seat away from the table. "Ah, yes, the advantages." He stood and crossed to her side of the table, looming behind her. "As I said, you'll reap every benefit. I'll make sure you have the finest of everything, and, of course, there are always—" he squeezed her shoulders and whispered in her ear "—the sexual benefits."

She froze beneath his touch. Her mouth went dry, and

sweat gathered on her palms. "In other words, I'll be your high-end call girl." She slid away from his hold and rose from her chair to face him.

The ancient vampire frowned. "Call it what you like, but I assure you that you will be receiving the better end of the deal."

He leaned closer, and a feeling of dread crashed hard in her chest, turning her breathing labored. This was going south, and fast. She wouldn't show her fear, but she wouldn't allow him to have any more of a physical advantage, either.

She held her voice steady. "What exactly would those benefits be?"

He stepped closer, and she took a matching step back. Slowly, they circled the table, and the frown on Caius's face became a smile. He thought she was being playful, she realized. Better that than have him realize what she was really being.

"You're the one who asked me to meet you tonight, Tiffany, so don't play coy. You know *exactly* what those benefits are. Don't you?" His gaze narrowed, staggering in its intensity.

She glanced at the floor and up again, praying she looked flirtatious instead of terrified. "I'm really not sure. You may have to spell things out for—"

Before she knew what was going on, Caius had pinned her between her chair and his body. He moved so fast she barely saw him.

He grasped her throat. With one squeeze, he could crush

her windpipe. "Don't get cute with me," he snapped. "We both know what I want, and I intend to get it whether you're willing or not."

Her eyes widened. Heat rushed to her face as she fought to breathe. She strained for the panic button and gasped for air as Caius's grip tightened. With the tiniest snap, his fangs descended. His canines glistened in the light of the chandelier. He reared his head and prepared to sink his fangs into the delicate skin of her throat.

Damon stormed through the kitchen, shoving his way into the restaurant. The smells of simmering white wine and melted cheeses invaded his nose. Shouts echoed behind him. An angry cook yelled as he passed, "You can't come in here!"

Not a surprising reaction to a man in a ski mask. He ignored them all and kept going.

At the sight of him, a woman in his path spilled a large vat of what appeared to be pea soup. The liquid splashed over the steel toes of his boots.

But he didn't care—nothing would stop him from finding Tiffany. When he heard the panic button sound, her safety became his sole mission.

He burst into the restaurant. His eyes darted across the room. Shit. Where was she? His line of vision followed a waiter as he walked past a back hallway. She had to be in a private room. Damon slipped through the crowded room as fast as he could, before he bolted down the hallway. A faint whimpering sound carried through the only door. Something inside him snapped.

Pulling his gun from his belt, he wrenched the door open, stepped to the side and aimed, making sure Tiffany wasn't in the line of fire. He squeezed the trigger. The mix of music and voices from the main dining room drowned out the muffled shot. Silencers were a hunter's blessing.

Caius's body jolted before he spun to face Damon. Tiffany fell to the floor, gasping for air. A small trickle of blood ran down her neck from where Caius's fingernails had dug into her skin as he choked her. Rage coursed through Damon at the sight. A loud snarl ripped from his throat. Caius would die.

He fired another shot straight into the ancient bloodsucker's chest, blowing a massive hole in Caius's body, but at Caius's age, the skin and organs knitted together again in seconds. Damon tucked his gun away, and ripped a silver dagger and his wooden stake from his jacket.

Fangs already down, Caius hissed, and the two of them charged each other. They collided at full speed, meeting each other blow for blow. A normal man stood no chance against a vampire as old as Caius, but gifted with the speed and strength of his Execution Underground training, Damon held his own. Anger and rage fueled his every move.

No vampire hurt Tiffany and lived. None.

Raising his dagger overhead, Damon slashed the knife across Caius's face. The leech hissed in pain. Blood gushed down his cheeks, and the wound smoked as if Damon had poured acid into it, but that didn't deter Caius. He blocked the swing of Damon's stake and punched Damon in the solar plexus. Gasping for air, Damon rushed the vampire, hitting him straight in the midsection. They toppled to the ground. Caius grabbed for Damon's stake, but Damon held tight. No way in hell was that vamp getting it.

Rolling his body overtop Caius, Damon plunged his knife downward and nicked Caius's arm, but the vampire managed to roll out of his grasp. Caius jumped to his feet and gripped Damon's throat, lifting him into the air. Damon was over six feet, but Caius dangled him above the ground.

Tiffany screamed. Shit. She was unarmed.

She lunged for a piece of flatware.

Damon gaped. "Tiff—" he choked out.

With both hands, she jabbed a fork into the back of Caius's neck, and he whipped his head around to address the distraction. Exactly the opportunity Damon needed.

He twisted and kicked his foot straight into Caius's gut. Caius's grip faltered. Seizing the vampire's arm, Damon drove the blade of his silver dagger straight through the bone. A loud roar ripped through the empty room, Caius grasped at the dagger, pulling the blade out so his wound could heal. Blood spurted from his forearm as he threw the blade with expert precision straight into Damon's shoulder.

Pain exploded through Damon's flesh, and adrenaline raced through him. He fell to his knees. Warm blood gushed down his chest, and he faintly registered the sound of Tiffany yelling his name. Clutching the dagger by the hilt, he ripped the blade from his wound. His vision spun from the pain, but he would *not* falter.

A fresh wave of adrenaline-fueled energy pumped into his veins. Caius rushed forward, but Damon swept the vampire's legs out from under him. The bloodsucker toppled over, and they rolled in a heap on the ground, both fighting to gain the upper hand. Caius's fist slammed into Damon's face.

Damon hit the bastard with an uppercut to the jaw, sending him flying backward. Caius scrambled across the floor as Damon jumped to his feet. Using every ounce of strength he possessed, he gripped Caius by the throat, lifting him into the air and slamming him down onto the dinner table. Shattered plate shards flew through the air.

Damon lifted his stake over his head, then brought the wood down. Caius clamped both hands around Damon's wrist, struggling to hold off death. Blood dripped across Caius from Damon's injured shoulder, but Damon fought through the pain.

The image of Mark's face contorted with pain flashed through his mind. This leech had killed his fellow hunter, his closest friend. The filthy beast lying beneath him had robbed Tiffany of her brother.

He would pay. He *would* die.

Damon shook as he shoved against Caius. Losing blood, and fast, he felt the wooden stake being raised as Caius gained the upper hand.

No.

Damon's vision blurred. Blood spurted from his wound,

and he felt the color drain from his face, but he refused to give in.

Caius. Would. Die.

He released one of his hands from the stake and saw Caius grin. The dumbass thought Damon was losing the fight. No chance in hell. With his free hand Damon pulled his gun from his belt. A bullet to the chest wouldn't deter Caius, but he knew what would. Looking up, he aimed his gun straight for the fragile hook that held the chandelier in place. He squeezed the trigger.

The bullet blasted into the plaster of the ceiling, and the chandelier teetered before plunging toward the ground. Damon jumped back. The gold bars and crystals of the chandelier exploded on top of Caius's body.

Writhing beneath them, Caius squirmed to release himself from their weight.

Now.

A loud battle cry ripped from Damon's throat. Running forward, he lifted his weapon over his head and stabbed the stake straight through Caius's heart.

The ancient vampire burst to pieces. Blood splattered in all directions, coating Damon in the thick crimson liquid.

"Damon!" Tiffany ran to his side.

Damon crumpled to his knees, wiping the blood off his face. Tiffany fell to her own knees beside him. Specks of blood covered her face and her sparkling dress. Dots of black clouded his vision. Tiffany examined his wound.

"Shit." She pressed her hand onto the hole to gauge its depth. He let out a low hiss from the pain.

She grabbed her now blood-covered shawl from the chair and wrapped the material tight around his shoulder to slow the bleeding. Man, she looked like an angel as she cared for him. His heart thudded against his rib cage. He couldn't be sure whether it was Tiffany or the blood he'd lost that was making him delirious.

"Damon, we have to get out of here. All you have to do is make it to the car. All right?"

He clenched his teeth and nodded. With her help, he stumbled to his feet and hobbled from the room as fast as he could, though he was teetering on the brink of passing out. Loud gasps and shrieks filled the restaurant as Tiffany led him out the front door, holding his arm around her shoulder to help steady him.

The sweet smells of food faded from his nose, and the fresh air of the cold Rochester night blasted him in the face. He coughed, fighting to breathe. "S-s-sorry I ruined your dinner." He was trying to joke even as his vision spun. He wanted to be strong for her, show her it was okay.

Tiffany joked back. "Oh, yeah, I was really looking forward to some of that pink Himalayan crap." She forced a small smile.

But hard as she tried, even in his fading consciousness, she couldn't fool him. Her eyes told him everything. He knew how she felt…and she was terrified.

Chapter Ten

A large mountain of sailor-level profanities wouldn't have been enough to express the deep shit Tiffany was in. Damon slumped against her shoulders more heavily each minute, quickly losing blood. He needed to get to a hospital as soon as possible. The bleeding wasn't slowing, despite the makeshift pressure bandage she'd placed on it.

As if that wasn't enough, pure horror clutched her hard as she stared at the familiar face looking at her from inside Caius's Bugatti Veyron, the metallic finish of the limited edition Pur Sang glaring beneath the orange streetlights. Damn it all to hell.

Caius had brought his vampire chauffeur.

Carl looked at her and Damon, taking in all the blood. His eyes widened, and she could practically see the light-bulb flicker on inside his head. Once an average man who'd served as Caius's Host back in N.Y.C., Carl flashed his elongated fangs. He'd been a vampire for two years, and there was nothing average about him any longer. A fiery blaze lit behind his eyes. His master was dead, and he knew it.

If Carl reported Caius's murder to the local nest, the death would infuriate the local vamps. With every vampire in the city on their tail, Tiffany and Damon would be dead within hours. And apparently Carl knew that, as well, because he ripped his gaze away from them and shifted the Bugatti into Drive.

Shit.

Damon groaned and swayed, barely holding himself upright as Tiffany released his weight. Pushing aside his leather trench coat, she snatched the Desert Eagle and her stake from his belt. She wasn't bad with guns, but she sure as hell wasn't a sharpshooter.

Still, she had to try.

Carefully but quickly aiming, she shot at the passenger-side rear tire. Her bullet hit the diamond-cut finish of the hubcap and ricocheted

Damn.

She squeezed the trigger again, hitting closer to the hubcap.

Come on, just a little closer.

She held her arms steady as the Bugatti rounded a corner.

Last chance.

One eye closed for a more accurate aim, she pulled the trigger for a third time.

The rear tire of the Bugatti exploded. Rubber flew in all directions. The awful scrape of metal against concrete hit her ears, more nerve-racking than nails on a chalkboard. She gripped Damon's elbow and pulled him forward.

"Come on, Damon. You have to run."

She kicked off her heels and bolted full speed toward the damaged car. Like a champ, Damon jogged behind her despite his bleeding wound. Carl threw open the door, briefly locked eyes with her then ran full speed down the nearest alley. A grin crossed Tiffany's face. He was fast, but not fast enough. He might be strong compared to what he'd been like as a human, but he wasn't nearly as strong and fast as an ancient master like Caius. Having been the star of her high school track team never failed to be useful when hunting.

A loud groan echoed from behind her. She glanced over her shoulder and saw Damon crumple to his knees. All the color had drained from his face, leaving his lips a pale white. He gasped for air. Tiffany skidded to a stop. Should she give up the chase?

The image of the victims' mauled flesh seared its way to the surface of her mind. If she didn't stop Carl, the news of Caius's death would race through Rochester like wildfire, and there would be no way in hell she and Damon could ever destroy the viral bloodsuckers before the virus spread out of control.

Damon was a hunter, a member of the Execution Underground. His wounds would heal.

She ran after Carl.

Bursting into the alley, she spotted the vamp racing along the far side, in the shadow of an office building. She launched herself into a full-on sprint. The muscles of her legs burned in protest, and the freezing concrete tore through the bottoms of her feet.

But she had an advantage: Carl didn't think she could take him.

When the leech reached the end of the alley, instead of rounding the corner onto the next block, he halted. Spinning to face her, he bared his fangs and hissed. The bastard was fooling himself if he thought she was scared. Two minutes of sitting with Caius across the dinner table was scarier than this guy threatening to kill her. The man couldn't weigh more than one-seventy soaking wet. It wasn't him she was scared of, it was what his words could do.

Before she stopped running, the vampire lunged. He knocked her to the ground, snapping viciously at her neck as he writhed on top of her. Really? That was all he could do?

She jammed her elbow upward and clocked him straight in the jaw. His head flew backward, and before he could return to attack she pulled the Desert Eagle and fired a shot straight into his forehead. The kick from the larger-than-average gun slammed her shoulder against the pavement. The wind rushed from her lungs. That was going to hurt in the morning. The monster screamed, falling onto the ground in pain as blood and brain fluid seeped from his head. Though the wound sealed itself within seconds, he clearly wasn't used to being shot in the head.

Wimp.

As he clutched his healing skull, she threw her body weight forward and landed on top of him, her stake held tight. He gripped her neck, cutting off her breath and holding her off him, but not before she positioned the stake between her breasts. With all the strength she possessed, she contracted her abs and shoved the weight of her chest downward. The sharp end of the stake pierced his skin and into his flesh.

He released her throat and grabbed her shoulders in an attempt to push her off, but it was too late. One more good shove and her weapon sank through to his heart. His undead body shattered in a burst of blood, and she flopped onto the concrete. Her elbows scraped the asphalt, and fresh blood coated her hair, face and dress.

For a moment she lay sprawled on the pavement. She squeezed her eyes shut. Her heart thumped, and she felt a slight soreness in her chest where she'd braced her weapon as she stabbed Carl. There was sure to be one hell of a bruise there later. The skin of her elbows burned, and she let out a small groan.

Her lids shot open.

Damon.

She scrambled up from the pavement and ran back down the alley. A small cry ripped from her lips as she rounded the corner. Damon was lying on the cold winter ground, unmoving. She rushed to his side. Her heart stopped, and bile rose in the back of her throat. She couldn't tell if he was even breathing.

Dislodging his arm from beneath the dead weight of his body, she fingered his wrist, searching for a pulse. A faint beat still remained, though she could tell it was quickly fading.

Somewhere in her mind, she was vaguely aware of the sound of her own screaming as she pulled his phone from his pocket and dialed 911. She tried desperately to lift him. They needed to get out of there so the cops, who were surely headed to the restaurant already, couldn't find them. All she needed was an ambulance. Tears streamed down her face, clouding her vision. She couldn't think straight. Only one thought held firm in her mind.

She'd left B to die....

An incessant beeping noise echoed in Damon's ears. It sounded in rhythm with every thump of his heart. The pounding in his head matched his pulse.

Man, he felt like shit.

A blinding light hovered overhead, but his vision was so blurred that he couldn't tell what it was. He squeezed his eyes shut. It felt as if there was tubing in his nostrils. Though his arm weighed a thousand pounds, or at least it felt like it, he gripped the thin tube and ripped it away from his face.

"Damon, no!" a panicked voice cried.

The smell of antiseptic assaulted his nose. It smelled as nasty as a...

His eyes shot opened, and he frantically scanned the hospital room. He was wearing an awful white hospital gown, barely long enough to cover his upper thighs. Before he could say anything, the smell of Tiffany's sweet vanilla perfume wafted into his nose and her arms were wrapped around his neck. The smell was comforting, bringing to mind memories of the perfume-scented letters she used to send him.

Her body shook as she cried into his shoulder.

He blinked, taking it all in, before he gripped her by the waist and dragged her from the chair beside him onto the bed. She sat next to him, tears filling her honey-colored eyes.

"What in blazing hell is going on?"

Her lip trembled before she burst into another round of tears.

Damn it.

Pulling her into his arms, he cradled her against his chest. Though she'd obviously washed herself off, her gown was crusted with blood, but damn, the slinky thing still looked good on her. "Shh. Shh. Stop with the waterworks and tell me what happened."

She let out one last sniffle and sat up again.

"Are you all right?" he said.

She stared at him for a long moment, then blurted out, "I almost killed you."

He stared at her as if she'd grown six heads. "What do you mean, you almost killed me?"

He racked his brain, but the last thing he remembered was the pain of his knees hitting the restaurant's marble floor after he'd killed Caius.

He'd killed Caius.

If he hadn't been lying in a hospital bed, he might have done a victory dance. Hell, yes. The bloodsucking bastard was dead.

Tiffany wiped her eyes. "After you killed Caius, you'd lost so much blood. I managed to get you out of the restaurant, but then Carl was there."

"Who the hell is Carl?"

"He is—was—a vampire. He was Caius's chauffeur."

"What kind of a vampire name is Carl?" Damon scoffed. He tugged the edges of the hospital gown to make certain he didn't expose the family jewels for all the world to see. Not that he minded the gorgeous woman next to him getting a full-frontal view.

She gaped. "Who cares how stupid a vampire name Carl is? You almost died!"

Given the pounding in his head, Damon didn't feel in the mood to bicker. "But I'm not dead, so that's all that matters."

Swearing under her breath, Tiffany stood and paced to the other side of the room. Immediately, he wished she hadn't. The warmth she'd provided slipped away fast, replaced by the coldness of her absence. Why did she have to be so stubborn? He wanted her with him.

He grumbled, "If you want to make up for almost killing me, get back over here where you belong and lie down with me."

Her whole body stiffened, but she crossed the room and sat back down on the bed. Before she could protest, he lifted her legs onto the mattress and tucked her against his side. She nestled there as if they did this every night. Though he knew he would never have that, at that moment he couldn't bring himself to care.

"I think that's the morphine talking," she whispered. The heat of her breath brushed over his chest like a soft caress.

Morphine? So that was what was giving him that relaxed feeling.

"Nope, it's that dress. You're lucky every man in this place hasn't come on to you. *I'm* too much of a gentleman for that."

She giggled, and the swell of her full breasts pushed against his side. Oh, shit. He yanked the covers up to his waist. Whoever thought flimsy hospital gowns were a good idea needed a strong kick in the ass.

"Back to Carl," Tiffany said. "He would have ratted us out. Every vamp in Rochester would have known we were responsible for Caius's death, and then, even if we managed to survive, we never would have been able to stop the virus and the murders. I couldn't let that happen. I was so focused on stopping him that I chased him and left you behind. I staked him, but then, when I came back for you, your heart was barely beating and I had to call an ambulance."

She twirled a single finger to indicate the room around them. "That's how we ended up here." She let out a long sigh. "I thought you would heal quickly—you know, with all the extra Execution Underground abilities—but you didn't. Joseph said when Caius stabbed you he nicked your brachial artery, which is why you lost so much blood."

Damon mulled over the current situation. Him in a hospital with all his extra abilities was *not* good, and that begged the question how Tiffany had explained his injuries, not to mention what she would do about any fallout from what had happened at the restaurant. But most importantly… "Who is Joseph?"

"A guy I knew in undergrad. He's a couple of years older, so he's already doing his residency. He's kind of sweet on me."

Damon frowned. It didn't matter whether or not she was his, whether or not she still hated him for what he'd done to Mark, he didn't want any other man looking at her. He eyed the way she was nuzzling into him. Did she still hate him? He shook his head. The morphine must have hit him harder than he'd thought if he imagined she would ever forgive him for what he'd done.

"Don't worry," she said. "I told him we were mugged, but I asked him not to call the cops until you woke up. I figured if the cops showed, you'd know how to handle them, but I think we might be able to slip out of here unnoticed before they arrive. I don't think Joseph bought the mugging explanation for a second, but he's eager to please me. Plus, I offered him five hundred bucks to keep his mouth shut."

Damon rubbed the base of his neck to ease the tension. "Where are you going to get that kind of money?"

Shrinking in on herself, Tiffany looked away from him. She was flat broke, and he knew it from the way she'd talked in her letters. Now, with Mark dead, all she was living off of was Mark's E.U. accidental death insurance.

She bit her lower lip. "Well…I figured you would pay for it."

He chuckled. "I suppose I can file for reimbursement with the E.U. I'll make sure to list it under bribery."

She frowned. "I was trying to help. If I hadn't brought you here, you would have died. But then…it was my fault you were almost dead to begin with."

He lifted her chin with two fingers. "As you said, if you hadn't brought me here I'd be dead, so I'm thankful for that. The E.U. will pay for your friend's silence *and* the hospital bills. Not much to worry about." He paused. "Aside from getting me out of this hellhole."

She smacked herself in the forehead. "Oh! I forgot you told me you hate hospitals." She scrambled off the bed and pulled out his clothes from the small closet. "I made sure the EMTs didn't cut them off you." She tossed the clothes to him.

"Thanks."

She glanced at the floor, refusing to meet his eyes. "You're welcome."

She wouldn't meet his gaze. What was that all about? He could tell she was upset, but he wasn't sure why, and he wasn't sure how to ask, either. Had he done something awful in his sleep?

He swung his legs off the bed and stood. An IV dangled from his arm. Ugh. There was nothing worse than the poking and prodding of annoying hospital staff. Without flinching, he pulled out the needle. When he faced front again, Tiffany stood in silence, staring at him as he untied the back of his robe.

A sly grin snaked across his face. "Admiring the show?"

Her embarrassed grin coupled with her deep blush was priceless. Her voice came out in a near squeak. "Sorry." She turned in the opposite direction.

He dropped the hospital robe and examined the bandage across his shoulder. The wound beneath it was probably healing over already. With the extra help from the hospital to keep him breathing, a nick in his artery felt like nothing.

He pulled on his jeans. "You can turn around now. I'm dressed."

Tiffany faced him, and her blush deepened at the sight of his bare chest. "I thought you said you were dressed?"

"Tiff, you've seen a *lot* more of me than this."

She bit her lower lip and stared at the floor again. "I know."

As he pulled on his shirt, he eyed the beautiful woman in front of him. "Do I look anything like you imagined?"

Her head shot up, and she gaped. "Who said I ever imagined you?"

Damon rolled his eyes. "Come on, Tiff. You wrote to me for years. You're telling me you never once wondered what I looked like?"

She shrugged. "Yeah, I guess I imagined a few times."

"And…?"

She shook her head, flustered. "I don't know. I guess

I imagined you shorter and with more hair. But I was wrong—wrong in a good way."

He would chop off part of his legs and grow his hair longer if it pleased her. That was the sort of thing he used to say in his letters. As far back as he could remember, he'd always been a quiet person. But over time, when he'd written to Tiffany, he'd begun to confess things to her, to speak to her in ways he'd never spoken to anyone else. In ways he now knew he couldn't speak to her in person. With the morphine no longer dulling his pain and with all that had happened between them…how could he be the man she'd once cared for when he no longer had her faith to support him?

"What about you?" she asked, interrupting his thoughts. "Am I anything like you imagined?"

In his head, he told her she was more gorgeous than he could possibly have imagined, that the soft curls of her hair and the honey color of her eyes rivaled the divine, that when she smiled it was like God raining down blessings from heaven. And on a sexual level? Sir Mix-a-Lot would've drooled over her backside, and he himself would love to hold those sweet cheeks all night long and grab on to them while he—

"Well?"

"I had a vague idea what you looked like. Mark showed me a picture from when you were seventeen."

Tiffany looked as if she were about to be hit by an on-coming train. "Oh, man. You don't mean the one where I'm wearing the Gru—"

"Grumpy Bear Care Bear T-shirt," he finished.

She stuck out her lower lip in a pout. "If Mark were here, I'd smack him upside the head for showing you that. What an awful photo."

He chuckled. "I never thought you looked bad." If he was honest with himself, at twenty-five, when he'd first eyed that picture, the only thought that crossed his mind was that she was total jail-bait. Seventeen-year-old him would have tapped that for sure.

Of course, an overwhelming urge to pound his own head against a wall had immediately hit him. Even back then, he'd hated himself for thinking about Mark's sister that way.

Tiffany stared around the room, as if she were too uncomfortable to meet his eyes. "So Caius is dead." She met his gaze at last, and something flickered behind her amber irises, something he couldn't identify. "I guess it's time for you to take me home, then. No more stalking me."

Damon's fingers clenched into fists, and he struggled not to throw whatever object was in reach. Why the hell had he ever promised to leave her alone?

Because she's giving up hunting, and because she doesn't want you in her life.

Her safety and her happiness, that was why.

He gave a single nod. "I'll take you home."

Chapter Eleven

Damon trudged up the stairs of the apartment building, following Tiffany. Though Caius was dead and Mark's death avenged, his stomach twisted into knots, dreading what lay before him. Damned if he hadn't sent himself to hell…

He swallowed hard, lifting one foot in front of the other, trying to act as if his one chance at happiness wasn't about to walk right out of his life. His heart pounded in his ears. Whoever the hell had come up with the bright idea that traumatic moments moved in slow motion could eat one of his fists. He would rather climb this stairway for eternity than face the next step—and, man, the climb was going fast.

Their goodbye had only lasted this long because he'd insisted on seeing her to her door.

They reached the final landing. She crossed to lucky

apartment number seven. No, there was nothing even remotely lucky about that number. It would be the last trace he would see of her once she closed—or, more likely, slammed—the door in his face. She seemed all too eager to get this over with.

Pulling her keys from her purse, she reached for the knob before turning toward him. "This is it," she said. "Are you satisfied now?"

He bit his lower lip. Hell, no. He would never be satisfied until she was his, until he knew that every morning when he woke up she would be lying right by his side, her face as peaceful and gorgeous as it had been during their night together.

The night she'd given him her virginity.

He wanted to tell her that, no, he *wasn't* satisfied. He wanted to tell her that she needed to be at his side. A sharp pang hit his heart, but he nodded to say that, yes, he was satisfied.

It couldn't have been further from the truth.

How could he have let this happen to him? How could he have fallen so hard? The thought of her staying with him sent pulses of ecstasy and elation beating through him. But as he stared at her beautiful face, knowing he would never see it again, all he felt was pain the likes of which he'd never known before.

He would willingly have suffered death a thousand times over rather than see her walk away from him.

She let out a long sigh. "I never thought I'd be saying this to the man I thought was responsible for Mark's death,

but thank you. Thank you for helping me to kill Caius."
She flashed him a weak smile. "I know it's probably not
much consolation, but after what happened in the alleyway,
when I left you behind, I understood why you left Mark.
I got caught up in the hunt exactly like you did, and if I'd
been in your place the night Mark died, I can't say I would
have done any differently."

Damon exhaled a long breath. He wasn't sure what to
say. All he managed to choke out was, "Thanks for telling me that."

Another weak smile crossed her full lips. Then she slid
her key into the doorknob and twisted until it unlocked.

His mind raced, and every function in his body seemed
to shut down and come alive all at the same time. Was he
really going to let her walk away?

Say something, asshole!

Finally he forced her name out. "Tiffany?"

Turning toward him, she met his gaze, a slight look of
happiness and hope in her sparkling honey eyes. "Yeah?"

*Say something. Say something. Say something—any-
thing.* "Uh…you should get a stronger lock than that. I'll
send someone over to install some extra enforcement.
Don't worry about the cost, it's on me."

Fuck! That was all he could say?

Within an instant the spark in her eyes faded. "Oh,
okay." Pausing, she met his eyes one last time. "Well,
thanks again. Good luck with your hunting. I trust you'll
destroy all the viral vamps." She turned away from him
and opened the door.

He was a weak man. The woman he loved, his one chance at happiness, was about to leave him and he was going to let her. His heart stopped.

The woman he loved... His breath caught. Did he really love her?

Who was he kidding?

Stepping over the threshold, she began to pull the door closed behind her.

He raced across the hall and pushed through the doorway.

Tiffany spun around. "Da—"

Lifting her into his arms, he kissed her before she could utter another syllable. Her tongue met his, and they crashed together hard as he held her in his arms. Her hands snaked over his shoulders. Her touch sent pulses of energy through him. His body stiffened to attention and pushed against her soft stomach as he pressed her against him.

Quickly, he slammed the door behind them and pushed her up against the door frame. She gasped as he lifted her and wrapped her legs around his hips. He longed to feel her hot and tight around him. She was beautiful. She was intelligent. She was driven, kind, forgiving—and he couldn't think of a single reason not to love her. Never before had any woman driven him to his knees, but he would willingly have begged her not to leave if he'd had to. Nothing could keep her from him.

He shoved his hips harder against hers, and she let out a small cry. Her lips brushed against his before he pulled his mouth away from hers to trail soft but desperate kisses across her collarbone. A moan escaped her lips. The delicious scent of her warm vanilla and cinnamon-scented skin filled his nose, and she tasted just as sweet.

He kissed her neck one last time before whispering softly against her lips, "You didn't think I'd let you walk away that easily, did you?" Cupping her cheek with one hand, he captured her lips again.

Several small tears trailed down her cheeks, and he prayed they were happy ones. He pulled away and whispered in her ear again. "Will you let me make love to you?"

She nodded, and a rush of adrenaline flooded every inch of his body. She giggled softly as he carried her toward the bedroom. A more angelic noise had never graced his ears.

Walking into Tiffany's bedroom was like stepping back into a dorm. Then again, despite all her maturity, she *was* still a college student. He chuckled as he laid her down on her pale green comforter. From the brightly colored lamp shades lined with small fake crystals to the bookcases stocked with textbooks to the fluffy white carpet beneath his boots, Tiffany's room shouted her spirit from the hilltops.

Damn.

He was pushing thirty, and here he was with his best friend's baby sister. He stared down at her. The swell of her ample breasts lifted with her quick breaths. He ran his hand over the soft curve of her hips, admiring every feminine detail. For someone who tried so hard to appear tough and callous, beneath the surface she was anything but. And right now she was staring up at him with pure sexual hunger.

Without a word, he dragged her dress off over her head, unhooked her bra with one hand and drew the pink tip of one nipple into his mouth. She moaned beneath him as he teased her breasts with his mouth and hands. She rocked her hips against his, eager for him to take her.

He released her from his grasp and stood before her. He shrugged his coat off and threw it onto the nearby desk chair before kicking off his boots. She pulled herself up and knelt on the bed in front of him, then toyed with the hem of his shirt before slowly lifting it over his head. She tossed it to the side and unbuttoned his jeans.

Pausing, she leaned her head back and gazed into his eyes. She wrapped her arms around him, hugging his middle. "My heroic B." A small smile crossed her lips. Then she unzipped his pants and thrust them down around his ankles.

He was on top of her within seconds, straining with need as he positioned himself outside her entrance. She was already so wet for him.

She ran her fingers over his naked chest, then wrapped her arms and legs around him. "You have no idea how many times I dreamed of this," she whispered.

A lump filled Tiffany's throat, and she fought back tears. She hadn't exaggerated. She'd dreamed of lying beneath B, beneath Damon, countless times. He was even more handsome, even more incredible, than she had imagined. A shiver ran down her spine.

Their first time turned out to be nothing compared to the intimacy she discovered in his touch now. She didn't wish it any different. This time there would be no pain, no fear or reluctance.

In one quick push, he penetrated her. Her warmth wrapped around him as he slid deep inside. He filled every inch of her core, and she cried out. With strong but sensitive movements, he thrust into her, the rhythm sending waves of pleasure through her. Every nerve, every inch of her skin, was alive and on fire.

The scent of his skin filled her nose. He was everywhere. His hands, his mouth, his tongue reached every part of her, leaving no spot untouched, as if he was discovering her body for the very first time.

But the faint scent of antiseptic from the hospital still lingered on his skin, a crude reminder of his still-healing shoulder. A tense knot gathered in her chest. How could she have been so stupid? She ran her hands over the muscles of his shoulders. Because of her negligence, she'd nearly lost him.

Propping himself up on one arm, he suckled on her lower lip, then kissed her long and deep. The sweetness of his tongue sent a rush of heat straight to her core. A gruff moan escaped his lips as she slickened against him. His pleasure empowered her. The man holding her was a fierce warrior who fought against the strongest supernatural beings in the world. He could massacre monsters with his bare hands, but she longed to be the one to make him as weak in the knees as he made her.

Slipping his hand between them, Damon fingered the soft flesh between her legs. She cried out as he rubbed against her soft, sensitive folds. Pressure built inside her until she teetered on the brink of ecstasy.

He ran his lips over her ear, his hot breath sending shivers down her spine as he whispered to her, "Come for me, Tiffany."

He drove into her in a hard thrust that launched her climax.

She cried, "Damon!" Heat rushed to her core. She bucked against him as wave after wave of pleasure rolled over her. Grabbing his face with both hands, she met his eyes. "Kiss me, damn it."

He smiled and playfully nipped at her neck. "Only if you come for me again."

She gasped. He didn't have to ask twice. He continued to pump into her as he kissed her so hard her head spun with desire. Another pulse of heat flooded through her, igniting a blazing fire.

As she finished riding the last remnants of her climax, she pushed hard against Damon's chest, fighting to roll him over onto his back. He grinned at her feeble attempt before wrapping a single arm around her waist and rolling her on top of him. He lay back as she straddled his stomach.

Her eyes widened as she drank in the sight of him. The toned muscles of his arms and chest flexed as he reached out to cup her behind. She squealed and wiggled against him as he tickled her. She fell forward, her breasts pressing against his pecs before she moved up and gave him a short kiss on the lips that was so intimate in its familiarity it made her breath catch.

Slowly she drew herself down the length of his body, her skin sliding over the hard ridges of his abs. Resting her head on his stomach, she snaked her fingers over his mouthwatering hips and belly, a delicious triangle of muscle with a small trail of dark hair leading down to his erection.

A low growl escaped his lips as she continued to move downward. "What mischief are you up to?" he purred.

He groaned as she brushed her lips against his arousal. "You pleasured me," she said. "Now it's my turn to pleasure you." She ran her tongue over the length of him, and the sound of his deep moans filled her ears.

Crawling up the length of his body, she left tender, soft kisses around his bandage. But a tinge of pain filled her heart. The image of his pained face, his unmoving chest and the paleness of his cold lips were seared into her mind forever. His pain had shattered her. Something inside her crumbled to pieces at the thought of losing him.

Not again.

Twice she'd nearly shoved him from her life forever, but now, after seeing him so close to death, she knew she would never be able to live without him. She would show him pleasure and entice him to stay. Though deep down, she knew she shouldn't worry. B would never abandon her.

After trailing kisses across his collarbone, she followed the line of his chest to the muscular curves of his abdomen. Her mouth practically watered at the sight of his abs. She imagined all the hard work, the training, the dedication it had taken to tone his body. He was perfect, like a piece of art.

He moaned as she massaged and caressed every inch of his body, from the crook of his neck and the bulk of his shoulders, all the way to his legs, hips and feet. He melted beneath her touch, and the look of ecstasy that crossed his face sent a rush of heat between her legs. She snuggled her body against him, her head resting on the tightness of his belly.

She whispered to him, allowing the heat of her breath to brush against his skin. "What can I do to please you? I'll do whatever you wish."

Tangling his fingers in her hair, he played with her long curls. "Your pleasure is more than enough." His ice-blue irises blazed in the dim light of her bedroom. That fire told her exactly what he wanted, though he refused to ask. He was too sweet, too much of a gentleman, to express desire for anything but *her* pleasure.

Another moan escaped his throat as she stroked her hand over his shaft. "Tiffany…"

She placed a finger over her lips and hushed him. "Shh. No protests." She placed her lips on him, and it was his turn to buck beneath her mouth. "I want to make you come," she whispered.

Damon groaned as Tiffany's lips wrapped around him. The warmth and wetness of her mouth enveloped him despite his considerable size. She slid her lips up and down the length of him, her hands working in tandem with her sweet, sweet mouth. When she finally released him, he was so close to finishing that the delay was pure torture.

She straddled his hips, rubbing her soft flesh against him. He ran his hands over her porcelain skin from her breasts to her narrow waist, all the way down to the delicious expanse of her hips.

The perfect hourglass.

A low feral growl grumbled deep in his throat. One single curl fell into her face, highlighting her gorgeous smile. She looked so good it hurt. He couldn't take it anymore.

"I need to be inside of you."

She flashed him a coy smile and bit her lower lip. That was all the answer he needed. He spread her legs to reveal her sweet pink center, then wasted no time. He filled her, and she threw back her head and cried out. She rocked her hips against him as he continued to pummel into her. A shiver shuddered through his body as he neared his finish.

Tiffany ran her hands over his arms. Her glowing honey eyes locked with his. She was barely able to speak through her labored panting. Her chest heaved in and out, and she moaned as she neared her own peak.

But a mischievous grin crossed her lips as she mimicked his words. "Come for me, Damon." The sound of her whisper drove him wild.

In one final thrust, he emptied himself into her. They both cried out; ecstasy the likes of which Damon had never felt before billowed through him in a mind-blowing release.

She collapsed on top of him, and he wrapped his arms around her and pulled the coverlet over him. Elation filled him as she nuzzled her head into the crook of his neck.

Gently, he kissed her forehead before he buried his nose in her hair. They lay there in silence as the energy subsided. His heart thumped hard against his chest. Several times he opened his mouth to speak, but no words came as she relaxed into sleep.

If he'd told her then that he loved her, that he wanted to spend the rest of his life with her in his arms, he wouldn't have been lying....

Chapter Twelve

If bones could talk, Tiffany's would have groaned and said, That. Was. Amazing. She stretched and twisted herself out of the tangle of bed linens, grinning like a fool as she mentally replayed the passion she had shared with Damon. She inhaled deeply, the scent of his skin filling her nose. He lay on his stomach next to her, mouth cracked open and arms spread, one over his head, the other dangling off the side of the mattress as he slept. She listened to the sound of his breathing, and watched his chest rise and fall.

Her fingers itched to run over the brand across his shoulders. The dark black ink contrasted with his lightly tanned skin. Watching him sleep, seeing him so totally relaxed, sent her heart racing faster. He was so sexy, so perfect. She bit her lower lip and fought to restrain herself from waking him, from pushing herself against him, kissing him deeply and seeing if what she'd heard about a man's sex drive upon first waking was true.

Before she could stop herself, she brushed the smooth skin of his face with her thumb. The sharp chiseled lines of his cheekbones and face stunned her. Even while he slept, he was breathtaking, beautiful in his intensity. But when he was awake, nothing gripped her more than the icy-blue depths of his eyes. They pierced through her, wild and ferocious, and sent chills down her spine. Like an angered Siberian tiger, both hypnotic and terrifying.

Still dead to the world, he responded with a low grumble. He leaned into her touch, then settled into sound sleep again. She smiled. Being with him for a second time had been so different from the first. When she'd given him her virginity, the pain had been minimal, and he had impressed her with how quickly he'd assuaged her fears. But the second time had blown her away with how familiar it had been in its intimacy. And unlike the first time, this time she'd known that the man she lay with was her B, the man she'd dreamed of for years.

Rolling to her side of the bed again, she stared up at the ceiling. For someone so distant, calculating and sometimes downright cold, Damon's capacity for tenderness had touched her, revealing the man behind the mask, the man she'd come to know through letters. There was no doubt in her mind that he cared for her. The same feelings coursed through her when they touched.

Whether he knew that or not, she wasn't certain.

She clenched her jaw. Anger built inside her as she

thought of how stupid she'd been. How could she have been such an idiot? She should have known that the man she knew, her B, wouldn't intentionally have left Mark for dead. Damon still blamed himself, but after nearly losing him in the same way, *she* didn't blame him anymore.

Her mind wandered to all the letters she'd never answered. How deeply had she hurt him?

Swinging her legs over the edge of the bed, she stood and padded across the room to her desk. She slid the bottom drawer open and dug underneath the piles of school papers until she found what she was looking for. She pulled out the large stack of envelopes—not a single one opened.

She set the letters down, then quickly cleaned herself up and got dressed, then pulled on a black pea coat. Finally she grabbed the letters, walked through to the living room and stepped out onto the fire escape.

The cold winter air stung her cheeks. She sat down on the top step, her favorite quiet place. She glanced at the sky. Not a single star in sight thanks to the overwhelming lights of the city. She exhaled a long breath.

She had to know.

After removing the rubber band holding the letters together, she shuffled through them, reading the dates. One letter each day for over a month. A large lump caught in her throat. Her breath swirled around her face as she held the last letter Damon had ever sent her.

Tucking the rest of the pile under one knee, she opened the envelope. The paper made only a small ripping noise as it tore, but in her ears the sound was amplified by a factor of ten, a noise nearly as painful as a blaring alarm clock during an awful hangover.

Her hands trembled as she removed the single piece of paper, and pain filled her heart at the sight of B's familiar handwriting. She paused. For a moment she almost released the paper into the wind. It would be so much easier not to know.

But she had to.

Hands still trembling, she unfolded the letter and slowly read the scrawled words.

Dear Tiffany,

I have so much to say, but little time to say it as I start to search for Mark's killer. I doubt you will even read this letter, since there's been no response to the others I've sent for the last month. But I have to write this in the hopes that maybe someday you'll open this envelope.

No matter how much you may hate me, no matter how much you may wish me dead, you will always hold a place in this cold heart of mine. I never intended to care for you, but I do. We both know I do, and for that I have no regrets.

Losing Mark, and now you, has driven me to the brink of insanity, and the pain is more than I can bear. You know how difficult it is for me to admit this to you, but I'm not okay.

I can never be okay.

Nothing I can say or do will ever express to you

how sorry I am. I'll bear the guilt of what I've done for the rest of my life.

This isn't something I can just get off my chest, and as much of a relief as it would be for all the pain of what's happened to be taken away, I don't deserve any relief. I wish there were something I could confess to you that would turn this around, something that would make this better. I wish I knew the perfect lie.

Tiff, I'm begging you.

Tell me what it is you want to hear and I'll make sure you hear it. I'd say and do anything to have you back in my life again. I've got no family to fall back on, and my heart is so rooted in our friendship that even if I did, their love would never be enough to heal me without you in my life.

It's amazing how we got this far, how a one-line letter could turn into these feelings I have for you. Maybe it's meant to be this way, because Lord knows I don't deserve a woman like you in my life.

We both know what I want to say. It's always been on the tip of my pen, waiting for me to write it. But I'm too much of a coward.

You know how I feel, and if I could just say it to you in person one time...I could die knowing I'd had something meaningful in my life.

Yours always,

B

With still shaking hands, Tiffany attempted to refold the letter, but it was no use. Tears blurred her vision and spilled over onto the paper. She trembled at the thought of what she had to do.

He has to know.

Damon sat straight up in bed, heart racing as he gasped for air in the aftermath of the dream. His pulse beat in a heated rhythm, and he clutched the sheets in his hands. His eyes darted around the room. Tiffany. Where was Tiffany?

He launched himself from the bed and threw on his jeans. Rushing into the living room, he spotted a hunched-over figure on the fire escape. He ran back into the bedroom and threw on his shirt and boots before he strode to the living room window.

In his dream, Tiffany had changed her mind and decided that she *did* blame him for Mark's death. She'd said she'd been wrong to forgive him.

He wrenched open the window and climbed onto the fire escape. A blowing northern wind hit his arms like hundreds of small needles pricking his skin. Damn, it was cold outside. Tiffany was sitting on the top step, completely still.

"Tiff?" he said.

When she didn't respond, he walked up behind her. His heart stopped as he saw what she held in her hands. His letters. He brought his hand to his mouth and lightly bit his thumb so a string of profanities wouldn't fall from his lips. One letter lay open on her lap, and it was *the* letter, his final letter.

The letter that told her he loved her.

Shit.

He opened his mouth several times to speak but couldn't find any words.

He was *still* too much of a coward. Every time he tried to find the right thing to say, his mouth went dry and the words dissipated. What the hell was wrong with him? Why couldn't he tell her? For fuck's sake, he knew exactly why. Because admitting he loved her would make him vulnerable. Though he'd often refused to admit it to himself, he'd been in love with her for years. They both knew it. She already held his heart.

But if he said he loved her, he would be defenseless and exposed. She would have even more power to hurt him than she did now, and damn if that wasn't the scariest thing he could ever imagine.

Tiffany patted the spot next to her, motioning for him to sit. He sat down, resting his elbows on his knees, completely unable to speak. The pain in his chest overwhelmed him. Everything inside him wanted to grab her, tell her that he loved her and kiss her senseless, but he just couldn't do it.

She let out a long sigh. "I don't think I need to tell you that I was wrong. I think you already know it."

Damon's stomach churned. Suddenly nothing else mattered but the words that had just left her lips. The cold weather ceased to chill him, and the wind stopped burning his cheeks. She wasn't saying what he thought she was…was she?

"Here." She pushed an overstuffed, unstamped envelope toward him.

"What is this?" he choked out.

She bit her lower lip and stared straight ahead, refusing to meet his eyes. "The letters I wrote you. I never sent them."

He watched her in disbelief. She'd written to him?

She turned toward him. Tears streamed down her face, staining her porcelain cheeks. Her voice cracked as she spoke. "You need to know—I need you to know—that I never stopped loving you, not for one second."

Damon tangled his fingers into her hair and encircled her waist with his arm. He pulled her into him so fast that he barely realized what he was doing before his lips crashed against hers. He kissed her deep. Their tongues swirled against each other, the heated passion radiating over both of them. The feel of her body pressed against his sent his heart racing into overdrive.

Slowly he released her hair but never stopped cradling her head. His lips brushed against hers as he spoke. "I never stopped dreaming of you," he whispered.

A single warm tear slid onto his cheek, falling from her face as he kissed her again. He scooped her into his arms and carried her into the warmth of the apartment toward the bedroom. If he couldn't say he loved her, he could at least try his damnedest to show her in whatever way he could.

Damon couldn't have been more content. Tiffany lay against him with her head nestled into the crook of his arm. His eyes ran over her naked form. She was so damn beautiful. Angels couldn't compare.

He allowed his head to sink into the softness of the pillow. He closed his eyes and pinched himself, but when he opened his lids again he was lying in the same exact spot. Was this really happening? Was this what lay in his future? His nights spent protecting the innocent, with Tiffany there to lie in his arms when he arrived home at the crack of dawn?

For once in his life he hoped for the best. He prayed God wasn't playing some cruel, sick joke on him. After they'd returned to the bedroom, he'd tucked her letters inside the pocket of his jacket. He was still in a state of disbelief. She'd written him letters. He couldn't decide whether he was looking forward to reading them…or dreading it.

A sharp buzz sounded from the bedside table as his cell phone vibrated. Tiffany stirred, blinking lazily as her eyes opened. The phone continued to buzz.

He looked at the caller ID. Shit. The E.U. calling never meant news about flowers and rainbows.

He snatched the phone from the table, flipped it open and placed it to his ear. "Hello?"

Chris's voice on the other end of the line sounded desperate. "Have you seen it already?"

Tiffany met his eyes, listening to Chris, whose voice was loud enough to carry.

"Seen what?" Damon asked.

Chris swore. "You'd better get to the nearest computer."

Without hesitation, Tiffany darted to her desk, where

her too-old laptop sat closed and asleep. She opened the screen and hit the power button.

"What's going on, Chris?" Damon asked. He pressed the button to switch the phone to speaker.

Chris spoke at the speed of light, his nerves clearly getting the better of him. "There is a viral video online. You need to see it before H.Q. gets it taken down. Search for 'zombie apocalypse Rochester.'"

Damon gestured to Tiffany. She typed in the search terms and hit Enter.

Damon shook his head, trying to wrap his mind around what seemed to be happening. "Please tell me this isn't what it sounds like." He could hear the sound of Chris's fingers flying across his keyboard in the background.

"If by 'what it sounds like' you mean dumbass teenagers getting video footage of the bloodsucker who's orchestrating your virus transitioning a dead guy into a viral vamp, then, yes, it's exactly what it sounds like."

Adrenaline shot through Damon's veins. "What are you talking about, Chris? We killed Caius last night."

"We? Who's we?" Chris rasped. "Who do you have working with you? And whoever you killed last night clearly wasn't the right vampire."

"Never mind who—"

Tiffany beckoned Damon. "Found it." She clicked Play.

The rustling sound of movement near an unsteady camera echoed from the speakers. The shaky video phone pointed down a dimly lit alleyway. A hooded man with his back to the camera over an unmoving form. A disgusting slurping sound carried through the video. Damon's heart raced.

After nearly a minute of continuous slurping, the figure pulled away.

"Fuck!" Damon roared.

The camera showed what was clearly a freshly dead corpse. Fang marks marred the victim's throat, plain as day.

"Holy sh—" The whispering of a teenage boy's voice was cut off as, judging by the sounds, one of his friends clapped a hand over his mouth.

Shit. Shit. Shit.

Damn teens these days and their freaking video phones.

A trickle of blood ran from the man's neck before the shadowed figure hunched over the body again. Reaching into his pocket, the faceless vamp removed a small syringe.

Tiffany mumbled under her breath. "Holy crap."

The shrouded figure lifted the arm of the corpse and injected the serum into the deadened vein. When it finished, the figure stood and stepped away, looming over the body. The corpse twitched, jerking to life. The dead man's eyes snapped open. The irises glowed a pulsing red.

The hooded figure disappeared into the night.

One of the teenage boys swore. The newly turned leech's head snapped in their direction. It opened its mouth and bared its fangs. A loud hiss ripped from its throat, and with unnatural jerky movements it scrambled into a crouched position, ready to pounce.

"Fuck! Run!" one of the boys yelled. The video blurred

and jerked as footsteps pounded the ground. Seconds later the video cut abruptly to black.

Chris cleared his throat. "We are in some deep shit."

Chapter Thirteen

An hour later Damon sat facing the rows of monitors in his home control room. Tiffany lingered outside the doorway, pacing. Sweat gathered on his palms, and a dry feeling filled his mouth. The last time he'd spoken with the Sergeant had been directly after Mark's death. The E.U. designated all accidental deaths as "under investigation," and Damon had been the Sergeant's lead witness.

One of the highest-ranking officers in the Execution Underground, Sergeant James Winfield took shit from no one and commanded respect without even batting an eye. He was one of only a handful of men in the Execution Underground who Damon absolutely refused to spar with, because he was *not* about to embarrass himself by having his hind end handed to him on a platter. With years of experience, age was nothing but a number to the Sergeant. Fifty-six years old and he could still kick some serious trainee and field operative ass. Aside from his salt-and-pepper hair, the gruff bastard didn't look a day over forty, and he didn't fight like an old man, either.

The green light on Damon's switchboard flashed, and the alert alarm sounded throughout the apartment. Tiffany jumped at the sound. On first moving in, Damon had rigged the sound system to blare in case of emergencies, and the Sergeant calling him definitely qualified. With a deep breath, Damon pressed the button to accept the call.

A small beep sounded, and then the Sergeant's stern face appeared on the nearest monitor, with Damon's own image boxed in the lower left corner of the screen.

The Sergeant's lips made a tight line, and he cast a frustrated glare at Damon. "What the hell sort of trouble have you gotten yourself into now, operative?" he barked. "Your town's little vampire-turned-zombie video bullshit is raising holy hell, operative. Do you know how much damage control that cost the security department?"

When Damon didn't respond, the Sergeant yelled, "Answer the damn question, operative!"

"No, sir. I don't know how much damage control it cost."

The Sergeant eyed Damon up and down. "A hell of a lot. That's how much. I don't give a flying shit if the video had nothing to do with you. It originated from your division area, so therefore you're responsible for it. Understood?"

Damon nodded. "Yes, sir."

The Sergeant glanced down at a stack of papers lying in front of him. "Your nerdy tech tells me you believed you killed the son of a bitch who was injecting these bastards, but it appears you were wrong. Is that correct, operative?"

"Yes, sir," Damon replied.

Sergeant James frowned. "You want to explain to me how the hell that happened, operative?"

Damon dug his fingers into the armrests of his chair. At the moment, there were very few things he wanted less to tell the Sergeant about than his failure to follow code and his misconceptions. He really hoped it was a rhetorical question.

No such luck.

The Sergeant banged his fist on his desk and glared at Damon. "Answer me, operative."

Damon inhaled a deep breath. "I received misleading information, sir. I was under the impression that the vampire at large, Caius Argyros Dermokaites, was responsible for the spread of the virus, and as a result I sought his death. I was mistaken."

The Sergeant shook his head as if Damon blew it on a regular basis when it came to protocol. In truth, never once had Damon been admonished for a protocol infraction. If there was one thing he knew how to do, it was play by the E.U. rules.

"From whom did you receive this faulty information, operative?"

Damon fought to keep his face impassive. "An outside informant, sir."

"And who is this outside informant, operative?"

"A family member of a former E.U. operative who is

highly knowledgeable about the current vampire situation in Rochester, sir."

The Sergeant let out a long sigh. "Dear God, Brock. This doesn't have anything to do with Operative Solow's sister, the one you always daydreamed over, does it?"

Damon didn't respond. There was no point. The Sergeant had busted him more than once for reading Tiffany's letters over and over when he should have had his mind on his training.

Damon heard steps behind him.

Oh, no.

Tiffany stood behind his chair, posture perfectly straight and confident as she smiled at the Sergeant through the screen. "That would be me you're talking about, sir, and yes, Operative Solow was my older brother."

The Sergeant appraised Tiffany. "Your brother was a good hunter, Miss Solow, and from what I hear you seem to be following in his footsteps, becoming quite the free-lance huntress yourself. Perhaps if the Execution Underground ever allows women to join I'll contact you."

Tiffany grinned from ear to ear. "Thank you, sir. I'd like that very much."

"Brock!" the Sergeant barked. "What is the fine young woman doing with your sorry ass?"

Damon opened his mouth, but Tiffany spoke first. "With all due respect, sir, the misconception was my mistake. I overheard Caius speaking on the phone about something spreading throughout the vampires in Washington State and how it was following suit here. I assumed it to be the virus."

The Sergeant paused and looked over his paperwork. "From what we've heard from our division in Seattle, there appears to be some sort of vampire governmental organization forming, a whole separate can of worms from this viral issue. The shit is about to hit the fan with these bloodsuckers. We need to get this under control as soon as possible." He folded his hands and leaned toward the camera. "This is what's going to happen, Operative Brock. With her consent, and since her place in Caius Argyros Dermokaites's inner circle means that she will be expected to maintain contact with his subordinates, Miss Solow will wear a tracking device that will lead us to the local vampire nest. Our best plan of action is to learn from the inside who is responsible for the spread of this virus, destroy as many of these monsters as we can and scatter their organization. I'm rushing in a team of hunters who will be under your command in this mission. Is that understood?"

Damon nodded. "Yes, sir."

The Sergeant looked at Tiffany. "Miss Solow, do you agree to act as an extension of the Execution Underground on this occasion and uphold all the same oaths as a true member of the organization agrees to, including putting your life on the line to save those of innocent civilians?"

"I do," she replied.

The Sergeant gave a single nod. "That is all, then. Operative Brock, your team will be there in three hours." He pointed a finger at Damon. "Don't fuck this up, Brock. And hurry up and build your permanent division. I want to get in the request to create your division before the shit hits the fan with all these supernaturals crawling around your city. If anything goes wrong with this vampire raid, H.Q. will blow off the request until these damn bloodsuckers are taken care of, and I don't want to risk innocent lives because you didn't do your job. So choose your permanent team and then prep for the raid." Without another word, the Sergeant logged off.

Damon released the breath he hadn't realized he'd been holding and slumped into his chair. Really? Pick his team *now?* A video had gone viral—bringing *way* too much attention to his city—somewhere out there a rogue vampire was hell-bent on spreading an infectious bloodsucker disease, he was expected to use Tiffany as a means of locating said psycho vamp, and yet the Sergeant wanted him to waste valuable time scanning résumés?

He let out a groan. Whether it made sense to him or not, an order was an order.

Tiffany placed her hands on his shoulders. "Are they all like that?"

Damon shook his head. "No, that's just the Sergeant. He's an ex-Navy SEAL commander turned E.U. hunter after his granddaughter got killed by werewolves."

"Oh, wow." Tiffany released him and stepped toward the door. She paused. "And what's this about you day-dreaming of me?"

Leaning his elbows onto his knees, Damon rested his face in his hands. "I can't believe he mentioned that."

Tiffany laughed as she leaned against the door frame. "Well, since you have very little time before a group of vampire hunters starts knocking on your door…" She stood as straight as possible and pointed an accusing finger at Damon. Twisting her face into a scowl, she mimicked the Sergeant. "I suggest you get your worthless behind to work, operative!" she yelled.

Damon leaned back in his seat and closed his eyes. "Fine. But I'll never get any work done with you in here taunting me."

Tiffany crossed her arms over her chest and shrugged. "All right. I can take a hint, but get to work."

She left the room, and Damon watched as her deliciously round behind and hips swayed down the hall. He got up and closed the door so he wouldn't go chasing after her, slam her against the nearest wall and take her hard. Clenching his hands on the desk, he thought about what lay ahead of him. Another raid with him as leader? Was he prepared to do that again, so soon after Mark's death?

So many things could backfire. Though they did have one advantage this time, which they hadn't had previously: an informant inside the nest.

He didn't like the idea of Tiffany going into a nest of vampires alone, but what other choice did they have? There was no other way for them to track the nest, and the vamps weren't stupid enough to allow her to bring an outsider with her. It was the only way.

As much as he could, he pushed his worries aside. There were too many things he needed to do.

He typed in his security codes, and within seconds Chris's face greeted him from the monitor.

"Hey, Damon. How's it go—"

Damon met Chris's eyes. "Do you have the résumés the Sergeant asked me to go over?"

Chris spoke while he typed nonstop on his keyboard, the clicking sound of the keys forming a strange robotic rhythm. He paused and emphatically jabbed the enter key. "Done."

Damon's side monitor flashed as dozens of images loaded. The faces of the finest hunters the Execution Underground offered filled the screen. "You've got to be kidding me. That's even more than I expected." With everything else on his plate, narrowing down this list was going to demand hours of work he couldn't afford to spare.

Chris cleared his throat. "And lucky for you, you have a contact at H.Q. who, despite your often grouchy demeanor, has taken the liberty of assembling a program for you, so you can refine the search and avoid having to read every single profile. What would normally be two or three hours' work has been narrowed down to less than an hour." He pointed at himself. "And that amazing contact to whom you owe your undying gratitude is me."

Damon glared at Chris. "Remind me the next time I see you in person to give you a nice big kiss on the lips."

"Considering the mood you're in, I'll take that as a thank-you." He reached forward to press the off button on his web camera. "Get to work."

In seconds the monitor transitioned to black.

Utilizing his touch screen, Damon slid the images onto his main monitor and started his search. It appeared his best option was to organize the candidates by hunting specialty first, before narrowing his search in each category. He glanced over the list of supernatural groups in Rochester and their current status. He needed a lot of manpower.

With the E.U. efforts intensely focused on N.Y.C. for years, Rochester had slipped under the radar. But now, with the N.Y.C. division finally gaining control of all their unruly boroughs, focus was shifting. Damon's division would not only secure the city, it would do it quickly. He would make certain of it.

First things first. Unrest in the Were community due to a possible change in packmaster.

He typed "werewolf" into the search box and roughly twenty profiles surfaced. He started mentally listing the attributes he wanted on his team. Young, able-bodied men, either fresh out of the academy but with lots of field training or only several years seasoned.

Though older hunters held the advantage of being wiser and more precise, he wanted to assemble a team that wouldn't disband anytime soon. Men near his age who possessed a drive, a fire, that too often faded over the years.

He typed in an age range and came up with three profiles, complete with photos. The emerald eyes of the hunter in the middle photo blazed with intensity.

He pulled up the man's stats, skimming for the important information.

Name: Jace McCannon
Hometown: Honeoye Falls, New York
Specialty: Werewolf
Experience: Three years field training
Current location: Atlantic City, New Jersey

Interesting. Honeoye Falls sat right outside the city limits. McCannon was practically a Rochester native. Damon's index finger hovered over the mouse. The hunter's burning eyes made him wonder if the man would be resistant to following orders.

After an extended moment of debate, he clicked the button to add the hunter to his roster. If he was unruly, Damon would whip him into shape. After all, he'd dealt with countless unruly trainees while he led raids during his field training. McCannon would listen, or Damon would send him straight back to H.Q.

Next up: demonic possession. There were two types of demon hunters: those who could kill demons and those who could exorcise the demon from a human's body, saving the innocent civilian. Looking at the numbers of possession reports on his sheet, he wanted somebody who could do both. He typed "Demon Hunter/Exorcist" into the system and prayed he would get a hit.

Yes! One hit.

Name: David Aronowitz
Ethnic Origin: Jewish
Hometown: Rochester, New York
Current location: Brooklyn, New York
*Requesting transfer near hometown for family issues

* * *

Perfect. Damon clicked the "add to roster" button without a second thought. No way would he pass up having a guy like that on his team.

Next in line: newly discovered occult activity and the possible formation of a Dark Wiccan coven.

Witches were extremely intelligent and cunning, and their relationships between covens could be immensely complex. Handling the occult wasn't black-and-white. It required someone with a level head. Figuring out the complex dichotomies of the witching world demanded patience. He tapped his fingers on the desk. He needed someone smart.

He narrowed the search to people with B.A. degrees or higher. The highest on the list was Shane Grey, Ph.D.

Bingo.

Three down, two more to go.

An increase in hauntings.

For the most part ghosts, while terrifying to humans, were nonconfrontational. But an angry Poltergeist wreaked havoc and terror. Damon wagered that the many abandoned asylums of Rochester contained a shit-ton of pissed-off Polters.

He typed in "ghosts and poltergeists."

A lone profile popped onto the screen. The haunted gray eyes of the hunter stared at him from the monitor. Damon could tell that some seriously traumatizing shit had passed in front of that man's eyes. A small red flag flashed near the profile picture.

He clicked on the flag and the screen flashed "Post-Traumatic Stress Disorder." Damon raised a brow. Damaged goods weren't generally listed. Why the hell were there so few ghost hunters? He widened the search.

Damn. The majority of them were already assigned to the Florida Keys and Saint Augustine.

He hit the return button to the single profile.

Name: Ashley (Ash) Devereaux

Current location: New Orleans, Louisiana

*Transfer required (Post P.T.S.D.)

New Orleans? Now there was a city with one hell of a ghost population. He hit the add button, and hoped the guy wouldn't freak out on him. If he was still listed after a P.T.S.D. diagnosis, then the E.U. saw something in him that went beyond his stats.

Last one.

Several new species of non-werewolf shifters reported.

After entering "non-were shifters" into the search engine, he pulled up roughly ten profiles. His gaze shot to the profile of one hunter immediately. Two different colored eyes, not a common trait in anyone. Intrigued, he opened the stats.

Name: Trent Garrison

Experience: One year field training, two years full-time off-site operative

Current Location: Jersey City, New Jersey

*Transfer requested (Post-facial injury)

* * *

He eyed the man's features. The E.U. had yet to update his profile shot. He respected someone who fought post-injury, and since non-werewolf shifters had been rising in population over the past two years, this man had been a pioneer in the field.

A muffled knocking sounded from the other side of the door.

"Damon?" Tiffany called.

He punched in the door code, and the latch clicked open.

Tiffany stepped inside. "You'd better get a move on. We have to prepare."

In his mind, the walls he erected during every hunt snapped into place. A level head would be the key to the success of this raid. He would *not* have a repeat of Mark's death. Come hell or high water, every member of the team the E.U. provided him with would come home safe. But his main concern, far and away more important than anything else, was ensuring Tiffany's safety.

He nodded. "Okay, I'm ready."

Her eyes darted to the main monitor. "Are these the hunters you're picking for your team?"

He didn't respond. Was that really what was sitting in front of him? His future team that he'd handpicked? A sur-real feeling washed over him. He should have felt honored to lead an entire division, but the tight knotted feeling in his gut refused to subside. After what had happened with Mark, did he deserve to lead?

A low whistle escaped Tiffany's lips. "Daaanng. Are all

the guys in the Execution Underground hot or what? Is that a requirement? Every single one of these dudes is frickin' gorgeous."

Damon grumbled in response. What was so fantastic about the men pictured on the screen? He didn't see it.

Tiffany grinned as if she were picking out her favorite Mr. February calendar pin-up. "They're all easy on the eyes, though I'm kind of partial to that one. He has awesome hair." She pointed at the golden-blonde from Louisiana with the haunting eyes, and then to the werewolf hunter. "But he's definitely my favorite."

He scratched his head and looked away. He tried to ignore her comments.

"Jace McCannon," Tiffany read from the hunter's statistics. She bit her lower lip. "He is one fine piece of—"

Damon hit Power-off on the monitor. The men's faces were gone in a second. Damn. It bothered him when she even looked at other men.

Tiffany hmphed, but a small grin crossed her face. "Jealous, much?"

Damn right he was jealous. He was jealous of any man she found attractive, and he would shove his fist straight down the throat of any man who made a move on her. He wasn't about to confess that, though.

"We'd better prepare for the raid," he said.

He stood to leave. Before the other hunters arrived, she needed to arrange the meet-up with the vampires, and he needed to prep his weapons. Preparing their plan of entry would have to wait until she led them to the location via the tracking device.

She crossed her arms over her chest and smiled. "If it's any consolation, I think you're sexier than all of them. You've got the whole tortured-soul thing going on. It's in your eyes. Women love that." Without another word, she brushed past him and walked out of the control room.

He raised a single brow. Tortured soul?

Chapter Fourteen

After mulling over the plan with Tiffany, Damon stood in his room, arranging his array of weapons. Tiffany was downstairs, preparing to make her call. Everything was planned to the full extent it could be.

The incoming hunters would provide the tracking device for Tiffany to wear. His contact in the police department had ensured that word of Caius's and Carl's deaths and the abandoned and—much to Tiffany's chagrin—now-impounded Bugatti was never released to the press, and somehow the mess at the restaurant had been entirely hushed up. Without evidence of Caius's and Carl's deaths, the other vamps would be confused as to their sudden absence. Everyone knew of Caius's obsession with her, and luckily, it gave her a higher standing in the hierarchy. She was going to request a private meeting at the nest to discuss his disappearance. She'd prepped to play the role of the grieving, overly attached human.

Once she met up with her contact, she would be escorted to the nest. Damon and the other hunters would monitor her movements from a safe distance and follow her to the location. Damon had instructed her to play it cool once she was inside and not draw too much attention to herself. Caius's subordinates would undoubtedly engage in a power struggle if they assumed he was dead. She needed to encourage them in the direction of declaring him missing, instead. Ideally she would also find out who was behind the zombie virus.

While Tiffany distracted the vamps, the tech specialists would map a layout of the building and use a high-powered heat sensor to detect where all the beings in the residence resided. It was Damon's job to make the call on when to enter and to direct their routes of entry.

Tiffany promised him that once the hunters were inside, she would seek safety in the van with the tech team.

The hunters' objective was simple: annihilate as many vamps as possible, particularly the ones showing any signs of viral infection. With luck all the Rochester vamps would be in attendance, including the bloodsucker orchestrating the spread of the disease.

No matter what, they hoped to effectively control the situation by destroying the source of infection, even if they were unable to identify him, which would free Damon to hunt down any remaining infected vamps—should there be any left—as quickly as possible.

He finished tucking his weapons into place, with one last piece to go. With care, he removed a long black case from the top shelf of his weapons closet and laid it across his bed. Damn, it had been a long time since he'd opened this thing.

He unhooked the latches and opened the lid to reveal his father's pure silver slaying sword. The sword had passed through the past ten generations of Damon's family, a treasured possession even before the Execution Underground's formation in the late 1600s, uniting freelancing hunters who were newly settled in the Americas into one central group, a group which would later become international. The beautifully crafted piece of weaponry had served his ancestors in slaying thousands of vampires over the years, and now he intended to use it for the very first time.

He strapped the custom scabbard on his back and slipped the sword in. Assessing his mental check list, he made certain he'd prepared. He glanced at his watch. Ten minutes before the Sergeant's chosen hunters arrived.

He grabbed his jacket from the bed, felt something in a pocket and realized what it was. Tiffany's letters.

A tight feeling constricted his chest.

Before he could change his mind, he snatched the letters from the pocket and opened the single envelope holding them.

Tiffany was right. He needed to know.

He had ten minutes. He sat down on his bed and opened the pages. The first letter was dated three weeks after Mark's death.

Dear B,
Your letters are piling up. I've re-
ceived one every day for a week now.
I haven't read a single one.

Damon stopped breathing. Deep down, he wasn't surprised she'd never read them, but it still hurt.

But she *had* read his letters now. One, anyway.

The letter.

He flipped to the next letter.

Dear B,
I wish you'd stop sending letters. Every
time I see the return address of the
Execution Underground, my stomach
churns because I know it's either a
check that's meant to pay me off for
the brother I lost, a check I have to
cash if I don't want to be homeless...or
a letter from you. I don't know which
makes me feel worse.

He bit his lip. Shit. That one stung.

Dear B,
Why?
All I can think is why...?

A sharp pain stabbed at his heart as he read the words. The next was merely a single sentence.

I feel nothing...

God help him. He had to keep reading. He couldn't pause to think. It hurt too much.

Dear B,
I tried believing this today.
Everything is normal. Mark is not dead. You are not the cause of any pain in my life. Life is the way it used to be. I'm a happy college student, preparing for med school.
Yeah...it didn't fool me for a second, either.

And the next:

If you were here, I'd stab a knife straight into your back, just like you did to Mark. What worthless excuse for a man betrays his friends? What kind of pathetic human being leaves the ones they love to die?
You do.

Next:

I wish I hated you. Things would be less complicated if I hated you.

He hated to keep reading, but he had to.

Dear B,
I'm addressing this to you, because though I know I'll never send it, I don't know who else to write to. It's strange that the only person left in this world who I feel a strong connection to is the man responsible for the death of my brother.
*   I'm all alone now. I have no family left. My grandparents are dead. Aunt Cecelia's dead. My parents are dead. Mark is dead. And now you might as well be dead, too.*
*   I must be next....*
Tiffany

He had to force himself to keep going.

Dear B,
I realize now that not only is my brother really dead, but so is the friendship you and I had. I've run

through endless possibilities of ways
to fix this, ways we could reconcile,
but there is no way.
Tiffany

He wanted to stop, but he couldn't.

Dear B,
I need to move on, to forget about you
and put the past behind me, but your
letters just keep coming.
   I tried to burn them. I built a small
fire out behind my apartment building last night. As I watched the flames,
I held your letters—all of them, the
ones I've read and the ones I haven't—
over the fire. But even though I will
never read them again, no matter
how hard I tried, I couldn't burn a
single one.
Tiffany

And finally...

Dear B,
This is the last letter I will ever write
to you. I'm moving forward with my
life.
   I wish I could say what we once had

between us was good, but I question whether a relationship built entirely on letters is really a relationship at all. The bitter, cynical side of me says it was never really anything. The nostalgic side disagrees and insists that at one point in time we did have something good, but that the goodness was just lost.

On most days, it feels as if I'm at war with myself about what to make of what we once were and what we are now. Was it good? Bad? Worth it? Not worth it? I don't know if I'll ever fully come to terms with either feeling. Perhaps that's because it's a little of both.

All I can hope for is that in the future I'll be able to go a day, maybe a week, maybe even a month or, finally, years without thinking about you, because at the current moment...

You occupy my mind every second, and without you, life doesn't feel worth living.

Yours truly,

Tiff

Damon folded the letters and placed them back inside the envelope. Mechanically, he tucked them inside his pocket again. A knock sounded at the front door. The team had arrived.

Tiffany called out to him from downstairs. "Damon?"

For a long moment he couldn't breathe, couldn't speak. His heart pounded, and adrenaline pierced through him. He could feel her pain, her grief within every word, but…

Damn. Despite everything she'd said, her feelings had never faltered. They were back to where they'd been prior to Mark's death. He sucked in a deep breath. A massive weight lifted off his shoulders. They were back to where they'd started, as if they'd continued writing all along. Back to both of them knowing but never speaking it aloud.

She loved him…and God help him, he loved her, too.

Tiffany stood stock-still as Damon attached the tracking device to the clasp of her bra. Despite all her nerves, the feeling of his fingertips brushing her skin sent chills racing down her spine, and heat rushed between her legs. The last time she'd felt that feeling, he'd been on top of her, pushing inside her. Pure ecstasy.

She barely noticed the small device rubbing against her skin as Damon lowered the hem of her shirt. With gentle movements he moved her long hair to hang free down her spine. She bit her lower lip. She didn't know why, but since right before they left his apartment with the E.U. team, he'd been more tender with her than ever, similar to how he'd been in bed, but…different.

Not that she was complaining.

"Are you ready?" he whispered in her ear.

She nodded. "Yeah, as ready as a girl can be for playing in a vampire nest." Nerves built inside her again. A light sheen of sweat covered her palms. She always felt a little clammy before meeting vamps, even when fully armed, with her gun hidden beneath her jacket as it was now. But the feeling always subsided when she encountered them and her hatred for what they'd done to her family rose to the top.

It was the anticipation that raked her nerves, not the mission itself.

"Repeat to me what you're going to do again. I want to be completely certain we're on the same page," Damon said.

She let out a long sigh and faced him. "I've already repeated this to you twenty times, but all right. I'm driving to Club Fantasy and meeting up with Janette. I'm riding with her to the nest, and when we enter, I'll stall the discussion of Caius's disappearance for as long as I can. When you guys burst in, I'll hightail it out of there to the van."

He gave her a single nod. "Good." He met her eyes as he placed his hands on her shoulders. "We'll be close by the whole time. Nothing will happen to you. I swear it."

She smiled as much as she could, considering her nerves. "I trust you to keep me safe."

He circled his arms around her waist and pulled her flush against him. Pressing his lips against hers, he kissed her deep. A small round of catcalls and whistles echoed from his fellow hunters.

He released her and shot a glare in their direction. "All

you morons shut your gaping mouths and get back in position before I put you there," he commanded.

The other operatives snapped to attention. Their mouths slammed shut.

Tiffany planted a kiss on her palm, before pressing it against his lips. She grinned. "For you to keep."

She longed to hear him utter three words to her. But she knew how hard that would be for him. For a man who'd been taught to bottle up his emotions, to be distant for the sake of the job, telling her how he felt would be torture. He wasn't prepared for that yet, not while he still bore the guilt of Mark's death.

He opened his mouth, trying to force words out, but she placed a single finger over his lips.

"You don't have to say it. I already know." She ran her hand over his arm before she sighed. "Let's go massacre some leeches." She turned away and walked toward the door.

Fifteen minutes later she sat in the passenger seat of Janette's silver sedan, cruising away from the city. She had no idea where they were going. She assured herself that there was nothing for her to be afraid of; Damon and the rest of the Execution Underground team were right behind her.

Once the vamps had accepted her suggestion of a meeting, entering the nest should have been a piece of blood pudding, but a mounting feeling of dread crept through her. She couldn't shake the feeling that the night wasn't going to go as smoothly as planned.

After thirty minutes of silence, Janette parked her car outside what appeared to be an abandoned warehouse. Tiffany nearly scoffed. What a cliché. Was it just her, or did all drug dealers, gangsters, monsters and the general underbelly of the population operate from inside old warehouses?

She and Janette exited the vehicle and slipped inside the freezing cold building. Tiffany almost choked on her own tongue. The inside held more vampires than she had ever imagined resided in Rochester. Nearly thirty bloodsuckers filled the room, along with only a small scattering of the humans she knew to be Hosts.

With twenty members of the Execution Underground at Damon's side, the vampires outnumbered them. She tried not to think about that. Few of the vampires were very old, of that she was certain. She prayed the E.U. hunters could handle the extra monsters.

All eyes turned to her and Janette as they entered the room. Tiffany scanned the crowd and recognized several faces. The closest in rank to Caius was Lucas. The regular bartender at Club Fantasy, Lucas had been on this earth since the mid-1800s, when he'd been working as a scientist, or so Caius had told her. The vamp wasn't nearly as ancient as his egotistical Roman superior had been, but in age he trumped all the other vamps in the room. Caius had told her that Lucas was the second-eldest vampire in the city, another migrant from N.Y.C.

"Finally our absent leader's pet is here," Lucas said with a grin.

From the look on his face, she already knew he couldn't

have been happier about Caius's disappearance. With Caius gone, it was highly likely power would fall to him. Others might try to battle him for the position, but considering his age, his defeat would be highly unlikely.

He eyed her up and down. "You don't look to be grieving very deeply over the death of your master."

Master, my ass. In her head, Tiffany pulled her gun and shot Lucas point-blank solely for the disgustingly smug grin painted across his face. She fixed him with a hard glare. "I'm not grieving because Caius is not dead," she said.

A murmur of whispers ignited throughout the small crowd. So much for not drawing attention to herself.

Lucas raised a brow. "That's quite an assertive claim. Do you know something we don't?"

She shrugged. "Perhaps. It depends on what you know. Gentlemen first."

Lucas frowned. He didn't like being sassed by a lowly human. His lips remained shut.

Janette answered instead. Her ghostly face reminded Tiffany of a skeleton. And, man, was the red lipstick freaky against that pale skin. Janette glanced in her direction. "All we know is that Caius, Carl and the car have disappeared. Perhaps you know something more than we do?"

Tiffany continued to stare straight at Lucas. "Actually, I don't. But why Caius going missing would cause all of you to believe he is dead is beyond me." She scanned the crowd, meeting several pairs of eyes along the way. "There is nothing pointing to Caius's death, and knowing him as

I do—as we all do—it seems quite likely to me that he's putting a plan in motion, something he doesn't want anyone to know about until he's ready to reveal it. It sounds to me—" her gaze locked with Lucas's again "—that some may be all too eager to declare him dead."

His jaw clenched. "Don't get too cocky, human," he spat.

She feigned an innocent look. "Too cocky? I'm just trying to protect Caius's interests...exactly like everyone else here who is loyal to him."

Many vampires and Hosts alike nodded.

She cleared her throat. She had to keep this situation under control. "Rather than bickering about whether or not Caius is dead, I think it would benefit all of us to come up with a strategy to search for him. Until it's proven otherwise, we should proceed as if Caius is alive and well. I'm quite certain he left to attend to pressing business."

Lucas chuckled. "Without informing you or any of his fellow vampires?"

Tiffany shrugged innocently. "Who am I to question the motivations of my master?" Her stomach churned. The word tasted disgusting on her tongue.

He crossed his arms over his chest. "Perhaps you're correct."

What? Tiffany's eyes widened. Where was he going with this? Why was he agreeing with a human?

A devious grin spread across Lucas's face. "May I have a word, Tiffany? While the others create possible action plans, you and I can discuss the finer details of Caius's disappearance in private."

Damn it all to hell. With everyone standing there watching, she couldn't refuse or she would appear insubordinate, a deadly sin for a human, as if she had something to hide or a reason to fear. And as Caius's favorite, she was somewhat safe—hurting her would be as blatant as attacking Caius himself. So if she wanted to appear as if she truly believed he was still alive, she couldn't act as if she feared Lucas in any way. But she wouldn't put it past him—or any powerful vampire, for that matter—to attack her in Caius's absence, if only to strike a blow at Caius if he sought the elder's position.

She flashed a fake smile. "Of course."

Lucas gestured for her to follow him down a nearby hall. Voices erupted in open discussion behind them, heatedly debating Caius's disappearance, as she walked toward what felt like her doom.

She followed Lucas to the end of the hall, where he held open a door to what had probably once been an office. She walked inside, and he followed suit. Adrenaline raced through her. When he closed the door behind them, the distinct sound of a dead bolt clicking into place sounded in her ears.

Shit-tastic sign number one.

Damon rode in the first of four E.U. vans. He sat next to the tech team leader, staring at the tracking screen. From what they could tell using their maps, a few minutes ago Janette had parked outside an abandoned warehouse near Brighton, a nearby suburb.

Courtesy of the silent hybrid engines, they surrounded the warehouse undetected. Though Damon's feelings regarding the raid remained steady and focused, his nerves circled around the thought of Tiffany in danger. He couldn't push their earlier moment from his mind. She'd known exactly what he'd been struggling to say, and despite that the words had still refused to leave his mouth, she cared for him, anyway.

Damn his stupid emotional inhibitions. If something happened and he'd never told her he loved her, he would never forgive himself. His failure would haunt him for the rest of his days.

No.

He couldn't allow himself to think like that. Nothing would happen to her. Her safety was his highest priority.

"All units secured," a muffled voice sounded over Damon's handheld radio.

Damon pressed down the button for confirmation. "Copy. Tech unit establishing ground layout."

Careful to not make any sound, one of his tech hunters slid open the side door of the van. He and two other hunters hopped out, the high-powered heat sensors in their hands. The three of them rushed around the building, hooking their equipment into place.

"Operative," a voice whispered from outside the van.

Damon turned.

Shit.

The Sergeant was standing outside the van, dressed in full gear and—from the bulges underneath his short leather jacket—fully armed. He climbed into the vehicle and crouched next to Damon.

Damon gave a single nod to his commanding officer. "Good evening, Sergeant. With all due respect, sir, may I ask why you're here?"

The Sergeant fixed Damon with a look that was half annoyance, half "What do you think I'm here for, idiot?" After a long moment, he said, "To make sure this goes smoothly, operative."

Damon met his eyes. "With all due respect, sir, I can—"

The Sergeant jabbed his finger into Damon's chest. If he'd been speaking above a whisper, he would have been barking at Damon, as usual. "Don't tell me what you can and can't do, Brock. I know you can do this or I wouldn't have put you in charge, would I? I'm here to make sure you don't call 'go' too soon. I can't have you getting trigger-happy. I'm no imbecile. You think I'm forgetting this is your first raid since we lost Operative Solow? Not to mention Operative Solow's sister is inside there. That's the woman you love, Brock. Don't think I don't know that."

Damon frowned. Damn. The Sergeant had always been so friggin' perceptive. It pissed Damon the hell off, but at the same time he respected the man for it. The Sergeant grated on his every nerve, but he was the man who'd made Damon into the hunter he was, and for that he looked on the Sergeant almost as if he were a second father—and the Sergeant acted is if Damon were a surrogate son, always giving him a hard time because he expected more of him.

Static crackled over the radio. "All secure."

Damon flipped three switches connected to the second monitor. A shadowy green layout of the building appeared on the screen. Damon's eyes widened.

"Damn. Don't know if I've ever seen more bloodsuckers in one place," the Sergeant said as he shook his head.

Damon scanned the screen. There had to be nearly thirty vamps in the main area and...

He paused. Three on the far side of the building? His breath caught. Shit. This was not good.

"Prep your team, operative, and remain calm. We'll get her out of there safely," the Sergeant said.

Tiffany's heart raced as she faced Lucas. Her pulse thumped in her blood, and she could feel the rhythm all through her body. Standing tall, she glared at the bloodsucker. She wouldn't show her fear. "What is this about, Lucas?"

An evil grin twisted his face. "That worthless hunter of yours, Damon Brock." The way he said Damon's name sounded as if he considered Damon the scourge of the earth.

Tiffany froze. It took everything she had to hold her face completely still. How did he know about Damon? She met his eyes and decided to bluff. "I don't know what you're talking about."

Lucas snarled. "Don't be cute with me, human. You know exactly what I'm talking about. Your vampire slayer lover and his brigade of Execution Underground cronies positioned outside this building." He stepped closer. "Lie and pretend you don't know again, and I'll sink my fangs into your throat."

She held her breath, holding her face still and stern.

He walked toward the wall and leaned against it. "I know you killed Caius."

All the neurons in Tiffany's brain fired. How the hell was she going to get herself out of this? She tried to steady her breathing. Damon and the other E.U. members would rush in soon, and when Damon saw she wasn't in the main room, he would come looking for her. Could she hold Lucas off until then?

Lucas went on. "But it's not Caius's life I care about. It's my master, Apophis."

Tiffany stared at him as calmly as she could. "If you expect the name to mean something to me, you're going to be disappointed."

A low growl escaped Lucas's throat and a shiver rushed down her spine. "Apophis, named for the Egyptian God of chaos and war, my master—the ancient vampire your hunter murdered."

She held her position. "Damon has destroyed hundreds of vampires, and you expect me to know the name of one in particular?"

Lucas chuckled. Moving faster than she could comprehend, he came to stand behind her, grasping her throat in one hand and her hair in the other. He led her toward a closed door that she assumed led into another room. "Perhaps you'll put two and two together when you see what I've saved as a surprise for the two of you."

Still gripping her hair, he wrenched the door open. A dark form loomed in the shadows. Lucas shoved her forward. She stumbled inside, and he flipped on the light. Her eyes locked onto the sight before her, and her heart stopped. Her stomach churned, and her whole body shook violently. Tears welled in her eyes as she choked down a scream.

Chained against the wall by his wrists stood her brother. At the sight of her, his irises flashed red and he hissed. His fangs descended as he fought against his restraints.

Bile rose in her throat. Unable to scream, she doubled over and vomited the entire contents of her stomach onto the floor. She panted, attempting to catch her breath, but to no avail. Her brain refused to process what stood directly in front of her.

Mark wasn't dead. He was a vampire.

And he was infected…

"No doubt that hunter of yours told you that your brother's body burned in the fire from the raid, and believe me, until this day he still thinks that to be true. But there's one problem with fires…." He stepped up behind her, and the warmth of his disgusting breath brushed against her neck. "There are no bodies to be found."

As fast as she could, Tiffany withdrew her stake from its hiding place and lunged toward Mark. But Lucas grabbed her midmovement. He dug his fingers into her hand, and the stake fell from her grasp as she felt the bones of her hand crushed beneath his fingertips. She crumpled to the ground.

Lucas kicked her spine, knocking the wind from her,

then put his foot between her shoulder blades, holding her down. She prayed he wouldn't move his foot low enough on her back to find her gun. "See, here's what happened. That hunter of yours murdered my master, Apophis. Caius, being the coward he is, stabbed your brother with his own stake, then left to save his own skin. When I saw your brother lying there on the cold ground, bleeding, I saw my window of opportunity."

He stomped harder on her spine. She reached for her stake, but the lacquered wood had landed just beyond her reach.

Lucas continued. "To make your hunter suffer, I turned your brother. I knew that to a vampire slayer of the Execution Underground, the only thing worse than death is being transitioned into one of the creatures they hunt."

Foot still on her spine, he bent and picked up her stake, then released her. She gasped for air.

"At first your brother was a normal vampire—under my direction, of course, seeing as I'm his master. But, well…a little experiment backfired on us. As Caius may have told you, other than the master I lost, science is the one love of my life. When the new vampire movement asked me to create a serum that would allow us to walk by day without weakening, I decided to use your brother as a test subject."

He paused to break her stake in two as if it were nothing more than a twig. "Turns out because it's been tampered with, the DNA of the hunters of the Execution Underground doesn't mix well with my vaccine, and, well, you know the virus that resulted."

Tiffany stared up at her older brother. Mark hissed and spat like an animal, fighting to be freed. If he hadn't been restrained, he would have torn into her flesh without hesitation.

"With the help of your brother, we were able to spread the virus and create a new strain of vampires by letting the newly turned feed on the humans he devoured."

Tiffany's stomach churned. If she'd had anything else there, she would have been sick again.

"Now I've combined the Execution Underground serum and my anti-sun vaccine into a single shot, and one injection can turn a new vampire into a flesh-eating monster. But for one special dose—" he pulled a syringe from his jacket pocket and held it up for Tiffany to see "—I've reversed the effect. Injected into the arm of an Execution Underground hunter, this will turn him into a ravenous flesh-hungry monster in minutes." A smirked crossed his face. "And guess which hunter I've saved it for."

Her eyes widened. Adrenaline raced through her body. Tears poured down her face. Dear Lord, no.

No, not Damon. She couldn't lose him, too.

"When the hunters storm in here any minute, your hunter will come straight here, looking for you. One injection." He grinned and raised the syringe into the light. "Or I can crush it now, and you won't have to go through the horror of seeing the man you love murdered, like I did. I'll give you a chance to save him—if you agree to sacrifice yourself."

Tiffany lay on the cold concrete of the warehouse floor,

her whole body trembling. All the warmth drained from her face. "Only if you get rid of the injection first." She fixed him with a hard stare. Nothing was more important to her than Damon and his safety. She couldn't take risks.

Lucas placed the syringe on the ground and positioned his foot overtop it.

Then she nodded. She would do anything to save Damon. Anything.

"What do you want from me?"

He crouched and prepared to lunge for her. "Don't hold back." He met her eyes. "I like it when my victims put up a fight."

Happy to oblige, she pulled her Smith & Wesson from her lower back, aimed and fired.

The sound of a shot from somewhere inside the building rang in Damon's ears. His heart stopped. "Go!" he yelled into his radio. He and the Sergeant lunged from the van, hitting the pavement at full speed.

The hunters rushed from their positions and burst into the warehouse. Shots were fired, the sounds echoing off the metal walls, followed by the clatter of ricocheting bullets. Damon unsheathed his sword and launched himself through the main entry. He didn't think twice. He swung the heavy weight of the silver sword in front of him, slicing the head of the vampire in front of him clean off.

The vampire exploded in a burst of blood. Shrieks and cries of pain filled the room, but a steady constant buzz filled Damon's ears.

Tiffany.

Nothing would stop him from getting to her.

Brandishing his weapon, he cut savagely into vampire after vampire, destroying any and all of the monsters standing in his path. A male leech rushed him from behind. Spinning, Damon brought down his sword and chopped through the monster's skull. Blood splattered his face.

He drew his sword back, only to have the weapon wrenched from his grasp as something huge tackled him from behind.

Spinning to face his attacker, Damon snatched his stake from his side and plunged the sharpened weapon downward. Huge hands caught his wrist, and he locked eyes with his opponent. His breath caught in his throat as he stood nose to nose with the shell of what had once been his best friend.

A blazing red pulsed in Mark's eyes. He hissed and twisted Damon's arm, trying to get him to release the stake. Damon gritted his teeth and pushed forward. He would not allow the pain constricting his chest to deter him. He would kill Mark, releasing his friend from the fate he'd always dreaded.

The two men met each other punch for punch and kick for kick. It was just like sparring class, where they'd always partnered to fight against each other. Being older and stronger, Damon had always won. He intended to win this time, too.

Mark stepped closer, and his fist collided with Damon's gut. It was the one move Damon always caught him on. It was as if Mark was handing him the fight. Damon stepped into him, clutching Mark's arm and using the weight of his body against him.

With the help of his hip, he dropped Mark onto his back, but Mark quickly shifted to his knees.

Damon brought the stake down with all his might. Mark grabbed Damon's wrist, but he was at a clear disadvantage, on his knees with Damon standing over him. A loud yell ripped from Damon's throat, releasing a fresh wave of adrenaline. He channeled all his energy into his biceps, struggling until he positioned the stake directly in front of Mark's heart.

The vampire bared his teeth, battling with all his strength, but Damon held firm. One small shove and he could end this. He would keep his promise to his best friend, his fellow hunter. His whole body shook as he tried to force himself to do what he needed to.

Sweet Lord, help him. He had to murder his friend.

The pulsating red in Mark's eyes flickered and for a quick moment his face slackened. The rage and fight disappeared from his expression completely.

"D-do it, Damon," he stammered, before his eyes blazed crimson again.

Damon gritted his teeth and didn't think twice. He plunged the wood of his stake straight into Mark's heart. The blood of his only friend, his fellow hunter, of Tiffany's brother, covered his face.

"Everybody out!" he heard someone scream.

A loud explosion sounded from his right, and a wave of

heat washed over him. The force of the explosion knocked him to the ground. Fire spilled through the building.

With shaking hands, he wiped the crimson liquid from his eyes.

"Brock!" The Sergeant's muffled yell carried from behind him.

Damon looked up and everything stopped.

For one long second he couldn't move, couldn't breathe, couldn't function.

Amid the smoke and flames, a large vampire stood silhouetted on the opposite side of the room, his arm around Tiffany's neck in a choke hold. She writhed against the bloodsucker's grip, struggling fruitlessly against him.

Damon launched himself from the ground and sprinted full speed toward her. Several of his fellow hunters and the Sergeant hooked their arms through his and tugged him back. Damon fought against them with every ounce of strength he possessed. They struggled to hold him back.

"No! Let it go, Brock! No!" the Sergeant yelled in his ear.

As the vampire disappeared into the smoke of the building, carrying Tiffany with him, her head snapped in Damon's direction.

No!

A loud cry ripped from Damon's throat as Tiffany's eyes flashed crimson and she bared her fangs.

* * * * *

Acknowledgements

A huge thanks to all of the following people:

To my super agent, Nicole Resciniti, for dealing with all my neurotic tendencies and having the most awesome agent editorial chops I've ever encountered. Nic, thanks for taking a chance on this young, inexperienced writer and being my greatest cheerleader every step of the way. Having you for an agent has been a true blessing, and has changed my life for the better. You are both a great business partner and a great friend. I know we're both in this for the long haul. I couldn't have done any of this without you. I'll be forever grateful.

To my lovely editor, Leslie Wainger, and to the head of the HQN imprint, Tara Parsons, thank you for championing my work and for believing in the heroes of the Execution Underground. Leslie, thank you for giving me the final polishing touches on my manuscripts and for being my guide through the crazy publishing process. I couldn't ask for a kinder editor to help me through my journey.

To my first writing mentor, Mark Powell, for telling me I was good enough to build a writing career and for making me believe it. Mark, I may not be writing literary fiction, but I hope you're proud of me and enjoy this book all the same.

To my writing friends and mentors at Spalding University: you all rock! Special thanks to Rebekah Harris for reading this before it was polished. Rebekah, you're a fantastic friend and hopefully I will find myself in the acknowledgments of your debut YA novel in the near future.

To Dr. Thebaud and Dr. Romain, thank you for restoring my health when I needed it most and for always keeping my well-being in mind. You've seen me at my worst but lifted me to my best. My family and I are beyond thankful.

To the best author girlfriends I could ever ask for, Cecy Robson and Kate SeRine. Thank you for holding me up every time I need it. I hope to always call you both my friends. And to my good friend and dance guru, Hollie Ruiz, for being such an enthusiastic fan and cheering for me: shimmying equals happiness. You're a great friend and a beautiful person. You inspire me.

To one of my best friends on the planet and the most awesome critique partner ever, Britt Marczak. Thank you for being there for me every step of the way. You read about Jace and the E.U. heroes when they weren't decent to see the light of day, but you loved them nonetheless. I don't know if I would have pushed through Jace's book without you.

To my pets: Sookie, Olivia and Elliot, for keeping me company in my office and being my favorite lazy editors—writing isn't the same without you interrupting me every five seconds and walking across my keyboard.

To my family (both immediate and extended) for supporting me in every single endeavor, I know that at the end of every day, no matter what has happened, you will all always love me and continue to support me. Mama, you believed in me. You believed in my writing way before it was any good, from that first butterfly book we made when I was little, to my sixth grade stories, through the first drafts of my first novels, all the way to where I am now and beyond. You're my best friend. You brought me into this world, and you've been the one to hold me up ever since. I love you.

To my husband, Jon, for sticking with me through all the ups and downs of the deadline for this book, for cooking dinner and cleaning the house when I'm too stressed out to do so, even in the face of a forty-hour work week. More importantly, honey, thank you for teaching me what it's really like to fall in love. I'm looking forward to spending our lives together, for better and for worse, until we are old and gray. I love you more with each passing day.

And greatest thanks be to God with Whom anything is possible. You rain down blessings on me every day, Lord.

SHADOW'S CARESS

PATTI O'SHEA

Chapter One

Cass glanced at her watch—another half an hour until she escaped. Tonight, the store was nearly empty. She didn't get how an 80s boutique stayed in business, but hey, it *was* Los Angeles. The appeal of the clothing was lost on her, but she didn't have to like it, just sell it.

The Twisted Sister video on the flat screens gave way to "Girls Just Want to Have Fun" and Cass winced. It was the third time since her shift started that she'd heard that song. She might need to look for a new job. Again.

Immediately, she rejected the idea. She'd have to live with the music. She could already claim a dozen former positions and she needed to remain somewhere longer than a few months or weeks.

The only job she'd managed to stay with for more than a year was the one she'd held right out of high school—vampire hunter. Her lips curved as she imagined the reaction if she added it to her résumé, but the amusement faded quickly. Right, like she could ever admit to *that*.

Cass looked around, but Genevieve, her coworker, was helping their lone customer. It was going to be a long half hour.

She bent over, tugged her black capri pants below her knees and pulled up the slouch socks…which promptly fell back down. Cass huffed out an impatient breath. Did she really have to dress like it was 1985?

Before she could work up a good mad, the hair on the nape of her neck stood on end. She jerked upright, but it took another moment for her to feel it. The presence.

He was back. This was the first time, though, that he'd shown up while she was working. She'd never believed in ghosts. Really. But the last four days had changed her mind.

Before she could decide how to handle his unexpected arrival, he trailed a finger over her bare shoulder where her oversized red sweatshirt fell to expose the strap of the tank top she had on under it. A shiver went through her that had nothing to do with fear.

Why did she have to like his caresses?

And how lame was it that she got heated up by a ghost anyway? When he'd first made his existence known, she'd been disconcerted. That had changed to rattled—he shouldn't be able to arouse her, damn it. Now, she could mostly take him in stride. At least until he touched her and made her cells short circuit.

Stepping away, she turned her back on him and fussed

with the T-shirts on the rack she faced. Cass felt his heat as he moved behind her and then he kissed her nape. Her nipples tightened and she almost melted as his lips moved along her skin.

She clasped the metal bar, the hangers biting into her palms, and closed her eyes to savor every tingle. The man knew how to use his mouth.

Blood roared in her ears, and while she didn't exactly forget she was at the store, the knowledge didn't stop her from enjoying this. His warmth surrounded her and she wished she could lean back into his body. Okay, she wished he *had* a body.

He kissed his way over to where her neck met her shoulder, licked farther forward and then nipped at her pulse point. Cass gasped and her knees buckled.

"Are you okay?" Genevieve called.

"Fine." Cass's voice came out thick and she could feel her face burning. She sidled away from him, and trying to appear nonchalant, headed for the registers.

She was an idiot. Not only was she at work, but he was also a phantom, a wraith. How pathetic was she?

Her sort-of-imaginary boyfriend followed on her heels and she was aware of him with every step she took. Awesome, now he didn't even need to touch her to get her warm. "Back off," she warned, keeping her voice soft.

The gap between them widened a few steps, and perversely, Cass felt immediate disappointment. She had to start dating again. This was her body's way of telling her that it wasn't normal for a twenty-one-year-old woman to live like a nun. But the idea of her ghost tagging along while she was out with some other guy… Well, talk about weird.

When she was behind the counter, the presence safely on the other side, she looked around. Genevieve was over by the dressing rooms talking with the customer and Cass turned her back to them. "Listen," she whispered, "you have to go away." Inspiration struck. "Go to the light. That's what you should do, okay?"

He didn't leave and she sighed. How long would he stick around? It wasn't like a ghost had any reason to haunt her, so eventually he'd drift out of her life.

A memory of vivid blue eyes staring up at her made Cass flinch. Vampires didn't become ghosts. Did they?

Of course they didn't, she assured herself. With all the training she'd had to hunt and kill them, someone would have mentioned it. But—she swallowed hard—she'd asked questions constantly that no one had been able to answer.

Maybe this one had come back to haunt her because their gazes had been locked as she'd driven the stake into his heart. He was the only vampire who'd ever awakened like that and he'd shaken her to the core. Maybe it had made the difference.

"Look, I'm sorry," she murmured. "Killing you is why I quit being a hunter."

Cass aligned the items lying on the counter between the registers. "If it makes you feel better, I still have night-mares about that day, so really, you don't need to haunt me.

My memory is doing it for you. Go to the light, have a nice afterlife and I'll see you in another seventy years, okay?"

For a heartbeat, she thought he was speaking and she could nearly make out what he said, but then her coworker laughed and Cass lost the almost-words. It had probably been her imagination anyway, just like it was imagination that she was talking to the ghost of a vampire she'd killed. The odds against it were astronomical. It was her guilty conscience, nothing more.

"Maybe I should become a nun for real," Cass muttered. "Then I could spend the rest of my life atoning for that year I was a hunter."

"Nuns probably have better health care coverage than we do," Genevieve said as she breezed behind the counter. "I didn't realize you hunted. Aren't you a vegetarian?"

"Yes." She didn't know what else to say, so she left it there. At least Genevieve thought she'd hunted animals, but then the majority of the world didn't believe vampires or demons existed. It was Cass's misfortune to know better.

The customer came up with an armful of clothes, saving Cass from more explanations, and when Genevieve finished ringing her up, it was time to close for the night.

It went quickly. They'd worked together long enough to cruise through the process of shutting things down, and with the ghost finally gone, Cass wasn't distracted.

Genevieve's boyfriend picked her up, but they waited until Cass was in her car before they drove off. She gave them a quick wave as they left and reached for the ignition. Nothing happened. Her heart sped up. It was dark, the parking lot was deserted and the idea of being stuck here didn't give her the warm fuzzies.

Cass turned the key again. Still nothing.

Reluctantly, she popped the hood and opened her door. She didn't know much about engines, but maybe something was loose and she could slide it back into place. She gingerly jiggled a few cables, but everything seemed connected.

"Piece of crap," she said and slammed the hood shut. For an instant she considered giving the tire a kick, but her sneakers wouldn't keep her from breaking a toe.

A shimmery warmth filled her and she realized the ghost had returned. "You know," she told him, "you could be useful and wield some poltergeist powers to get my engine started." Nothing. "Yeah, that's what I figured."

Leaning her hips against the grille, Cass tried to remember whether any of her friends had brothers or boyfriends who knew how to fix engines. The squeal of tires made her straighten and look up. She turned in time to see a pickup truck come skidding around the corner of the big department store.

Cass hurried around the hood. *Get in the car.* She needed to be inside with her cell phone, ready to call 9-1-1.

The other vehicle's headlights were off. That wasn't good. Her stomach knotted.

The truck passed beneath a light and a glint caught her eye. What made her freeze, though, was the man on the passenger side. He looked familiar. That couldn't be—

Hands pushed her to the ground and Cass felt a warm weight settle over her.

Gunfire erupted.

She flinched and the man on top of her curved his body around hers.

Something—a bullet maybe—hit asphalt near her face, sending a spray of debris her way. She closed her eyes and brought her hands up to shield herself.

Tires squealed again and the engine roared as the driver gunned it. Cass lifted her head and saw the shooters leaving at high speed. She started to shake. So she'd been a vampire hunter, big deal. No one had ever shot at her before. If this guy hadn't shown up and pushed her to the ground, she might be dead.

His weight eased off her and Cass got to her hands and knees. "Hey, thanks. I guess I locked up there for a second." She climbed to her feet slowly, giving her legs a chance to stop trembling. "But when I saw that gun and the man holding it—"

Cass stopped short, blinked hard and looked again. Her savior wasn't some passing good Samaritan, it was her ghost. She recognized his energy—only he wasn't looking quite so spectral at the moment. He remained mostly translucent, but she could *see* him. She took in the tousled light brown hair, the handsome face, the vivid blue eyes, and gasped.

The last vampire she'd slain had just saved her life.

Chapter Two

Cass drove through the darkened streets of L.A., her hands clenched around the steering wheel. One of the police officers who'd responded to the shooting had gotten her car started, but that was the only good thing that had happened since she left the store tonight.

What did she do now?

The vampire hunters wanted her dead and she knew how they worked. They'd be watching her apartment. If she were stupid enough to go there, they'd pick her off. Cass had no clue what she'd done to anger them, but she'd recognized Quentin as the shooter.

The name made her shudder. She'd had one run-in with him when she'd been part of that group, but that encounter was enough for Cass to realize the guy was psycho. And he was after her. On orders. It had to be on orders because he was a follower, not a leader. It wasn't comforting news. The organization wouldn't stop until the mission was completed.

Turning to her friends was out. None of them were aware she'd been a hunter and she couldn't tell them. Besides, it would put them in danger. Her former coworkers didn't care about collateral damage and the biggest risk any of her friends had faced was driving on the freeways.

The police weren't an option, either. What could she say? *Hey, you're wrong about it being a random drive-by shooting. That guy with the gun? Yeah, he and I were both vampire hunters.* Sure. They'd think she was a whack job.

Maybe if she were a better liar, she could tell the cops some story and they'd believe it. Problem was she sucked at lying. She always had.

Cass eased the car to stop at a traffic light and tried to beat back the panic. She had nowhere to go, no one she could ask for help, and to make things extra difficult, she didn't have much money. Her emergency credit card wasn't an option. It could be traced and the hunters had the resources to do that.

Another car pulled beside her and her anxiety level skyrocketed. When the light went green, Cass hit the accelerator so fast, her sedan lurched into motion. She had to get a hold on herself. If she let her fear get the upper hand, she'd make it easier for the hunters. They'd have—

"Where are we going?" a voice asked from beside her.

Cass cut herself off midscreech and jerked her gaze to the passenger seat. Her ghost was back. Relief flooded her.

"Watch the road!" he ordered.

His urgency registered. She yanked the steering wheel, bringing the car back into its lane and narrowly missing the oncoming vehicle. Cass got a long honk for her efforts. "You scared the hell out of me!"

"Sorry."

He didn't sound sorry, but she took a deep breath and let it go. She had bigger problems to worry about. "Go away. I don't have time for you."

"You don't really want me to leave."

"Yes, I do. Really."

"If I do as you ask, who helps keep you alive, Cassandra?"

"Cass. I don't like being called Cassandra. And right, like I'm supposed to believe you want to help me. I killed you, remember?" A sudden realization dawned on her. "You're here for revenge, aren't you?"

"No. In your case, retribution would be wasted energy. You were young and I've seen no hatred in you. My assumption was that you obeyed orders, nothing more." He didn't wait for her to respond before continuing, "Besides, I'm not dead."

Relief flooded her. Maybe she was being stupid, but Cass believed him about not wanting to hurt her. And he *had* saved her life earlier. Then the last thing he said registered. She shook her head, but kept her gaze on the road. "You are dead. I read about ghosts and you guys hang around because you *believe* you're still alive, but you're not. Trust me. I drove that stake into your heart."

He was quiet for a long moment and Cass was torn between hope that he'd believe her and go away and fear that he'd do exactly that. At least when he was around, she wasn't on her own, and right now, the last thing she wanted was to be alone.

"What were you taught about killing vampires?"

Cass didn't get why he was asking, but she didn't see any reason not to answer. "That there are four things I had to do—stake you, put garlic in your mouth, behead you and bury your body separately from your head."

"And did you follow all those steps?"

She swallowed hard. The only time she'd chopped off a vampire's head had been while her trainer had been watching. It had taken her forever and she'd had to stop to puke. More than once. Even now, the memory made bile rise in her throat.

"No," Cass admitted quietly. She sounded normal and that was good. "But what difference does it make? Beheading vampires is an old wives' tale and it's not easy to cut off heads, you know."

"As slight as you are, I imagine not."

He shifted in the seat and Cass glanced over briefly. The translucence of his body threw her when he sounded so...normal, but he was more solid than he'd been in the parking lot after the shooting.

The ghost licked his lips and the memory of his mouth on her throat made Cass heat up. Damn, she was glad the car was dark and even happier that she had to watch the road otherwise he might figure out how easily he aroused her.

"The thing is," he said, and she heard reluctance in his voice, "beheading isn't a myth. A stake alone doesn't kill a vampire."

Right. "I don't know how to break this to you, but you're a ghost and you have to die to be one those."

"Wrong. I'm a shade—a shadow, if you prefer—not a ghost."

Cass frowned. "What does that mean?"

"It means I'm in limbo. I've been in limbo for two years, and in that time, you're the only person who's been able to see me or hear me."

A hint of an accent crept into his voice. English, she thought, and Cass realized she knew nothing about him. All her boss had told her that day was where to find the vampire. "What's your name?" she blurted out.

The weight of his gaze felt heavy, but his tone was neutral when he answered. "Malachi James."

She bit her lip and tightened her hands on the wheel. "You're thinking I should have known who I was killing."

"No, I'm not." Their gazes locked briefly when she glanced over and he must have read her confusion. "It's easier to commit murder when the target is impersonal. A name makes me real. And you did *not* kill me, no matter how much you insist otherwise."

Murder. The word made her cringe. "I'm sorry. Really, truly, totally sorry, okay? I wish I could have a do-over, but we don't get those."

"In this case you do—in a fashion."

The only way to change things was to go back to that

day, but that was impossible. Wasn't it? "Vampires can time travel?"

His chuckle sent a shiver of awareness down her spine. Why did he have to be so sexy? She wanted to write off her desire as vampire charisma, but she couldn't. It was him. "Didn't you ever learn it's not nice to laugh at someone?"

"Sorry."

"Yeah, I heard that before and you weren't sincere then, either."

Malachi put his hand on her leg and squeezed gently. That sent more tingles through her, but it also felt like an apology. A real one, not that offhand *sorry* he'd tossed out. His hand stayed above her knee and she reached down, covering it with her own. Cass half expected her fingers to pass through his, but they didn't and his heat made her palm burn.

She couldn't let the way she responded to him sway her into doing something stupid. "Look, I'd like to help you, but I can't. I have my own problem to deal with." Problem—that was an understatement.

"I know." He gave her another squeeze. "But if we work together, we can solve both our difficulties."

Cass put her hand back on the steering wheel and steeled herself against Malachi's touch. "That sounds good in theory, but aside from pushing me to the ground, how can you help me?"

"For a start, I know why they want you dead."

That stunned her enough that Cass nearly missed the light going yellow. She slammed on the brakes and gaped at him. His expression was serious, his blue eyes urged her to trust him, and she wanted to. Wearing faded jeans and a black T-shirt, he looked like some guy her own age, but appearances were deceiving. Malachi wasn't twentysomething, he was a vampire, and for all she knew, he might be thousands of years old.

"How can you have that information?"

"I walked into their headquarters and searched for everything I could find about you." When she didn't reply he added, "You're the only one who can see me, remember?"

His fingers moved higher on her thigh, and if Cass didn't need to keep her foot on the brake, she would have let her legs fall open to give him more room. She was *such* a sap. Malachi was trying to divert her…and was succeeding. Reaching down, she grabbed his hand and put it back at her knee.

"If you want me to believe you, don't use my attraction to you against me."

It wasn't as if she could deny what he did to her. Every time he'd touched her over the last four days, she responded. He'd have to be a complete moron not to register that.

"That wasn't my intent. And the need goes both ways, don't doubt that."

"Because you haven't had sex in two years."

The light turned green and Cass was grateful for the distraction. His gaze had made her feel vulnerable.

Malachi took his hand off her leg and crossed his arms over his chest. "I could have stopped you that day, you know. Vampires are much faster than any human. Much stronger, too. If I'd reacted as soon as I awoke, you wouldn't have stood a chance. But when my eyes opened, they met yours and the surge of desire was powerful enough to blind me to your intent. By the time I saw the stake, it was too late to grab it."

Unsure what to say to that, Cass kept quiet. She wanted to believe him—maybe a little too much—and that made her wary. "Why did you want information about me?" she asked softly.

"Because you're the one who staked me, only you can pull it out and return me to my life."

Her brain struggled to process what he said and what, exactly, it meant. "What if someone else removes it?"

"I remain in limbo." Malachi started to reach toward her, but brought his arm back before making contact. "I loathe limbo. Imagine being surrounded—humans or vampires, it makes no difference—and yet no one hears you or sees you. Imagine having no one to talk to, no one to touch or who touches you in return. It's a lonely, empty existence."

His voice sounded choked and Cass put her hand on his knee, giving him the same reassuring squeeze he'd given her. It would be a nightmare to be that alone. "So," she said, clearing her throat, "why do my former bosses want me dead?"

The silence would have unnerved her except that he put his hand over hers and laced their fingers. It was a few minutes before he said, "They're aware that you didn't be-head the vampires you were assigned to take down. Don't ask me how they found out, that I don't know. They don't want to chance you restoring any of us to our lives and the easiest solution is to kill you."

Cass mulled it over and another option came to mind. "The hunters could dig up the vampires and behead them. They know where the bodies are buried."

"No, they don't." He must have sensed her confusion because he explained, "I destroyed all the files about your jobs, including the location of the graves."

He didn't say more and she glanced briefly at him. The tilt of his lips was totally smug male. Cass almost hated to burst his balloon. "They'll know the general areas where I left the vampires even if they don't have a precise map."

"How could they?"

"Hunters don't dig the holes themselves, there were men who did that for us. All the bosses need to do is identify the spots that were used while I worked for them."

"That still leaves a lot of ground for them to cover and would waste time and resources. It's easier to kill you."

"Yeah," she agreed glumly. "I'm blaming you for that."

"I am sorry." Malachi brushed his thumb across the palm of her hand, sending warm shivers through her again and Cass gave up fighting the sensations. Didn't it figure? The first guy to interest in her months and he was a sort-of ghost.

And she was an idiot. Cass worked on tamping down her attraction. She had men after her who wanted her dead and it wasn't only to keep her from pulling out a few stakes.

No, killing her served as a lesson to other hunters—do your job right or suffer the consequences.

Panic threatened to take hold again and Cass drew deep breaths. She needed control or she'd die sooner rather than later.

But Malachi had said they could help each other. "Okay, I get what I can do for you. How can you help me?"

"Dig me up, remove the stake and I'll be a vampire once more. That will allow me guard you until they decide it isn't worth the effort to murder you."

Nice and logical, but he'd missed an important fact. "You might become a vampire again, but these guys *kill* vampires and they'll take you out if that's what they have to do to get to me. I thought I'd killed you once, I don't think I could deal with being responsible for your death a second time."

But it wasn't only that. If she pulled the stake, it became personal. Killing her would become a crusade. Sure, she might return Malachi to his life as a vampire, but the hunters would take it as her declaration of war.

Chapter Three

Malachi shrugged off his disappointment. He'd never expected Cass to agree immediately to pull out the stake. Hoped, yes, but it was enough right now that she could see and hear him. There was time to convince her.

"Where are we going?" He'd asked the question earlier, but she'd never answered.

"I don't know. It's harder to hit a moving target, right?"

He grimaced. That's what he'd feared, that she had no one to turn to for help. He'd do everything possible to protect her, but as a shade, his options were limited. Where could he suggest they go that would be safe for her?

Shifting in his seat, Malachi studied Cass. Her dark hair was short, messed up by the wind and by the way she occasionally ran a hand through it. She wore thick black-and-white bracelets to go with her 80s-style clothing and it underlined how delicate she was. Cass wasn't fragile, though, and he had the stake in his physical body to prove it.

Her toughness didn't matter. He wanted to take care of her, defend her, shield her from all that was bad. Not because she was his only hope of regaining his life, but because she was Cass.

One side of his mouth curved. Cass Lanier was fun, full of life, and she made him feel real, engaged with the world, and she made him care. All things he hadn't experienced since becoming a shade. He liked her. Too much.

And he desired her too much as well. She'd be called cute rather than beautiful, but to him, no woman was sexier. His need went beyond her appearance.

His grandmother had claimed he'd been born with a touch of the sight, that he would simply know things. She'd been right and he hadn't lost it when he'd become a vampire. It was the knowing that had prevented him from taking action the day Cass had staked him. As his gaze had met hers, Malachi had recognized her as his destiny and the shock had paralyzed him. He hated the term *soul mate,* but the sense of connection he felt to her—

An unfamiliar sound stopped him midthought. Malachi tried to decipher what it was and where it came from, but it ended before he identified it. Whisper-soft, too quiet for Cass or any other human to hear, but it left him uneasy.

"You're frowning," Cass said.

"Just thinking." If that sound was something to worry about, he'd tell her when he knew more.

She glanced at him. "About what?"

"Safe places for us to hide." It wasn't a lie; he had thought about it for a moment before he'd lost himself in his fascination with her.

"You mean where *I* can hide."

"And me. I won't leave you alone." That surprised a quick peek from her. Malachi read awareness of him in Cass's gaze—and her uneasiness with what was growing between them. Keeping his voice conversational, he added, "If anything happens to you, I'm trapped in a world without human or vampire contact of any kind. Being isolated— it's worse than death could possibly be."

"I'm sor—"

Malachi held up a hand to stop her. "There's no reason to apologize. It's done."

The sound came a second time, jerking Malachi's attention from the conversation. Something electronic? Again, it didn't last long enough for him to figure out what it was.

"Your frown's become a scowl."

He nearly cursed because he knew Cass believed he hadn't forgiven her for staking him. "Because our options are limited on where to go. You're a known vampire hunter."

"*Former* hunter."

"That won't matter." His clan lord had ordered that no one hunt the hunters, but if Cass showed up on anyone's doorstep, killing her would be deemed self-defense. He needed someone who would give her a chance to talk.

"You can't come up with anywhere?" Her voice held more resignation than question and it was only then that

Malachi realized how much she'd been counting on him being able to provide her with a safe haven.

Shifting in his seat to see her more clearly, he said, "There are two possibilities. I'm merely trying to decide which one is the best choice."

Jet or Laurent—both men would allow her to explain. But Jet had a way with human women and Malachi wasn't letting his friend near Cass. Laurent, then. Once convinced of the truth, he'd fight to defend her almost as fiercely as Malachi would himself.

The mystery tone sounded again, but his attention was captured by the motion he discerned in his peripheral vision. Through the back window, he watched a pickup truck come up behind them on the street, fast. Too fast. Same color as the one—

The traffic light turned yellow and Cass began to slow. "No. Floor it." She hesitated. "Now!"

"Wha—?"

He moved, putting his foot on top of the accelerator and pressing hard. The car shot into the intersection on the red. Cass didn't stomp on the brake. Instead, she steered, avoiding the car coming on the cross street by inches. More than one horn blared, but Malachi didn't ease up on the pedal.

"Are you trying to kill me?" Cass didn't quite yell, but it was a near thing.

"Look in the rearview mirror and tell me what you see."

She muttered one pithy word. "It can't be the same pickup. We haven't been tailed, and in a city the size of

L.A., the odds of them accidentally finding us are minuscule."

But even as she was speaking, Cass put her foot on the gas pedal next to his. Satisfied that she wouldn't slow, he pulled back to his side of the car and turned to check on their pursuers. The red light and traffic at the intersection had impeded the truck, but it was free now and attempting to make up ground.

As a shade, Malachi had lost some of his vampire abilities, but he still had his enhanced senses. He could see the men in the truck despite the distance between the two vehicles. "It's them," he assured her. "Try to lose them."

"How am I supposed to do that?"

"Make random turns or something." The car's speed decreased and the pickup closed the gap. "Keep moving!"

"I can't turn going this fast."

True, but they'd shot at her with a semiautomatic weapon earlier tonight and Malachi didn't want Cass within range of that again. "Go through another light. That should give you time to slow and make a few turns."

She nodded, but she didn't look away from the road. Her body was rigid, her knuckles white where they gripped the steering wheel, and Malachi wished he could do more than sit. This was *his* Cass under threat and he was useless. Another reason to hate being a shadow.

The hushed sound from earlier filled the sedan, but Malachi ignored it. Ahead, the traffic light had gone yellow. Cass swerved around the car in front of them and blasted into the intersection.

More horns, but no near misses.

By the time the pickup truck reached the light, cars were moving on the cross street, holding it back. "They're stuck. This should buy us a minute or two."

Cass hung a right at the next corner. She continued maneuvering through the streets until they reached the road they'd been on previously, but a good half a mile from where they'd turned off. Making a left when the light became green, she headed in the opposite direction from their original course.

Malachi faced forward and smiled. Smart choice. Their pursuers might not consider that they'd doubled back, and even if it did occur to them, he and Cass should be long gone by then.

"We'll head to Laurent's home. He's a friend of mine and I trust him." His smile faded. A man should be able to protect those he cared for and Malachi couldn't, not as a shade.

"Okay," she said.

That easy acceptance improved his mood. Maybe Cass was simply desperate, but he preferred to believe she trusted him, that she shared the same sense of belonging that he felt.

He started to give her directions, but that electronic tone stopped him midsentence. This time it was enough to make the hair on his nape stand on end.

"What? Come on, give. Something is going on and I need to know everything you do."

Maybe she did. "There's a noise in the car. I've been

unable to identify it, but it comes at regular intervals and that bothers me."

"Crap, my engine has more wrong than the police officer said, doesn't it? This is all I need on top of being chased by—"

"No. It's something else, not the car itself." An itch began between his shoulder blades. He didn't know why his instincts were emitting warning signals, but he wouldn't discount them. "Turn off this street and avoid the major roads."

She didn't argue. She didn't ask questions. She simply moved into the right lane and did as he'd said. "Something's off." Cass held out her arm. "I have goose bumps."

"I feel it, too." Malachi put his hand on her leg and gently rubbed her thigh. "Don't stop or slow."

"I don't plan on it." Cass gave his forearm a light caress. Her touch was fleeting, a mere brush of her fingertips, but it sent shock waves coursing through him.

At least until that electronic hum interrupted. The sound was dissonant enough to drive the pleasure from him. This time he narrowed it down to the front seat. Malachi eyed Cass's purse where it rested atop the transmission tunnel, but it was zipped shut. "What do you have in your bag?"

"I don't know. Stuff." Cass shrugged. "You're not thinking the noise is in my purse, are you?"

"Possibly. Would—" Cass's heated curse interrupted him. "What?"

"I think our friends are back."

Malachi turned to look out the rear window. "It's them," he confirmed.

"They shouldn't have been able to find us this easily."

She was right about that. Cass had done a brilliant job after running that light. This was the second time the hunters had overcome the odds and located them. It shouldn't have happened.

As if on cue, that hum came and Malachi jerked. Realization dawned. "They've got a tracking device on the car. That has to be the sound I'm hearing—the GPS being pinged."

Cass skidded through a turn, the tires squealing. "Why would they put a bug on my car? They know where I work and where I live. It's not exactly like I've been hiding in the L.A. underground or something."

The point was valid, but it was the only thing that made sense. A decrepit-looking van pulled in front of them. Malachi braced himself, but Cass avoided a collision.

"Is that idiot talking on his cell phone?" She sounded angry.

Malachi shifted his focus from the pickup to the van before his brain made the connection. "Your phone."

"What about it?"

"Cell phones can be located by pinging them and tracking via GPS. The vampire hunters didn't have to put a bug on your car, they're following your phone."

"Providers don't ping just because someone asks them to."

"No," he agreed, "but what if the request came from

someone on their payroll who works for the police? Or what if the hunters have someone in their pocket who's part of the phone company?"

Another turn took them into an area filled with warehouses and with very little traffic. It made it easier for Cass to drive.

And easier for the hunters to kill her without witnesses.

Malachi reached for her purse, opened it and dug around until he found her phone. Cass swore again, this time at him, but he ignored it. There wasn't time to worry about things like privacy and asking politely. He needed confirmation and the next ping was due shortly.

He didn't have time to take it out of the case, but it didn't matter. His sense of touch was as highly developed as his hearing and vision. He felt the sound in his fingertips.

"I was right. It's your phone. We'll have to toss it."

"What?" Cass didn't exactly shriek the word, but it was close. "You can't throw my phone away. Turn it off."

"Off or on doesn't matter, it remains traceable."

The stubborn expression on her face made him sigh.

One final attempt, then he'd throw it and face her wrath. "Is this thing—" he held out the phone "—worth your life?"

Silence for an instant, then she grudgingly answered, "No. Toss it."

Malachi didn't wait. He opened the window and pitched it into the street.

It was then he realized he should have had Cass throw it even if she was busy driving. The pickup was close enough to know there was no one in the passenger seat, but that was the window the phone had flown out of and it was obvious that she hadn't been the one who'd disposed of it. Did the hunters know enough to guess there was a shade with her?

Probably, he decided. They knew the steps necessary to kill a vampire, they'd realized they could take out Cass and eliminate the problem she'd caused by not beheading her assignments, and they'd had too much success to discount them.

Cass squealed around another corner. She stopped the car's fishtail and zoomed forward. The truck was closing in now.

"No," she moaned quietly.

Malachi shifted his gaze forward. There was a railroad crossing dead ahead. Red lights flashed and the guard arms were lowered into position.

He scanned the area, looking for a way out. The road was too narrow to make a U-turn and there wasn't a handy cross street before the tracks. He would have added a few curses to the litany Cass was reciting, but he didn't have time for that.

His mind whirled, rejecting option after option. Nothing got her out of this mess. His fear spiked. The best choice he could come up with was to stop the car, get out and run.

Before he could offer the suggestion, Cass came up with her own idea.

She put the pedal to the floor and raced toward the tracks.

Chapter Four

The train blew its horn, but Cass didn't slow.

If she stopped, the men in the pickup truck would kill her. She'd rather take her chances playing "beat the locomotive."

Squaring her shoulders, she drew a deep breath. Malachi was a shade, his body safely buried in an unmarked grave. She wasn't risking him, only herself. Cass glanced quickly to her right, but he wasn't there. She was on her own then. Big surprise.

She pressed the accelerator to the floor.

The gate arm crashed against the car, the sound as loud as an explosion. Cass winced, but stayed steady.

The lights mounted on the front of the engine lit up the sedan's interior. The train horn blew long and with an urgency that felt palpable. She looked out the side window, but all she could see was metal roaring toward her.

And then she was on the other side, the vehicle shaking as the train passed directly behind the rear bumper. She kept driving. She didn't know how long the train was and she wanted to be gone before the pickup crossed the tracks.

Cass focused on escape, afraid that she'd break down if she spent even a second recalling how close—

"What the hell were you thinking?" he demanded harshly.

Tears welled. She wouldn't cry. She never cried. And it wasn't as if he had any reason to be frightened. Anger drove away the weepiness and Cass embraced it. "What do you care? You weren't here. I don't know why you disappeared since being hit by a speeding locomotive wouldn't hurt you a bit."

"Don't push me, Cassandra."

His cold control made her angrier. "Don't call me Cassandra."

"Then don't insult me."

Her hands trembled and she clutched the steering wheel firmly to hide it. "Oh, yeah, I forgot," she drawled, letting sarcasm drip from each word, "you need me to rescue you from limbo. Oops, guess you do care."

"Bloody hell! You believe I sat here worrying about myself? You think that's all you are to me, a means to an end?"

Malachi had lost his temper along with his American accent. *He* was pissed off? Well, too bad. "No, you didn't sit there worrying. You bugged out when the going got tough."

"You're calling me a coward?" His voice had taken on a definite growl to go with the heat.

"If the cape fits, fang boy." She grimaced at her lame insult. Well, whatever. Adrenaline aftermath didn't exactly inspire snappy repartee.

The sound he made was so far from human that Cass felt her mouth go dry. Maybe infuriating a vampire wasn't her best idea ever. But he was a shade, right? What could he do to her? And he needed her to unstake him or he was trapped in never-never land forever.

Besides, if anyone had the right to be angry it was her. She'd trusted him to stick by her, although Cass had no idea why. No one in her entire life had been there when she needed them and he was no different. The sense of belonging was a fantasy, something she'd built up in her head because of the circumstances. It wasn't real and it wasn't reciprocated.

"I was present for the entire ride. I went nowhere."

"Liar. I checked before I hit the tracks and you weren't here."

"And where do you think I went? The car was moving."

"Ghosts pop in and out all the time."

"I'm *not* a ghost, I'm a—"

"Yeah, yeah, I know. You're a shadow. I get it. That doesn't mean you didn't leave me on my own."

No reply and Cass turned her head to glare at him. The passenger side of her car was empty. Maybe she'd driven him away for good. Instead of feeling satisfaction, a stab of fear pierced her. What had she expected? Really.

"Slow down. You have to make a left at the next inter-section to get to Laurent's home."

"What?" She jerked her gaze toward him, but the seat remained empty. "Where are you?"

"Right beside you as I was when you played chicken with a train." Malachi's English accent was pronounced. "Left at the light. Do you hear me?"

That question and his tone made Cass grind her teeth, but she nodded and switched lanes.

He'd been invisible most of the four days since he'd started hanging around. Until tonight, she'd sensed him, felt him touch her, but she hadn't been able to see or hear him. Maybe Malachi wasn't lying about being with her when she'd raced the train.

She mulled that over. Cass realized she had a chip on her shoulder. She always jumped to the worst conclusion when it came to assuming someone had abandoned her, but she couldn't help that. Her mom had dropped her off at kindergarten and hadn't bothered to come back—that had made an indelible impression on her life—and being passed around foster care hadn't done anything to over-come her insecurities.

Malachi gave her another set of directions with less of an accent. Cass made the first turn and then glanced over. He was filmy, but she could see him again.

Ten minutes later when he provided the next instruc-tions, he sounded American. A quick check verified what she suspected—he was solid once more. When he'd been angry, he'd been invisible, but as his temper had cooled, he'd become real again. Okay, sort of real.

That gave her more to consider. She hadn't reached any definite conclusions when, a while later, he interrupted her thoughts.

"Park the car," he said. "We'll walk from here."

"Walk? Why?" But she did pull to the curb and turned off the engine. "You tossed my phone and no one has followed us since we lost the pickup."

"Better to be safe and they know what you're driving." He got out of the car.

Cass watched him round the hood, but she didn't move. Walk? In L.A.? Malachi opened her door for her and held out a hand. She stared at it a moment before unhooking her seat belt, grabbing her purse and letting him help her. No one had ever opened a door for her before. "How old are you anyway?"

Instead of answering, he made a bow, and when he straightened, offered her his elbow. "Milady."

Bemused, she took it and walked beside him. "Lady. Yeah. If I'd been born in your time—whenever that was—I probably would have been a scullery maid."

"Do you know what that is?"

"No," she admitted reluctantly, "but from the books I've read, it sounded like a lowly position."

"It was, but if it makes you feel better, I didn't rank much higher."

He didn't sound mad any longer and Cass ignored the sense of relief. Adrenaline—there was no doubt that's what had made them both feel combative earlier, but she was glad things were relaxed now.

Well, mostly relaxed. She was far too aware of the brush of his hip against hers as they walked, the play of the muscles of his forearm beneath her hand, and the way he made her heart beat faster just being beside her. "I don't know about that," Cass said. "Your accent came across pretty aristocratic to me."

"Many decades of practice." Malachi gave her a smile that had her stomach doing a flip. "If I'd spoken the way I did when I was alive, I doubt you'd have understood a word I said."

She looked around, studying her surroundings until she had a grip on her hormones. "Speaking of aristocratic, check out this neighborhood."

And she was dressed like a Madonna wanna-be. Malachi didn't look any better. His jeans had seen better days and his black T-shirt was faded and frayed. Cass stifled a groan. "We're going to get arrested for being here."

His grin widened. "You'll get arrested. I'm visible only to you."

"What? You're solid and completely seeable."

"Only to you," he repeated.

Oh, awesome. "So anyone who's looking out a window thinks I'm talking to myself. I'll end up in the psyche ward, not jail."

"The houses are set far enough back from the sidewalk, that it's unlikely anyone can see you conversing with me."

"Right. That makes me feel much better." Cass stiffened.

"Wait a second, no one can see you? Even now? Tell me that doesn't include your vampire friend."

"I would, but I'd hate to lie."

Cass groaned and pulled him to a halt. "Malachi! Why didn't you mention this before?"

"I did, but I chose not to remind you because you'd have refused to come. As a shade, I'm unable to protect you from much. I trust Laurent to take care of you while I can't."

She stared at him hard.

Malachi covered her hand with his and squeezed gently. "He's a good friend and isn't someone who will attack without provocation. I'll tell you what to say to convince him I'm with you." When she hesitated, he added, "Trust me."

The scary thing was that she did trust him. She wished she could believe it was because he wanted something from her, but Cass knew that wasn't the truth. And maybe it was part of the reason why she'd become furious when she thought Malachi had cut out on her earlier tonight. Somehow he'd become important to her.

"If this Laurent dude kills me," she grumbled, "*I* will come back as a ghost and haunt *you*, got it?"

"I'm not worried." He gave her a small tug to get her moving. "Come on."

But when they turned into a driveway a good fifteen minutes later, the house that stood at the end of it was completely dark. Vampires were nocturnal; there should be some sign of life.

He frowned, but led her to the door. "Ring the bell."

Cass did. No lights came on and no one answered. She looked up at him.

"I don't hear anyone moving around," he confirmed. "Laurent isn't home."

The immediate relief she felt at not facing a vampire in his lair was tempered by the knowledge that Malachi had admitted he couldn't protect her very well. Sure Los Angeles was a big city, but without money, how long could she hide before the hunters located her? One swipe of her credit card for food, gas, or a hotel and she was sunk.

"What do we do now?" she asked.

"Find the spare key and go in."

Cass stared at him. Let herself inside a vampire's house and have him arrive to find her there? After Malachi said she was a known vampire hunter? "I think Laurent might consider me being inside his home to be a provocation and a reason to attack."

"Then you'll have to stake him, won't you?" Malachi said with a grin.

"I thought he was your friend."

"He is, but you can explain the truth while he's down. Shades can hear, you know, even if no one hears us in return. Then, once you say your piece, yank out the wood. He'll heal."

"And no doubt be mad as hell."

"No doubt." But Malachi sounded amused at the prospect.

Cass shook her head. Vampires—who could understand them?

Chapter Five

Cass took one look around the entryway of Laurent's home and edged closer to Malachi. The place could have graced the pages of some decorating magazine and everything appeared hugely expensive. "Wow, your friend sure went all out."

Malachi laced his fingers with hers and grinned. "That's because Laurent de Brinay *was* born to the aristocracy and he's accustomed to his finery. Don't worry. His lordship isn't attached to these things and if we break something, he won't have us flogged."

She replayed his words. "You used to sweat about knocking something over, didn't you?"

His smile faded. "When I was human, I was a tenant farmer who always had dung on his boots. Until I became a vampire, I'd never dreamed homes such as this existed. It was difficult not to be intimidated—at least initially."

For the first time, she noticed that the hand she held was rough and callused. She liked that, and imagined his palms running over her body.... Cass shivered and watched the heat flare in his eyes. He knew what he did to her, knew and responded to her desire. Malachi had told her the attraction went both ways and now she believed it. He was as helpless against the want as she was.

"Why did you spend the last four days touching and kissing me?"

"Because I couldn't stop myself." His voice was deep, husky. Sexy. "I realize I had no right, but you can be assured that I didn't do more and I never invaded your privacy by entering your bedroom or bath."

That startled Cass. She hadn't considered that he might have watched her sleep or shower. "Good, because that kind of weird stalker behavior would have creeped me out."

His lips curved, not a full-fledged smile, but enough to make her heart beat faster. "I couldn't have gotten away with it had I tried. You reacted the instant I entered the room, and when I spoke to you, your brow would furrow as if you could hear me."

"I nearly could. I just couldn't make out the words."

Malachi gave her a gentle tug and pulled her deeper into the house. Cass drew a sharp breath as he turned on the lights in the...well, living room seemed too mundane, but she didn't know what else to call it. "Are those *real* Fabergé eggs lying out on the end tables?"

"It's likely," he said.

That meant the vases were probably genuine Ming dynasty and the paintings… "You might not have dreamed homes like this existed, but I never dreamed I'd be inside a house like this. Ever. None of the vampires I staked lived like— Oops."

He laughed and that good, shivery feeling went through her, making her tingle in all the right places. "I know you hunted vampires—you don't have to censor that part of your life. As for living in this manner, most of us go through a phase of collecting expensive things, but after a while, you realize it doesn't matter."

"Did you?" Everything about him fascinated her and Cass knew that spelled trouble.

"For a time, yes, but I never felt comfortable with it." Malachi drew her against his body and wrapped her in a loose embrace. "Once a peasant, always a peasant."

His light teasing added to the warmth she felt. Why him? Talk about a doomed relationship. She'd driven a stake into him, and if that weren't enough, she had people who wanted her dead. And Malachi, too, for that matter.

With a sigh, Cass put her arms around his waist and rested her cheek to his chest. "What do we do now?"

"Since you don't trust me to honor my word and protect you if I was a vampire once more, I suggest we hide here until we can think up some other way to keep you safe."

Cass stiffened and leaned back to meet his eyes. Hurt. She'd hurt him. "I trust you. I do," she said sharply when he would have disagreed. "That stuff in the car where I thought you'd left, that was about me, not you."

His gaze assessed her and Cass fought the need to con-

ceal her vulnerability. "I have a few abandonment issues."
She shrugged and tried to smile. She failed. "But that has
nothing to do with freeing you. They kill vampires, and
unlike me, they *will* chop off your head."

"There's more to it than that."

"Yes." The urge to look away was even stronger now,
but Cass refused to be a chicken. "If I unstake you, they'll
hunt me for the rest of my life. Are you willing to commit
to guarding me for sixty or seventy years?"

"If necessary, I would." He stopped her before she could
argue by brushing his lips over hers. "I loathe limbo. There
aren't words to tell you how much. For releasing me alone,
I'd happily spend the next hundred years protecting you."

"But—"

Malachi kissed her again, stopping her midprotest. Cass
kissed him back, savoring the feel of him. She had it bad
for this guy. Really bad. Opening her mouth beneath his,
she invited him to deepen the kiss. As his tongue teased
hers, her eyes drifted shut.

This wasn't adrenaline. This wasn't loneliness or gratitude for his help. This was about Malachi, about how he
made her feel when he touched her. About how she loved
touching him in return.

He ended the kiss and Cass moaned a protest as she met
his gaze. His lips were barely out of reach of hers when he
said, "I was born in the sixteenth century. Do you think
seventy years is a daunting length of time for me?"

"Probably not."

That half smile of his again, the one that made her breath

catch. "It's all moot, though, you know. The connection between us is strong enough to keep me at your side until you grow tired of me and tell me to leave."

Cass couldn't imagine that ever happening, but she didn't say it. Connection? Yes, she felt it. Scary? Hell, yes. But the lure of Malachi was stronger than the fear of whatever.

We hardly know each other. But Cass didn't say that aloud, either. She might not have every detail about him, but she knew who Malachi was at his heart. That frightened her, too.

And she was tired of being afraid to let anyone close. Tired of worrying there was something wrong with her, something that made people walk away. Tired of thinking. She pulled his mouth back to hers. "Kiss me, damn it."

He hesitated, peering into her eyes, maybe into her soul, and then he smiled. "I think we'd best find a bedroom before I kiss you again, yes?"

"Yes." Cass had a pang of embarrassment over how enthusiastically she'd agreed, but it didn't last long. Not when Malachi didn't waste any time getting her up the stairs and down the hallway to a guest room. His eagerness made her feel special, but it was the look in his eyes as he closed the door behind them that made her heart roll over in her chest. This wasn't going to be just sex. It was going to be more.

A lot more.

Her gulp was audible.

"I know. Look at my hands." Malachi held them out so

she could see them shake. "This is how much I want you, Cass."

She let her purse fall to the floor and started tugging off the chunky plastic bangles on her wrist. He watched with an intensity that made her burn and she wondered how explosive things would get when clothes started coming off.

Tossing the last bracelet on top of the dresser, she took a step toward him and stopped. "Are you going to want to bite me? Because I'm not sure how I feel about that."

"I've no fangs as a shadow." Malachi crossed the floor until he stood in front of her. Slowly, he brought a hand up and trailed the backs of his fingers along her cheekbone. "But even if I did, I'd honor your wishes. It will always be your choice."

He was telling her that he'd put her needs ahead of his wants. Cass fell a little further. A little harder.

She went up on her toes, kissing him. It started sweet and easy, but that didn't last. Malachi devoured her mouth as if he were starving for her and Cass kissed him every bit as desperately. She couldn't get enough of him, would never get enough.

A moan of protest escaped her as he stepped back, but when he lifted her sweatshirt, she raised her arms to help him. As soon as it was off, she reached for his T-shirt. He removed it and let it fall to the floor. His shoulders were broad, his chest muscular, and Cass felt her mouth go dry. Damn, he was beautiful.

"If this is what being a farmer does for a man, then *viva la*…" She couldn't come up with the Spanish word for peasant, and as Malachi tossed her tank top aside and reached for the hook on her bra, Cass decided it didn't matter.

He stared, and with a growl, she curled her hands around the waistband of his jeans and tugged him closer. "Gawk later," she told him and pressed her breasts against his chest.

They both groaned at the contact. Malachi wrapped his arms around her, bringing her tightly against him, and lowered his head to take her mouth. She ran her palms over his back, her fingers enjoying the warmth of his skin, the hardness of his muscles. So good. He felt so damn good.

Malachi slipped a hand between their bodies to cup a breast and his thumb teased a nipple. Cass arched, needing more contact, needing more of him.

It wasn't enough.

She reached for the button of his jeans, worked it free of the loop, and eased down his zipper. It was Malachi who broke the kiss and gasped as she cupped him through his briefs. Her smile widened as she saw how dilated his pupils were.

"I'm trying to show you how much you matter," Malachi said with some English in his voice.

"That doesn't mean you have to dawdle."

Okay, she sounded as breathless as he had, but it got her hot and achy to touch him. To know that she was eroding his self-command. It might have taken her some time, but she'd figured it out—Malachi James only lost his American accent when his control slipped. Being the woman who made him surrender that restraint? Major turn-on.

Malachi studied her before one side of his mouth quirked up in a lopsided smile. "I can move quicker." He stepped on the backs of his tennis shoes to get out of them, bent to pull off his socks and pushed down his jeans. "You're not keeping up. Is this too fast for you?"

"Hell, no." With a laugh, she kicked off her shoes and wiggled out of the capris. The flare of heat in his eyes as she stood in front of him in only her panties nearly made her squirm.

She laughed when he bent down and picked her up. Not romantically sweeping her off her feet, but a fireman's carry and Cass loved it because it told her how much he wanted her.

Yanking back the bedspread and blankets, Malachi put her on the bed and followed her down. He kissed her briefly before moving to her throat and then her breasts. She splayed a hand through his hair to keep him there. It worked for a moment, but then he was kissing her stomach, tracing the edge of her navel with his tongue and sliding lower.

Cass lifted her hips as he pulled her panties off, then pushed him onto his back. "It's my turn."

Ignoring his protest, even if it was made with that toe-curling English accent, she leaned over him and put her lips on his. She could kiss him forever and it wouldn't be enough, but there was more of him she wanted to taste.

His chest and shoulders tempted her. She let her fingers travel over his body, trailing openmouthed kisses behind them. Cass watched the way Malachi reacted to learn what he liked. If his hands fisted or he tensed, she repeated what she'd done. She stroked his erection through the cotton, squeezing his shaft gently.

Growling, Malachi tugged her up, turned her on her back and, after pushing off his briefs, settled between her thighs. Cass rocked into his hard-on, gasping at how good it felt.

It got even better when, gaze locked with hers, he slid slowly inside her. Cass moaned, but that changed to a gasp.

"What? Did I hurt you?"

"No." Her voice was ragged, but he sounded completely English, so she figured they were even. "I can see through you."

Bowing his head near hers, he said, "Sorry. Give me a moment." Malachi closed his eyes, and with a muscle jumping in his cheek, became more solid. "Better?"

"Yes." And now she understood. He had to concentrate if he wanted to be visible to her.

As he thrust, Cass let her eyes drift shut, immersing herself in the sensations. Everything seemed more intense, more brilliant because she was with Malachi.

It didn't take long before she dug her fingers in to his hips, demanding everything. They'd had four days of fore-play, how much longer did he think she needed? "So close," she managed to say. "Malachi."

He got the message and Cass arched into his strokes. Her orgasm slammed into her. All she could do was ride the waves and cling to him.

Cass was nearing a second orgasm when she heard him

groan and knew he was coming. She opened her eyes, wanting to watch his face, and stiffened.

Malachi had vanished. Again.

This time, she knew he was here. She could feel him against her body, inside her body. Cass closed her eyes, trusting touch rather than sight. His orgasm sent her soaring again.

Later, after he'd rolled to her side, Cass propped herself up on an elbow and brushed his hair off his forehead. The clutching she felt in her chest as he smiled at her made everything clear. This man had her heart. There was only one thing left to do.

"We have a few hours until sunrise," she said quietly. "Let's dig you up."

Chapter Six

Malachi winced as Cass forcefully drove the shovel into the earth. "Careful, sweet, you don't want to hack off some part of me that you'll miss later."

Her head jerked up and she appeared startled until she caught his grin. A spark of answering humor made her green eyes dance with mischief, but it was her smile that hit him square in the chest.

"If you did more digging yourself and less standing around, you wouldn't have to worry about losing your parts." Her dry tone made his grin broaden.

"I can't dig and extend my senses as far as I'd like. I want as much notice as possible if the hunters arrive."

Cass straightened and said, "You're presuming they know about shades, but there's no proof. No one ever told *me* about the possibility."

They'd been over this once when he'd informed her that

the men after them had seen an invisible person throw the phone out the car window. "I hope so, but in my experience what the foot soldiers are aware of and what the officers know are usually two different things."

She scowled. "Yeah. And the organization gets off on secrets." Cass looked around, but the wooded area remained quiet. "We should be getting close to your body—you weren't buried that deeply."

"More reason to take care." Malachi winked at her and returned to digging.

They couldn't waste time. Coming here tonight was a calculated risk. He hoped it would take the powers-that-be time to round up the troops to cover the general burial locations where Cass might have left her not-quite-dead vampires, but that's what it was. A hope.

Waiting a few weeks might have been better. That would be long enough for the hunters to question if there truly were a shade with Cass and give up on the graves.

But that meant counting on friends to protect her while he remained a shadow. He trusted Jet and Laurent, but neither of them would die to keep Cass safe. Malachi would.

With all that had transpired tonight, he didn't think she'd stopped to consider the ramifications of her situation. It would require a covert operation to recover her things from her apartment and she'd never be able to hold a job. It would be a hell of a life for her even with his help. Unless…

He glanced up briefly. Moonlight illuminated her face and he could see the determined expression there. Cass was young—how could he consider it?

You were but twenty-two when you were brought across.

True, but in his day that was near middle-aged. The world was a different place now. Still, despite her tendency to be flip at times, Cass was more mature than her years in many ways.

"I think I just hit your body," she said, breaking into his thoughts.

"I hope you used the word *hit* in a figurative sense. It's going to take considerable strength to recover from the stake without adding additional damage."

Cass ignored the teasing. "I was careful."

She put down her shovel and went to her knees, using her hands to move the dirt. Malachi tossed his own shovel aside and joined her. It seemed an eternity before he saw his face. With mock sorrow, he said, "I look so peaceful."

"You're on a roll. Getting laid must bring out your inner smart-ass."

That sobered him. "We made love. I know things were intense and that scared you, but don't diminish what we shared."

"I wasn't—"

"Yes, you were, but it's okay. I understand your reasons. Of course, that doesn't mean I won't call you on it." Her glare made him smile and Malachi kissed her forehead. "We need to clean the dirt from my eyes, nose and mouth before you pull the stake."

Without saying more, she did it quickly and thoroughly before removing the garlic. He'd forgotten that detail.

Standing, she put a foot on either side of his waist to

give herself leverage. Then she looked at him, asking wordlessly if it was okay.

Malachi reached out and took her hand in his. "As soon as you remove the wood, get out of the hole. Give me room to acclimate." She nodded, but he hesitated. "We've both been avoiding the words, but I've no idea what will happen once I'm back in my body. In case things don't go well, I want you to know that I love you, Cass." Without waiting for a response, he released her. "Now pull the stake."

For an instant, she gaped at him. Then with a short nod, she bent down, wrapped both hands around the wood protruding from his chest and yanked.

The world went black. Malachi had no sense of self, no sense of place, there was only an abyss of nothing.

Until he hit bottom hard enough to force a groan.

Where was he? Why did he feel so weak?

Injured. Severely, if the energy his body was using to repair itself was any indication. His brain was sluggish, his senses dulled, but he reached out with them anyway, needing information. There was a presence nearby. Human. Female. Malachi forced his eyes open.

A worried face peered down at him.

She had short dark hair, enormous green eyes and an elfin chin that wobbled as he watched. "Are you okay?"

He gazed up at her, but didn't answer. His body continued to mend, but something had caused the damage. Something or someone. Her?

Tears filled her eyes and her teeth sank into her lower

lip. Memory flashed of biting that lip himself while he'd kissed her.

"Malachi, please."

He'd heard those words before from her, he knew it. Closing his eyes, he tried to think. The visions that filled his mind were erotic enough to assure him it wasn't merely his fantasies. She'd been his lover.

"Damn it, Malachi, I love you, too, but I swear I'm jumping in that hole and putting that stake back in you. At least when you were a shade, you talked to me."

The tartness jarred his memory into sharp focus. "Give a man a chance," he said. His voice was raspy from disuse, but he ignored that and opened his eyes. "Even for a vampire, recovering from a major trauma isn't instantaneous."

She swiped at her cheek, ridding it of the tear that had dared escape. "You scared me."

"Sorry, sweet. I need a minute or two more."

It was closer to twenty before the wound was healed and he felt capable of moving. Cass was there to help as he hoisted himself from the grave and the feel of her hand at her elbow caused his fangs to descend. Damn.

Malachi staggered as she released him, but when Cass tried to grab him again, he stepped out of reach. He shook his head. "I need blood badly. You're safe," he assured her. "I'm old enough to have control, but it's easier if you don't touch me."

"You know, if you wanted like a pint or something, I could give you that."

Cass looked so earnest that Malachi smiled despite the

gnawing hunger. "No. I won't be able to stop until I've taken enough to heal completely. The blood loss would kill you. If you wanted to become a vampire, it would be all right because I'd have to take that much anyway, otherwise it's not a good idea."

She only stared at him, answer enough to his unspoken question.

He ignored the stab of disappointment. Becoming a vampire wasn't something to be done on impulse or because she was worried about him. "I'm feeling strong enough to walk to the car and we need to get out of here."

They started away from the grave. He knew Cass was worried, but he couldn't reassure her, not when it took every bit of concentration to merely put one foot in front of the other.

Car doors slammed and they stopped short.

"We got lucky; that's her car." The voice was soft, but clearly audible. More door slams. At least four men then, possibly more.

Malachi gestured behind them. "We'll hide."

Cass nodded and turned with him. His head swam. The timing could have been worse. They could have arrived while he'd been lying in the hole, but this was bad enough.

Without blood, a lot of it, he couldn't survive a fight. Not for long. And if he died, his Cass died, too. They wouldn't keep her alive, not even to chop the heads off the remaining vampires. Bringing him back was a clear announcement of whose side she'd chosen. He stumbled and started to fall, but she put an arm around his waist, propping him up until he regained his footing.

The second time he tripped, they both went down. "Keep going," he told her softly. "I'll catch up."

"That's bull and we both know it," she whispered hotly. "I'll be damned, Mal, if I'm leaving you here as some sacrifice to those bastards. Win or lose, we're in it together."

Instead of wasting energy arguing, he stood. Cass was stubborn, but she wasn't stupid. This area wasn't big enough or wooded enough to hide her for long. The best he could do by staying behind was delay them. Briefly.

"You need blood," Cass said when they'd managed to gain a bit of ground between them and their pursuers. "If you make me a vampire, will that be enough to give you a chance against them?"

"Yes, but—"

"If I'm a vampire, will I be able to fight with you tonight?"

"For a limited time, but then you'll need blood as much as I do now. Becoming a vampire is overwhelming at first. You won't know what you can do or what your restrictions are and finding out in the middle of—"

"Do it."

"You should know the pros and cons. You should have time to consider them and weigh how the change will affect your life. This isn't a minor decision."

"No, it's not, but there's no choice. If you don't bite me, we're both dead. Do it."

Malachi hesitated a moment more, then nodded. This

gave them a chance and it was the only thing that would. As weak as he was, he'd never get close enough to feed from any of the hunters. He picked a sheltered location and guided her to it. Half-falling, he sat and patted his leg. Cass settled on his lap.

His fangs were down before she stilled. She looked at him, her eyes apprehensive. He tried to think of something to reassure her, but only one thing came to mind. "I love you, Cass."

Her tremulous smile stayed in his mind as he leaned forward and found the artery he wanted. Slowly, taking care not to hurt her, he sank his teeth into her throat.

Need swamped him and he drew her blood in quicker. When Malachi realized how greedily he drank, he battled within himself. He had to pay attention, had to know the right moment to stop and give her his blood in return. To help focus, he chanted her name in his head.

He still nearly missed feeling Cass die.

Chapter Seven

Cass cringed as a cacophony of sound beat at her. She could hear the flutter of wings, detect insects crawling in the grass, pick up the footsteps of the hunters as they tried to move stealthily. And the scents!

Malachi hugged her closer and crooned against her ear. The sound was soft and soothing, and she concentrated on him to blot out the riot of noise. It only took a moment before she grimaced. "You smell like dirt," she said, her voice modulating immediately as her own volume made her wince.

"I was buried for two years. You're lucky I don't smell worse." His hand rubbed her back in comforting circles. "They're closing in on us. Open your eyes."

"Will my vision be as overloaded as my ears? And why am I talking with a lisp?"

"Yes, you'll probably find your new sight overwhelming, but we don't have time for you to acclimate slowly. As for the lisp, your fangs are down and you haven't learned to speak around them."

Cass immediately reached out with her tongue and hissed as a sharp point pierced her flesh. She really was a vampire, with the teeth to prove it.

"Open your eyes, sweet."

Knowing she had no choice, Cass did it. Her fingers dug into his shoulders. The moonlight allowed her to see as if it were the sun. Colors were brighter, outlines sharper, and she could look a long distance with utter clarity.

Gulping, she turned to Malachi, needing him to anchor her. His black T-shirt had a ragged hole and she could see each fiber. For the first time, she noticed slight lines between his brows, saw the three pale freckles over his right cheekbone, and she could count the flecks of navy in his eyes.

"Cass, get control."

"I'm trying." And failing. There was too much.

"I can help. Let me in your head."

She wasn't sure what he was asking, but somehow she opened and he was in her mind. Cass could feel his essence. Malachi built a screen for her, blocking some of the sensations. It was quick, taking only seconds, but Cass felt better.

When Malachi spoke again, it wasn't aloud. *They have us loosely pinned in and we need to find a more defensible position.*

Cass stood when he prodded her. *Can't we sneak past them?*

We can try, but there's enough of them and cover is so light here that I doubt we'll succeed.

I wish we could use mind control, but hunters are trained to be unaffected by it, Cass sent.

Malachi didn't comment, only gestured to the right and Cass fell into step with him. Remembering how weak he'd been earlier, she watched closely, but her blood seemed to have worked and he moved without trouble.

Her blood. Yeah. How long did she have before she stopped feeling as if she could leap a tall building?

Perhaps an hour.

His grimness registered and Cass guessed that meant it might take less time than that. Awesome. Once she crashed, she'd be a liability to him.

Win or lose, we're in it together, he told her, repeating her words.

Stop reading my mind!

Sorry, sweet. If I leave your head, you'll be deluged by sensation again. What if I pretend not to hear you?

Before Cass could decide what she thought of that idea, Malachi pulled them down behind a bush. She waited for what felt like forever before a man came into view. He crossed within feet of their position, stake in one hand, gun in the other. If it had been daylight, they'd probably have been spotted.

They stayed where they were for long moments after the hunter left. Cass fought the urge to move until Malachi took her hand and tugged her to her feet. They'd gone maybe ten yards when he stopped and whirled.

Cass's stomach twisted when she saw who stood there. Henry Votto ranked high in the hunter hierarchy and he always killed his vampire.

"I got 'em," he called. "Well, well, Cassie, it looks like you went over to the dark side. I guess I can put this away." He slid the gun into a shoulder holster.

She clenched her jaw tight enough to make a muscle tic. As much as she disliked being called Cassandra, she hated Cassie a bajillion times more. And it was such a stupid thing to get pissed off about considering the situation. How had he found them and why hadn't they known he was there?

Psi tracker, Malachi told her. *We won't elude him.*

"What's—"

He squeezed her hand hard enough to quiet her. Yeah, not now. The others converged on them, surrounding her and Malachi.

Five against two.

Cass recognized all of them, but she could only recall a couple of names—Jimenez and Quentin. "I didn't realize I rated some of the best hunters in the city."

And damn the lisp. She sounded like Cindy Brady, not a tough vampire chick. Cass tried to pull in her fangs, but failed.

Cass, they know you're a new vampire and what that means. How you speak doesn't enter into it. We'll fight back-to-back, that way no one can come up behind us. Don't take on the psi tracker—leave him to me.

Malachi was right. The hunters had enough experience that even if she sounded scary as hell, these guys wouldn't be rattled. She took up her position at his back.

Three of them charged before she could prepare herself.

She swiped at Jimenez's stake, knocking it loose. To her surprise, long talons came out of her fingertips. "Whoa!"

The weirdness made her hesitate and they took the opening. Cass barely had time dodge the blow from the second man before Quentin was on her.

With a twist, she evaded the strike and lashed out. She caught his forearm, but only scratched him.

Jimenez and Hunter Two immediately moved in.

Scuffling behind her told Cass she was on her own. Malachi had his own enemies.

She kicked out, glad her capri pants were stretchy. Too damn bad she wasn't wearing boots. Still, she managed to strike Jimenez's leg with enough force to tumble him to the ground.

Cass could see his pulse beating in his throat. Her mouth watered and she pulled her lips back. Fear filled his eyes and it startled her. Quentin and the other guy pulled Jimenez out of range and it was only then that she realized she'd salivated as if he were the world's best tofu burger.

In a distant part of her brain, Cass thought that should scare her. It didn't. She wanted to sink her fangs in. Badly.

Hunter Two rushed her. Cass reached up, caught his wrist in her hand and squeezed. He dropped the stake.

Bones snapped, but she didn't release him.

Motion captured her attention. A quick peek showed Quentin was attacking. She grabbed the guy's other arm and spun around, using him as a shield.

Quentin's stake penetrated the man's back and he screamed.

She flung him at Quentin. The smell of blood made her teeth ache. She wanted it. Craved it. Needed it.

Involuntarily, she took a step forward.

Control, Cass. Hold control.

Malachi's voice helped her rein in, and while she had the chance, she glanced over her shoulder to check on him. Blood ran from a gash on his cheek and there was a long, ugly scrape on the inside of his arm. Votto and his companion worked like a well-oiled team, putting pressure on Malachi.

A low growl that wasn't quite human escaped her, but before Cass could protect her lover, it went quiet behind her. Too quiet.

She spun around and saw Jimenez running at her from her right, Quentin from the left. Damn them, she wanted this over. She wanted to hold Malachi, make sure he was okay.

Instead, she had to fight these two.

One of the stakes grazed the arm she brought up. Cass kicked out again, but missed. Her momentum allowed her to pivot out of the way of Jimenez's strike, but she felt the wood whoosh past her ear.

"You killed Suzuki," Quentin said, mouth pulled back in a snarl. "You'll pay for that."

"You killed your friend, not me." But even as she spoke, she knew it was pointless. Quentin hated vampires, and in his mind, she was guilty. Not him.

Jimenez took advantage of her distraction and only extra-fast reflexes allowed her to get out of the way. She kicked again and caught him on the side of the knee as he went past her. The sound made her cringe. So did the angle of his leg and his scream.

Quentin's face contorted with rage. He didn't bother to raise his stake as he charged.

Cass swiped out with her talons.

Two of them caught his throat. The gurgle he made—not pretty. He fell to the ground, clutching his neck. The blood fascinated her, but a shout from behind her broke Cass's trance.

Malachi!

If anything happened to him—

She turned in time to see him rip open Votto's throat, a feral expression on his face.

The hunter didn't get up. The other man was already down and Cass thought his neck might be broken. Four dead, one whimpering. She took a step forward and staggered, suddenly feeling as if a breeze could knock her over.

Malachi immediately straightened, his talons and teeth retracting as he came to her. His arm went around her waist. "Let's get out of here, sweet."

Cass let him lead her away. "And go where? There are

hunters all over the world and they'll never stop coming after us. And why the hell can't I get these teeth to pull in when controlling the claws is easy?"

And then she felt Malachi more strongly in her head, walking her through how to retract her fangs. It was simple and she felt silly for needing lessons.

"Don't. Some things will be instinctive, but much won't. You're not the first fledgling to go through this and you won't be the last. As for the hunters, I know." Malachi tugged her closer to his side. "But we're not on our own. Now that you're a vampire, we can go to the clan lord. We'll be safe on his estate. Believe me, the enforcers won't allow any hunter within a mile of the property."

"Clan lord? Enforcers?" How much more was she unaware of?

"A lot, but what I know I'll share with you."

They reached her car, but instead of getting in, Cass leaned against the fender and took his hand. "It's—" She hesitated, but this was Malachi, she could share anything and he wouldn't think less of her. "It's scary. Being confined forever even on an estate and drinking blood. I'm a vegetarian."

"Not any longer." He said that gently, reminding her that she'd changed. "And we won't be forced to spend our lives at the estate. In a month or two, we won't be a priority to the hunters and we'll be able to go anywhere."

"After tonight? I doubt it. They'll be looking for revenge."

Malachi brushed her hair off her face and cupped her

chin in one hand. "The hunters will never know for certain what happened here. Enforcers are already on their way to clean up for us."

"What? How?"

"I sent a telepathic message. And no, I can't communicate with everyone that way. Not yet. Only those with whom I have a direct blood link."

Which raised additional questions, but Cass went in a different direction. "This clan lord, he's going to want me to dig up the other vampires I staked, isn't he?"

"Yes, but it will likely be when the furor has subsided and we'll have a team with us to guard our backs."

Us. This wasn't the right time or place, but Cass needed to know. "Things were pretty stressful. People say stuff…" Hell. "Is there really an *us?* After you train me in, I mean."

Malachi moved close enough that she could feel the heat of his body with her own. His other hand came up, framing her face. He met her gaze squarely and said, "It wasn't the situation. I've never used those words with another woman, no matter how intense the circumstances. I love you, Cass."

To her surprise, she didn't feel fear. Nervousness, yes, but it was the good kind where it was like champagne bubbles dancing in her cells. Putting her arms around his neck, Cass went to her toes and kissed him sweetly. "I love you, too," she told him.

Another wave of fatigue washed over her and she leaned on him. "Mal, I don't think I can drive."

He hugged her tightly. "I'll take care of it and I'll take care of you when you need me." It sounded like a promise.

By the time Malachi got her car started and drove away from the wooded area, the eastern sky had begun to lighten. Cass turned her head and stared at his profile. Before she could stop it, the title of one of those damn 80s songs jumped into her head—"The Future's So Bright, I Gotta Wear Shades."

Yeah, she decided. The future was looking pretty awesome.

* * * * *

HUNTER'S
SURRENDER

ANNA HACKETT

Mining engineer by day, writer by night, Australian-born **Anna Hackett** grew up a reader without dreams of being a writer. "I wasn't one of those kids who was always writing stories," Anna notes. "I was too busy reading." But in 2006, on a work trip to a gold mine, something changed. "I figured, I'd read so many romances, how hard could it be to write one? Little did I know!"

She bought some how-to books, joined some writers groups and started writing. "As a teen, I raided my mother's romances and my father's shelves of action-adventure books," she remembers. "So no surprise I love writing action-adventure stories with a strong dose of romance." Add in a lifetime love of ancient history and mythology (she's been to Egypt twice) and it became apparent that paranormal romance was a perfect fit.

Anna learned the importance of grabbing every opportunity that presents itself. In 2008 she entered a pitch contest and was selected to pitch her short story online. The story sold and she found herself with an editor.

After three years in beautiful Denver, Colorado, Anna and her English-American husband currently live in an isolated mining town in northern Australia. When she's not wearing her boots and hard hat, Anna is at her computer, working on her paranormal romances.

Chapter One

"He's here somewhere. Find him!"

Rand Wilder stood silent in the desert darkness. Despite the moonless night, his enhanced vision allowed him to see the six vampires hunting for him.

The thump of music from the run-down highway bar nearby sounded like a heartbeat in the night. The lights of Las Vegas shimmered in the distance. The warm desert air brushed over him.

As did the vampires' energies, prickling over his skin and pulsing under his heart.

Anaharta. Vampires ruled by the heart chakra. And ones who'd let their energy course out of alignment.

Unbalanced vampires were Rand's favorite prey.

"Come out, come out." The tallest vampire spun in a slow circle. "We know you're here, hunter."

One of the vampires came closer, his feet kicking up the

coarse desert sand. Rand's hand tightened on his stake—a shaft of pure titanium. The vampire's jagged energy was evident in the creature's jerky movements.

Come on, just another inch. Rand waited. His career as a vampire hunter had taught him patience. Against unbalanced rogues, it was his greatest weapon.

The vampire paused, lifting his pretty face to the star-scattered sky. It seemed a cosmic joke that such powerful, vicious beings were so beautiful. No doubt the Indian vampire goddess Kali had laughed when she'd created the first of her children thousands of years ago.

Vampires were ruled by the energy coursing through their chakras—energy they got from blood. Over time it improved their skin, trimmed their bodies and smoothed out their features.

But it didn't hide their rotten insides.

Dark memories of his father's blood running like a river across the floor twisted through Rand. A man who'd dedicated his life to protecting the innocent hadn't deserved to be tortured to death.

Rand tried to recall his father's deep voice and booming laugh, but the sounds were lost to him. His heart thumped hard against his ribs. Time, and the blood of all the vampires he'd killed, had dulled his memories.

Now he knew only rage and death.

The vampire inched closer, unaware his executioner stood within a breath of him. Rand thrust out his arm.

The stake sank into the vamp's heart, the executed seeing no more than a blur of shadow. He didn't make a sound as he crumpled to the sand.

Using his speed, Rand attacked the two closest vampires. They, too, died in silence.

"What the hell?"

"Alban and Jago are down!"

"Where is he?"

The frenzy of panicked voices echoed through the dark. Again Rand waited.

"It's The Darkness," one of the vampires moaned.

It was the name the vampire community had given Rand many years ago. The darkness hid him, was a part of him, one of his many hunter skills. He came from it when the vampires least expected him. It also filled his soul.

Long nights in the darkness had taught him that to fight the monsters, he had to become the monster.

But killing when he couldn't be seen was hardly a challenge. He wanted the fight to be personal. He wanted to see their fear, smell their terror, hear their ragged heartbeats…and if he got too close…well, it wasn't like there was anyone who'd miss him.

He strode forward, coming out of the dark like the predator he was.

"So, finally I meet The Darkness." The tall vampire stood flanked by his two remaining followers. His voice was composed, but his fear stained the air.

Rand didn't say anything. He didn't talk to those he executed.

The air between them hung heavy, tension thickening like building thunderclouds.

The vampires attacked.

For Rand, time slowed. He heard every solid beat of his heart. Felt the touch of cool steel in his hand. Sensed the spike of pranic energy from the vampires.

He blocked the strike from the first vampire with a forearm. Took down the second with a smooth thrust of the stake. A hard kick sent the tall leader tumbling back into the sand.

Spinning, Rand moved lightning fast until he was face-to-face with the first vampire.

"No, please—"

His father had begged for mercy. But no one had listened. That long-ago vampire had forced a teenaged Rand to watch as he'd ripped Brody Wilder apart.

Rand stabbed the stake through the vamp's chakra and didn't wait to watch him fall.

"Just you and me, *vishuddha*," the tall vampire said.

Rand straightened and eyed his final foe. The vampire had used the formal name for Rand's kind. He was a descendant of a pure-blood vishuddha, the rare child resulting from the union of vampire and human.

Gifted with enhanced strength and senses, and a much longer life than humans, vishuddha made the perfect hunters of vampires.

He was doing what he'd been born to do.

They flew at each other and went crashing to the ground. At six foot five, Rand was bigger, but the vampire was strong. They wrestled and Rand felt the scrape of sharp fangs on his cheek.

"I'll take your blood, Darkness. And I'll make it hurt."

Fangs ripped at the side of Rand's neck and he felt his flesh tear. For a second, he relished the pain. Then he thrust a fist at the vampire's head.

Rand had never let a vampire feed from him and he wasn't starting now.

He'd been hardened in the blood and pain of many battles. One unbalanced rogue wouldn't be his undoing.

Raising an arm, Rand rammed the metal stake into the vampire's back. The tip pierced his heart from behind.

With a garbled cry, the vampire slumped forward, heart chakra destroyed.

Sucking in a deep breath, Rand rolled the body off him. He pushed to his feet.

Another monster dead.

He stared at his bloody hands and the stake resting in them. It was all he knew. Blood. Death. Darkness. What would his father think of him?

Before Rand could clean his stake, headlights cut across the desert, blinding him. A car jerked to a halt on the rough ground, doors opened.

"Police! Stay where you are and drop your weapon."

Damn. Someone from the bar must've spotted them. He'd hoped when he'd lured the vamps out of the bar—and away from the humans they'd been planning to snack on—that no one would notice.

Rand didn't move. He tried to avoid humans, especially

the authorities. They knew nothing of the beings existing alongside them. And it was best it stayed that way.

Still, he wasn't going to hurt them. He dropped his stake into the sand. He was damned good at killing but he wouldn't injure an innocent.

"Cuff him," one of the officers said.

A shadow moved forward. Rand's eyes adjusted and he saw an older cop by the car, gun aimed at Rand's chest.

A younger one approached him with cautious steps. Rand saw the officer's eyes stray to one of the vampires. Dead, fangs retracted, they looked like humans.

How in hell was he going to get out of this?

The young cop swallowed. "You're under arrest—"

"Now, you don't want to do that, *chéri*."

The female voice floated through the night like an angel's song. It stroked over Rand's nerve endings like caressing fingers, setting his body aflame.

She came out of the darkness like an underworld goddess. Tall, slender, pale skin glowing in the dark. She wore a white leather catsuit, which should have looked ridiculous, but only accented slim curves and feminine limbs. A fall of raven hair reached her waist.

Light in the darkness. Rand blinked, unable to look away.

She stopped, pressed a hand to her hip and looked at the cops. "I believe you were leaving. You saw nothing here that concerns you." The older cop nodded. "Yes, ma'am. You're right. Let's go, Johnson."

The younger man stared at her with glazed eyes. "We were leaving. Nothing here that concerns us."

Rand fought his body's instinctive urge to follow the men.

The woman sauntered forward, moving with a liquid grace that mesmerized. She patted Johnson's cheek, then watched them get in their car and drive away.

Then she turned to Rand.

A searing pain hit him between the eyes. Her unearthly beauty struck him like a blow to the head and his body hardened. Her features were perfect—slim nose, sharp cheekbones, sensual lips and eyes the color of amethysts.

Eyes that held an impossible blend of experience and innocence.

Innocence? He snorted. The brow chakra belonged to the *ajna*. Those born to vampire parents, the equivalent to undead royalty.

The strongest and most powerful of all the vampires.

But even knowing what she was, his hands itched to run over her marble-smooth skin. She pumped off sensuality like heat off a roaring fire.

Unblinking violet eyes watched him. "I've been looking for you."

Rand watched her, his mind racing for a way to survive her attack. She looked young, but she felt powerful. Ajna were the only vampires strong enough to survive the rush of solar energy through their chakras and walk in the sun. They were damned hard to kill.

It'd been an ajna that had destroyed his father. Since

then Rand had tangled with only one in his career and even with his enhanced healing abilities, it'd taken two months for him to recover.

She tilted her head. "Don't you speak?"

"Not with vampires," he growled.

She crossed her arms under her breasts, accenting her already mind-scrambling cleavage. "Well, you will talk to me."

Used to giving orders, this one. What the hell did an ajna want to talk to him for? "You think so?"

Her nod sent a ripple through her shiny hair. "I have a deal for you, Darkness."

Dominique had never expected The Darkness to be so big, so broad or so...wild.

When she'd set out to find him, she'd never given any thought to what he looked like. She'd only cared about his reputation. Amongst vampires, he was known as the biggest and baddest of the vampire hunters.

And Dominique needed big and bad.

She studied his large form—massive shoulders, a wall of chest and roped muscles under his worn jeans and black T-shirt. Shaggy brown hair threaded with the glint of gold hung to his shoulders. His eyes were moss-green and filled with shadows.

A throb of heat went through her, weakening her limbs. Energy washed over her, clogging her throat—the chakra of the vishuddha.

Dieu, she'd never felt energy like this—scalding hot.

She swallowed and fought for control. She'd never realized how cold she'd been until now.

Dominique was raised to have exquisite control of her energies. Her calm, controlled parents never let their energies run wild.

The thought of her parents reminded Dominique why she was here. A shiver wracked her. The energy in her drained away, leaving her deathly cold.

Please let this man be the one who could save her and her family. Save her from the ruthless vampire determined to make her his possession and kill her parents if she refused. She resisted the urge to squeeze her hands together and forced them to stay at her sides.

"I don't deal with vampires." The hunter's deep voice was little more than a growl. It skittered down Dominique's spine.

She sensed the power vibrating off him. He wasn't pureblood, but if the rumors were true, his grandfather had been a full vishuddha, so Rand Wilder was still very powerful.

He'd certainly wasted no time dispatching the six anaharta.

But he'd let the last vampire close enough to wound him? Through the murky night she studied the blood staining his stubble-covered cheek and neck. Its scent was rich, strong.

She wondered what he tasted like.

Her heart thumped against her ribs. At the ajna court, no one fed from live hosts anymore. They were much too civilized. So why had that thought jumped into her head?

Remember why you're here, Dominique. She was a lawyer for the ajna and a damned good one. She knew how to get her argument across. "My deal is one you should find very pleasurable."

He grunted. "Not a word I use in conjunction with vamps, sweetheart."

She moved closer to him, watched him tense. She felt the heat pumping off him, hot against her cool skin. It drew her, made her wonder how hot his hands would feel running over her.

She smelled more than his blood now and breathed deep—sweat, soap and man. The muscles in her belly tightened. She'd come here in desperation, but now she realized she might get more than she'd expected.

She only hoped she could handle Rand Wilder.

"If you take my deal, you can drive a wedge into the ajna court. How do you Americans put it...flip them the bird?"

His green eyes narrowed. "Why the hell would I want to do that?"

Those eyes lasered into her and Dominique swallowed the knot in her throat. She wasn't afraid of this man. She was done being afraid.

Research was one of her best skills and she'd done her research on this man. "An ajna killed your father. The court and their Paladins did nothing to bring the killer to justice." She tilted her head. The fact that the Paladins—powerful vampires who policed the vampire world—had done nothing must torment him. "Wouldn't you like them to pay?"

His mouth firmed. "What do you want?"

She smiled now. "I want you to take my virginity."

Chapter Two

Rand felt his body tighten so hard it hurt. Brutal arousal flooded his system.

It'd been months since he'd taken a woman to his bed. He savored the desire for a moment before he clamped down on his traitorous body's reaction.

She was a *vampire*. He knew she was nothing like the out-of-control rogues he'd just killed. It'd been the first lesson his father had taught him—they only hunted vampires who willingly let their energies run wild. The others were left to live their lives.

But it didn't change the fact she had fangs and drank blood.

Despite vampires' sensual natures, he'd never been tempted to tangle with one before. He wouldn't insult his father's memory, what he'd fought for, by being with a vampire.

Rand let his gaze skim over her perfect lips, then traced over the smooth, white skin of her throat. God, he bet she'd be delicious. She'd feel silky and supple. And he'd be the first to slide his body into the warmth of hers.

Jesus. His chest heaved. "Sorry, sweetheart. I'm not interested in screwing a princess with fangs."

Heat seared along her cheekbones. "Watch it, hunter."

Time for him to get out of here. Before he did something stupid—like touch her. He stepped around her. "I'm leaving."

She sidestepped in front of him. "I haven't finished with you yet."

That silky voice stroked over him. Rand went to move around her, but found his feet rooted to the ground.

Damn! Usually a vampire's thrall didn't work on him, but this woman's voice was a powerful weapon.

She came closer and he smelled her scent. Fresh water with a hint of some flower he couldn't name. It wrapped around him. So clean in the blood-soaked darkness.

Her violet eyes widened. "You're so hot."

She lifted a hand. It hovered between them for a second before she pressed her fingers to his chest.

Lightning. They both gasped. Her fingers clenched on his shirt, then moved in a caress. She smoothed those long, elegant fingers over his muscles.

"So much energy, so much rage," she whispered. "How do you function with such chaos inside you?"

Rand had dealt with his frenzied emotions all his life. It

was the curse of the vishuddha to feel too much and deal with strong energies.

But with this woman touching him, he felt himself skate close to the edge of his control.

Her fingers slid down his T-shirt, stroked over the ridges of his stomach. Fire followed her touch, roaring through his body and arrowing to his groin.

But something else about her caught his attention. The wonder lighting her face.

"You're not what I expected, Darkness."

"My name's Rand," he bit out. For some unknown reason, he didn't like that name spilling from her lips.

She lifted her flawless face. "I am Dominique Valois."

Valois was the cream of vampire royalty. The blue-blooded family had been around for centuries. They were known for only breeding with other ajna to keep their line pure.

Now why would a Valois princess want a roll in the sheets with a vampire hunter?

Not his problem. "Let go of your thrall, princess."

"You must hear me out."

He gritted his teeth. The hint of desperation under her tone caught him. "Talk fast."

Her hand moved back up his chest, skirted the wound on his neck and stroked over his jaw. Flames licked down his body

"Why did you let the vampire do this? You could've killed him before he savaged you."

"He got lucky."

Her thumb brushed his lips. "I hear the lie in your voice." Her head tilted, exquisite black hair sliding across her shoulder. Her voice lowered to a seductive whisper. "Tell me."

He couldn't stop the words that tumbled from him. "I don't care if I die."

"You court death?" She shook her head. "*Non,* you flirt with it."

"Say what you have to say and release your thrall." He was already working to break her control over him. The fingers on his right hand moved.

"I told you, I want you to take me to bed and take my virginity."

Instant images flooded Rand's head. His big hands stripping away white leather. Dominique naked amongst his sheets, all marble-smooth skin and husky cries. He saw his body covering hers, her long legs wrapping around his hips.

Sweat broke out on his forehead. "Why's a Valois looking to slum it?"

She lifted her chin and for a brief second, he saw a flash of something dark in her eyes. *Fear?*

It couldn't be. She could snap his neck or command him to stab the stake through his own throat.

"That is my business. All I need is your cock."

Hearing the blunt words in her exotic, proper tone made his arousal thicken. His body yelled yes, the hunter in him told him no.

The fingers he could move curled. "I told you, I'm not interested."

Her eyes narrowed. "Really?"

That one word dripped with feminine challenge. Rand's nerves stretched tight.

Her hand moved across his chest, a nail scraping over his nipple. He swallowed a groan. Her hand inched lower and then even lower.

"I do believe, Monsieur Wilder, that you are lying again." Her hand cupped his rock-hard erection through his jeans.

Jesus. Pure electricity flooded through him, making his skin feel too tight and his muscles threaten to turn liquid.

She stroked him and savage hunger sang through his system, screaming for him to touch her, take her.

"Don't you want me?" Her husky murmur carried so many forbidden promises.

Her hand continued its torture, stroking the hard length of him. Her other hand curled around his neck and brought his head down. She was tall, but he was taller, and he felt her go up on her toes to press her crimson lips to his.

That luscious mouth moved like a whisper over his, small nipping bites that teased, barely giving him a taste of her.

But what grabbed at him was the trace of hesitancy. Like she hadn't kissed many men.

The thought fired through him. Emotions—hot, rich emotions—stormed through him and riding the wave was the strongest desire he'd felt.

It'd been so long since he'd felt pleasure, enjoyed anything other than killing. It'd been far too long since he'd held another against him. He needed to taste her.

With Dominique caught up in her seduction, Rand broke through her thrall. His hands gripped her hips, his fingers sinking into leather-slicked skin. He yanked her to him and took control of the kiss.

He plunged his tongue into her warm mouth and swallowed her groan. She tasted of fresh and sweet, cool spring water and natural honey. She tasted of innocence and desire, a combination that stole his sense. He dragged that taste inside him.

The force of his kiss bent her head back, but Dominique returned everything he gave. Her hand slid into his hair, clenching there. Rand slid one of his hands between them and pressed her other hand against the bulge in his jeans, crushing those elegant fingers against his heated body.

Right now, Rand didn't care who she was, or what she was. Right now, Dominique was a light in the darkness his life had become.

Mon Dieu, she was going up in flames.

Dominique felt the full force of Rand Wilder's arousal swamp her. Was amazed to feel her own energy rise up to meet his. Her fangs sprang into her mouth.

He tasted ruthless, wild and dangerous. What would it feel like to have him take her? To feel his muscled, iron-hard body move within her?

Her fingers clenched on his erection. It felt huge under well-worn denim. And it made her hunger.

She'd danced with men, kissed them, shared bold caresses, but at twenty-eight, she was young for a vampire and had been expected to keep herself pure for her marriage. She'd never felt what she felt right now. When the hunter known as The Darkness kissed her, she felt like she was necessary for his survival.

One of his big, hot hands slid down her thigh. He gripped her leg and lifted it around his waist. In a thrust of hips, he ground himself against her softness. Her belly exploded in wild flutters.

Energy rushed through her and over her skin. She'd always suspected there was more than the cool control she'd known growing up. She'd always yearned for more than the icy politeness of court.

And Rand Wilder was showing it to her.

"Please," she whispered against his lips. She needed more. She wanted this man to show her what had been missing from her life.

Suddenly he pushed her away. She stumbled, then caught her balance. Her head felt light, her body heavy.

They watched each other, chests heaving. She felt her energy straining for him.

When he lifted a hand and rubbed the back of it across his mouth, like he was wiping the taste of her away, Dominique's stomach contracted. The rejection hit her like a blow.

"I can't help you," he bit out.

He didn't want her. She bit down hard on her bottom lip and tasted her own blood on her tongue. The one man who could save her and her parents from Vilein didn't want her.

It seemed the only man who wanted her was one she was trying to escape from.

"Why?" She hated that even she heard the hurt in that word.

He shoved a hand through his hair. "I kill your kind."

Dominique pressed two fingers to her temple and worked to control the wild energy inside her. Slowly she felt her control cooling the rush. "You have vampire in you, too."

"Enough to make me good at killing those who get out of control." He shook his head. "I've never taken one to my bed."

"And I've never taken any man to mine."

Even though she'd come here to ruin herself with a man Vilein would consider the worst possible choice, Dominique now wanted Rand Wilder for a very different reason. One even she didn't understand.

Rand's stubbled jaw tightened. "Like I said, I can't help you."

Her stomach knotted. Lifting her chin, she pushed the unfamiliar emotions away. She had some pride. She wouldn't throw herself at a man who didn't want her.

She straightened her shoulders and tossed her hair back over her shoulder. "Fine." She shot a pointed look at the dead vampires scattered around them. "Death makes a cold, lonely companion, but it looks like the two of you are happy together."

He didn't say anything but his moss eyes darkened.

Forcing a sultry smile, she ran a finger down her chest, between her cleavage. "You aren't the only hunter in Las Vegas. I'm certain I'll find many others happy to accept my offer."

She turned and walked away into the night.

She'd find someone to ruin her. Someone with a bad enough reputation that Vilein wouldn't want her anymore. She sucked in a breath. Her plan *had* to work.

Bile rose in her throat. Cold, sharp fear ate at the edges of her sanity. Dark flashes of the things Vilein had done to her and worse, the things he'd promise to do once she was his, burst through her head.

She swallowed back the need to be sick. She was ajna. She'd been raised to know no fear. She was tired of being afraid and now she was doing something to save herself.

The lights of Las Vegas cast a golden glow on the horizon. There were plenty of vampires in the city.

And where there were vampires, there were hunters.

Her heart squeezed. Just not the one she wanted.

Chapter Three

Music pumped through the club. Multi-colored strobe lights twirled above the having dance floor.

Rand cursed. Short, pithy and loud.

Damn, Dominique Valois. His hand curled around the beer he'd been nursing for the last hour.

Someone bumped against him at the glossy bar yelling out drink orders.

Why the hell was he here? Shadows was owned by an ex-hunter and a popular haunt for those with any vishuddha blood.

Lifting his head, he scanned the crowd. He sensed the other hunters in the place, recognized some. There were even a few vampires among the dancers.

It wasn't Rand's kind of place. He preferred a quiet bar or, better yet, a solitary beer on the deck surrounding his home in the desert.

But he'd hoped the loud music and frenzied crowd would be a distraction. Stop him from thinking of Dominique. Naked. Moaning. Crying out his name.

He took a quick swig of the beer. Grimaced. It was hot. *She's a vampire. One of her kind killed your father.* It'd become a mantra to him. But no matter how many times he repeated the words, his body wasn't listening.

Had she found some nameless, faceless man to service her? Was she right now naked and entwined with the jerk? Rand slammed the bottle down on the bar. The bottom smashed into tiny amber pieces.

Was someone else being the first to show her pleasure?

As he signaled the bartender over to clean the mess, a prickle started at the back of his neck. The feeling crawled upward until he felt a burn between his eyes. His back tensed.

He opened his vishuddha senses. He sensed the mass of energy from all the vampires partying in the club. But ajna were rare and their energy strong. It didn't take him long to find her.

Turning, his gaze raked the mass of bodies grinding and swaying to the pumping Latin rhythm. Then the crowd parted and he saw her.

She'd changed since the desert. Now it was black leather hugging slim legs and riding low on her hips. A tight, bloodred tank top displayed toned arms, the deep V hinted at full breasts. The bottom of it left a strip of supple belly bare.

She sauntered toward him, her gaze locked with his.

The sway of her hips made his mouth dry. Damn her for being so beautiful.

The people crowding close to him at the bar shifted away. No doubt from a mental command from her. She leaned sideways, elbow on the glossy surface, and faced him.

"Didn't think I'd given up on you that easily, did you?"

Her siren-song tones seeped into him. He pressed his palms flat on the bar, anything to stop them from stroking what he shouldn't touch.

She inched closer, her silken hair falling forward. "I'm used to getting my way, Wilder."

"That doesn't surprise me, princess." He hated that his voice was jagged as glass.

Her red lips quirked. "I'm a lawyer, we hate losing."

So she was smart as well as sexy. "A lawyer? Figures." Most vampires were experts at hiding in plain sight of humans. They attended colleges, owned businesses and who knew what else. "Haven't you found someone who fits your 'take my virginity' bill yet?"

Violet eyes traveled down his body before drifting back to his face. "Only one."

Hunger ignited deep in his belly. Why her? Women came on to him all the time. Those with hunter blood were lured by his reputation. Those who knew nothing of vampires were drawn by his dangerous aura. But none of them set him on fire like this one.

Dominique moved between his thighs until her hips

bumped against his bar stool. Her palms slid up his chest. "Have you changed your mind?"

The music echoed around them—sultry and drugging. It'd be so easy to succumb. To give her what she wanted and take something for himself at the same time.

"Tell me why you want me?" Because he couldn't control it, he touched her. His fingers slid along black, shiny hair. "Why are you so desperate?"

She licked her lips, which made Rand's already hardening erection throb.

"It's best if you don't know." Her voice was quiet.

His gaze traced over her perfect features. She looked like a fantasy come to life—a vixen's body coated with an innocence he found irresistible.

God, he was confused. He was honest enough to admit he wanted her…but he couldn't forget what she was.

She dropped her gaze. "I'm running out of time, Rand."

Yes. The word quivered on his lips. He'd made a life out of saving others. Saving those who couldn't help themselves. Dominique was powerful. Confidence and intelligence shined in her eyes—that she was so desperate told him she was in deep trouble.

She pushed away from him. "I'll just have to work harder to convince you."

With a tantalizing swing of leather-clad hips, she headed for the dance floor. Even if he'd wanted to, Rand couldn't have looked away.

The crowd parted for her. She started to gyrate to the

blood-pounding beat. She moved with the liquid grace of a vampire, like the music was a part of her.

She raised her arms above her head, then turned, her violet eyes clashing with his. Her lips parted.

Two men materialized from the dancing crowd and flanked her. Both were big, brawny and had some hunter blood. One plastered himself against her back, the other moved against her front, his hands clamped on her hips. She swayed to the music, her hips pumping in time to the beat.

Rand's hands clenched into tight fists, hot emotion boiled inside him.

He knew it was crazy, but some part of him considered her his. She'd come looking for *him*. Not the idiots rubbing against her like randy bulls.

The two men moved closer, locking her between them. So attuned to her, only Rand saw the flicker in her eyes, the tensing of her muscles. He stood, his hands flexing.

She wedged a hand to one man's chest and pushed him back a few inches. Rand released his held breath. She could take care of herself.

When the hunter wrapped his burly arms around her and nuzzled her throat,Dominique went stiff.

Damn it to hell. Rand walked toward her. As he neared, he sensed the tinge of her fear in the air. *Who'd made her so afraid?* She could slam both these men against the wall with a single swing of her arm. This fear was something deeper.

"Wilder," one of the hunters said, although his eyes never left Dominique.

"Get out of here." Rand let his ruthless order sink into his words.

One hunter opened his mouth and Rand straightened to his full height, his knuckles burning with the need to slam into this guy's face.

Rand used the little compulsion he possessed. "Go now or this will get messy."

A muscle ticked under the eye of one man. Then they left. Obeying the command buried in Rand's voice and not willing to tangle with him.

Dominique moved close to him, pressing that tempting body against him. The fear on the air bled away.

Her hand touched his shoulder, a light caress. When her fingers brushed his neck, his throat, he felt the spark of energy between them. It ran like lightning through his body, firing his blood.

With a sigh of defeat, he put his arms around her and pulled her closer. She started to sway, rubbing against him while he remained motionless. He felt the wash of energy in the room.

He reached out and gripped her jaw. She watched him, gaze steady. His fingers ran along her cheekbone, moving closer to her brow. Her chest hitched.

What would happen if he touched her chakra? Rand had heard the rumors of the tantric sex of the vampires—the sharing of bodies and energy. It was said the sensations were mind-blowing. Beyond anything regular sex could promise.

No. He dropped his hand to his side. Disappointment flashed in her eyes before she hid it.

Her fingers clenched on his shirt. "I'm not giving up on you, Wilder."

He couldn't look away. The way she moved made him wonder how she'd move underneath him, with his hands on her.

Her seduction didn't only affect him. Every man on the dance floor watched her, eyes burning. Rand knew each one was imagining being with her, touching her, and rage welled inside him.

Dominique had no idea what she was doing. She didn't look away from him, couldn't know she was seducing every male who watched her.

Couldn't know he was drowning in her.

Dominique was lost in the music and Rand's dark green gaze.

She'd followed him from the desert, desperate to convince him to help her. She needed Rand Wilder.

Now he stood in her arms. All six foot five inches of wild male. And she was doing everything she could to entice him to show her what it'd be like between them.

She shimmied her body, imagining they were alone, just the two of them.

When his hands clenched at her waist, she smiled against

his shirt. *Mon Dieu*, he smelled so good. All man. Nothing like Vilein's cloying cologne.

She smoothed her hands over Rand's shoulders. "Dance with me."

"I don't dance."

What a surprise. "Fine, I'll dance for both of us."

He didn't move to the music, but he did slide one thigh between her legs. Rough denim rubbed against smooth leather, melding them closer together. That thigh rubbed against the aching part of her, making heated desire curl in her belly.

Dominique pressed her face against him, drew in more of his delicious scent. He was so big, so strong, and for the first time in a long time, she felt protected. Safe.

One of his hands smoothed over her bare shoulders and she shivered. His fingers were callused, the sensation on her skin amazing. What would they feel like on her belly, on the sensitive flesh of her thighs? Damp heat pooled between her legs.

Those fingers brushed her shoulder, shockingly hot. Then nudged the strap of her tank top aside.

She felt his body stiffen and her own did the same. His gaze was sharp on her skin.

"Who did it?" His voice was so black goose bumps raced over her arms.

She tried to pull away. "It doesn't matter."

He spun her and bent her forward. Her bottom nestled against his thighs, one arm was banded around her waist.

Oblivious of the crowd dancing around them, he pushed the back of her shirt up, leaving her back bare.

She struggled against him, didn't want him to see the ugly black bruises and red welts covering her back.

Her stomach revolted, her mind taking her back to those moments when she'd been helpless. She squeezed her eyes shut.

Rand's body quivered. Then a gentle hand skimmed down her spine. Warm lips pressed to the back of her neck.

Dominique felt tears well in her eyes. She'd told no one of her attacks, kept all the pain to herself. Now someone—this big, wild hunter—was showing her compassion.

He let her shirt drop and turned her. His gaze bored into hers. Sympathy was doused by something darker, dangerous. "Who. Did. It?"

Chapter Four

Dominique had thought luring The Darkness into bed would be easy. She'd never planned to tell him why. Or share what she was running from.

"Rand—"

A hand tapped Rand's shoulder. "Hey, buddy, time's up. I want a turn with the lady."

Dominique saw the glaze in the interloper's eyes. A quick scan of the room showed every male in the bar was watching her. Hot intent burning in their glassy eyes.

She groaned. She'd unconsciously let some thrall seep into her dance.

"Back off." Rand's voice held an edge of danger.

The man folded huge arms across his chest. "I think she's worth fighting for."

"You don't want to take me on," Rand warned.

"Rand—"

"Be quiet, princess." He didn't even look at her.

Dominique huffed out a breath. She was going to tell him she could command the man to leave. But apparently the macho vampire hunter had other ideas.

The big man swung out with a fist. Rand ducked, his move so fast he blurred. Then he slammed his own knuckles into the man's face.

He went down hard. His body hit the grimy floor and he didn't get up.

Rand wrapped tight fingers around her upper arm. Without a word, he dragged her to the door. The hard grip gave her a flashback of Vilein. An ugly taste choked her throat.

"Let me go," she insisted.

No response.

Heat welled in her chest. "You have no control over me, hunter. I'm not yours to order around." She hadn't come looking for another overbearing man to treat her like his possession.

Rand pulled her out into the warm Vegas night. He dragged her around the building and into an alley. He stopped beside a beast of a motorbike.

He leaned down, his face close to hers. "I'm not letting you go. You'll get yourself into trouble. You almost had every man in that club ready to strip you naked."

She stiffened. "I'm ajna. More powerful than you, vishuddha. I can take care of myself."

He moved closer, crowding her. Her pulse tripped. She backed up a step, the back of her thighs hitting the metal of his bike.

"Then why are you covered in bruises and whip marks?"

Banked fire burned in his green eyes. Dominique had never seen anyone so angry, so full of emotion. Especially not for her.

Shame ate at her insides. She didn't want this man to know what had been done to her. She wanted to be strong again. She wanted him to see her as a woman in charge of her own destiny, not a bruised, broken damsel.

She lifted her chin, gave him her best ajna look—superior, cool. "That's my concern. All you need to do is give me an answer. Will you take me to bed?"

He tightened his jaw. "No, damn it."

Her stomach lurched. She shoved at his chest. "Fine. Get out of my way."

His hands gripped her arms, surprisingly gentle for such a big man. "No."

Air hissed between her gritted teeth. "You don't want me, but no one else can have me, either, is that it?"

"Not want you?" Rand's hands slid into her hair, tangled. "I want you so much I'm going to snap." His mouth crashed down on hers.

Her brain short-circuited and her hands clenched on his T-shirt. Under it, she felt the rapid beat of his heart.

He nipped at her lips. "You taste so good, Dominique. Too good."

She loved the sound of her name on his lips. She pressed closer to his warm body. Vilein never said her name. He called her *ma petite* in an ice-cold voice. And it was worse when he said it with a whip in hand.

Non. She wouldn't let that man ruin this moment. With Rand touching her, she didn't feel afraid. She felt strong, whole.

"Touch me. Please." She'd never begged. Even in those pain-filled moments when she'd been helpless.

But she would if it got this man to touch her when she ached.

Rand's hand stroked down her body, cupped her bottom, shaping her. When he lifted her, she gasped. He set her down sideways on the bike.

His tanned hands slid up to cup her breasts. She closed her eyes against the sensations. When fingers slid inside her shirt, touched the silk covering her skin, she moaned. He brushed over her peaking nipples and she went damp.

With a curse, Rand leaned down and pressed his mouth to one taut peak, over lace and fabric. He sucked, strong and firm, and Dominique cried out. With an impatient hand, he shoved her shirt aside and pushed the cup of her bra down.

One pebbled nipple was free to him. He latched on to it, his teeth nipping.

Dominique sank her hands into his long hair. She never wanted him to stop. The sensations were enthralling.

Rand slid a hand over her quivering belly. He unsnapped her pants and, without pause, his fingers dipped inside.

"You make me crazy." His mouth was on hers again, hard and hungry. His clever fingers delved under silk and lace.

When his tongue brushed against her fangs, he paused.

Then, with exquisite slowness, he ran his tongue down the length of one throbbing fang.

Dominique jerked against him. When he touched the sensitive nub between her thighs, she shuddered. "Yes."

"Do you like that?" he asked, voice harsh. He nudged her legs apart and stepped between them. His finger circled her clit, stroking, teasing.

"Yes." Her hips moved against her will. "Show me what it should be like."

She'd never felt like this. Never felt the desperate coiling low in her belly, the liquid fire between her legs.

One long finger parted her folds. Her hips canted forward. He slid one finger inside her.

Her head fell back. That finger plunged in, out, in again.

"You're so tight, Dominique." His voice was serrated.

Another finger joined the first, stretching her. A cry caught in Dominique's throat. All the sensations were too much.

"Easy," he murmured. "I've got you."

The feelings grew, multiplied. When that thumb stroked her again, she shattered, her hands digging into his shoulders.

He moved, but she was too exhausted to care. Felt too good to worry about opening her eyes. Strong arms wrapped around her. Her head rested on his shoulder and she heard him sigh.

"Tell me why you need me?"

Thoughts of what—who—she was running from filtered through her pleasure. Her muscles tensed.

"Who are you so afraid of?"

Dominique's remaining lassitude evaporated. She lifted her head and stared into moss-green eyes. "My fiancé."

Fiancé. The word tore through Rand like an exploding bomb. She belonged to someone else.

He stepped away from her, his gut cramping, the scent of her desire still strong in his senses.

Dominique brushed her dark hair back from her face. "My parents betrothed me to another ajna the day I was born." She shivered. "Everyone believes Vilein is perfect... but behind closed doors..."

Helpless against the terror in her voice, Rand cupped her cheek. "He hurt you?"

She pressed her face against Rand's palm. "Yes." It came out a tortured whisper. "A preview of life once we're joined, once I belong to him." She wrapped her arms around her middle. The first few times I was too shocked to fight back. This last time I thought he'd kill me.... I flew to Las Vegas the next day desperate for a way to stop him." Her gaze was steady on Rand's. "To find you."

The shadows in her eyes made Rand want to wrap her up and take her away. She was stronger and more powerful than him, but it didn't change his feelings. "Tell me."

She bit her lip. "He likes games. Likes tying people up, ripping off their clothes and whipping them." She pressed a hand to her mouth. "I scream, I cry...but he doesn't stop. He enjoys it."

Rand fought the energy churning through him. He

wanted to find this bastard and shove a stake between his eyes. How could anyone want to break this woman? "He hasn't raped you?"

Her gaze dropped. "He's waitingfor our joining. He wants a pure wife."

Jaw aching, Rand choked down the fury. It wasn't what Dominique needed right now.

"I think he's killed some of his lovers. He's cold, controlled, ruthless, but my gut tells me he's unbalanced."

Most of the vampires who let their energies out of alignment were wild, filled with jagged, raging energy. But occasionally Rand had seen the ones who coated their unstable power with icy control.

Like the one who'd killed his father.

"Expose him at court. Surely your parents can help?"

She shook her head. "They don't know. Only see what he shows them." She breathed deep. "And he threatened to kill them if I say anything. I won't risk them."

Rand understood the need to protect. His father had died helping Rand escape the vamp who'd killed him.

"They're ajna—"

She shook her head, the move fierce. "Vilein is older than them. Stronger. He'll kill them."

Her hands gripped Rand's wrists. "I tracked you down because my only chance is to ruin myself for him. To lose my virginity to the most unacceptable person possible. A hunter." Her fingers brushed over his pounding pulse. "You."

Her words were a punch to the gut. She wanted him for his reputation. Because he was the best at killing her kind.

She wanted The Darkness, not the man.

He turned his hand around and broke her hold. "There must be another way. You should talk to the Paladins."

Surely the group of powerful vampires could help her. They took down unbalanced rogues, cleaned up any messes that bled into the human world.

Again she shook her head. "A risk I won't take. If something goes wrong…"

Damn. "You shouldn't have to open your legs for the worst hunter you can find." He wanted to yell the words, but he locked his jaw and fought to keep his voice even.

Her eyes flashed. "I'll do whatever I have to do to protect myself and those I love."

A part of Rand admired that. Dominique wasn't crying, wasn't playing the victim. She was sacrificing a part of herself to save her parents. "How do you know he won't hurt your family anyway?" "Because I'll make my ruination public." Her chin lifted. "If something were to happen to them, the court would look at Vilein."

There was a core of steel in this beautiful vampire. Rand knew then he'd help her. He'd keep her safe and together they'd find a solution that didn't involve her screwing a damned hunter—even if that hunter was him.

When someone showed her the delight of making love, it should be someone who cared about her, cherished her. Not a man drowning in blood and darkness.

"Come on, let's go."

Something bright ignited in her violet eyes. "You'll do it? You'll help me?"

"There's another way." There had to be. "You can stay at my place tonight. Tomorrow we'll figure something out."

He watched the light drain away. God, he felt like he'd kicked her. He settled onto his bike in front of her.

She shifted, slim arms wrapping around him, thighs hugging his and full breasts pressed against his back.

Rand closed his eyes for a second and fought for control. He'd spent enough time in the muck to recognize someone, even a vampire, who was untouched by it.

He was stained, his hands too rough, too bloody. Some part of him knew this woman deserved so much better than him.

He couldn't take Dominique to his bed. It would be a betrayal of everything he was, everything he fought for, of his father.

And not because she was a vampire.

Because she was innocent.

Chapter Five

Dominique pressed her face against Rand's back, her hands resting against his hard abdomen.

The big bike hugged the curves of the desolate desert highway, purring beneath them like a predatory cat. Dominique's hair flew out behind her, the wind in her face.

Her fingers flexed against the heat of him. The contrast of hot male and cool air was a distracting combination.

The throbbing of the bike and the rub of her legs against Rand's kept her desire on slow burn. What he'd done to her before…she shivered and rubbed her chin against his shirt. He'd given her the most intense orgasm she'd experienced and it'd been out-of-this-world amazing. She wanted more.

What if they could just keep riding? Her arms tightened around him. What if they just followed this road wherever it led? Far from Las Vegas, far from Vilein, far from whatever had put the shadows in Rand's eyes. Just the two of them.

She let the fantasy play for a minute, then she choked it off. Rand wasn't interested in running away with a vampire. And running wouldn't stop Vilein.

Staring into the darkness, she drew on Rand's warmth. She knew Vilein would come looking for her. She knew it in her blood.

A shiver wracked her. She needed Rand to take her virginity, then she needed to get far away from him.

If Vilein caught her here with Rand...her fingers clenched tight, her knuckles screaming. He was a vishuddha, strong and skilled, but Vilein was very powerful.

Strong fingers covered hers, squeezed. Rand sensed her agitation. Dominique worked to control the energy coursing in her.

Moments later, he turned the bike off the highway. They followed a track back into the desert and pulled up in front of a house.

Glass and wood nestled in the desert like they belonged there. On one side of the house was a large wooden deck, and beyond that the dark expanse of the Mojave Desert.

He swung off the bike. "Come on."

Dominique followed him inside. He flicked on some lights, illuminating a large open kitchen and living room.

Beautiful desert landscapes graced the walls. The furniture screamed male—oversized, leather, worn. Large glass sliding doors led onto the deck and his kitchen was compact, but looked well-used.

It surprised her that she easily pictured Rand in the

kitchen wearing low-riding jeans, shirtless, with a fry pan in hand.

And she pictured herself sitting on the counter, hair loose, wearing his shirt and laughing.

Dominique shook her head and walked toward the glass door. Where had that thought come from? She'd never seen any ajna share that kind of relationship. Certainly not her parents.

The ajna court was cold and ruthless. No one showed their true feelings for each other. No one dared show such weakness.

She stared out into the night. "You like the desert."

"Yeah. No one to bug me."

No one to kill. No one to care about. She pressed a palm to the glass. Rand surrounded himself with nothing, yet inside, this house was a home. A sanctuary.

"The guest bedroom's all yours. First door on the right. If you need me, my room's at the end of the hall."

She spun. He stood in the doorway to the hall, a shoulder leaning into the doorjamb. He watched her with hooded eyes.

She did need him, but so far the baddest vampire hunter in the business was turning out to be nobler than she'd thought possible.

"Do you need to feed?" he asked.

His question startled her. "No. Not yet."

She felt the first faint beat of hunger, but she could last the night.

"I don't feed off a host. I'll need to find a blood bank."

There were plenty who made their wealth off supplying blood to vampires.

"You never feed from the living?"

She studied Rand's blank face. "The ajna court believes they've moved past it." Although there were whispers that many did differently behind closed doors. Whispers of the pleasure. "I've never fed from a human before."

His green eyes registered surprise. "And I've never let a vamp feed from me before."

They stared at each other in the charged silence. Dominique eyed the tanned skin of his neck, heard the strong, steady thump of his heart. Her belly coiled. It was too easy to picture sinking her fangs into his skin.

He cleared his throat. "Well, I'm heading to bed."

Dominique rubbed her hands up her bare arms. Suddenly the thought of being alone terrified her. Since Vilein's savage attacks, her dreams had turned into twisted nightmares where she relived every single minute again and again.

She moved to a shelf on the wall. It held a small wooden carving of an eagle and one framed photograph.

Dominique picked up the photo. "Your father?"

"Yes."

How could one word hold so much emotion? She ran a finger over the faces in the picture. A very young Rand— no more than ten or eleven—wore a cocky smile and stood beside his father. He favored Brody Wilder, both of them big and broad, with rough-hewn handsome faces.

In the boy's eyes, Dominique saw adoration, love and

belonging. She turned her head, eyed Rand through her lashes. She saw none of the boy in the man. No doubt he'd died the night one of her kind had killed Brody.

"You look like him." She wished she could see Rand smile like that again.

"I have my mother's eyes." Rand moved closer.

Dominique looked up. His face was impassive but those ever-present shadows in his eyes flickered like smoke.

"What happened to her?"

"She died not long after I was born. My father grieved for her every day."

So Rand had only ever had his father, until even he was taken away. Dominique set the photo back on the shelf. "I'm sorry about your father."

Rand ran a hand up her arm, his fingers curling around her arm. "He died so I could escape. Zahn was too strong for him. The bastard made me watch as he tortured Dad. Burned him, cut him, ripped his skin off. Even after all of that, my father fought back long enough for me to get away."

She'd read the report on Brody Wilder's death. "I'm so sorry."

"The Paladins did nothing."

"Zahn was the son of one of the oldest court members. His father covered up the killing." Dominique raised a hand and placed it over Rand's. So much boiled behind his eyes. For a second, she saw the boy who'd lost his father. "By the time they found out, Zahn had been killed by another ajna whose wife he'd raped."

"I was closing in on him. I'd honed my skills and lived and breathed my need to end him." Rand's tone was soaked with his need for revenge. "When I heard he was dead, I decided to stop any other unbalanceds from taking another kid's father."

And so The Darkness was born.

The need to comfort was unfamiliar, but so strong Dominique didn't bother to fight it. She wrapped her arms around him.

He didn't move, didn't say anything. But it didn't matter. She held him—the lonely boy who'd watched his father killed, the hunter who dispensed death and the man who was still so alone.

His arms moved around her. Tightened.

"Is this the life your father wanted for you?" she murmured.

Rand pulled back. "This is the life he trained me for. He said we had a duty as vishuddha to protect the less powerful."

Dominique glanced at the photo. At the protective arm Brody Wilder kept around his son's thin shoulders.

"There's more than the darkness, Rand. There's more to life than dancing with death every hour of the night. One look at your father tells me he knew that."

Rand ran his fingers along her chin, his touch warm. "I have to work hard to remind myself you're a vampire."

Dominique felt the words like the slash of a knife. It would always be between them.

Pulling away from him, she swallowed the lump in her throat. "I'm going to bed. Good night."

The nightmare choked Rand, forcing his head under the murky water of his past.

He struggled, twisting in his bed. Like he was kicking his way to the surface. The sheets tangled around his body.

Horrible memories held him down like greedy hands. He was fifteen again and in the dirty basement where his father had died.

Chains dug into Rand's wrists, but still he fought, blood running down his arms. His father's screams echoed around him. Rand tried not to watch Zahn's evil handiwork, but as blood splattered the walls and his father's screams turned to tortured moans, Rand couldn't look away.

His father's back was raw, the skin gone. Now Zahn picked up a whip with a wicked cat-o'-nine-tails head.

Crack. His father jerked. *Crack. Crack.*

Rand yanked at his chains. Metal dug all the way to bone but held strong. He was helpless. Useless. He squeezed his eyes closed.

The screams changed. Higher pitched, feminine. His eyes flew open.

It was Dominique tied down and fighting against her bonds. Her naked back gleamed, her hair falling over her face like strands of midnight.

The whip fell, she screamed. A welt scored her flesh, welling with blood.

"No!" Rand roared.

The vampire holding the whip turned. Zahn was gone, replaced by a man who looked like he'd stepped out of a dinner party. Except for the blood covering his silk shirt. A cold ruthlessness edged his hawkish face.

Dark, twisted energy pounded at Rand. This vampire had definitely taken the slippery, dark road of the unbalanced.

"You can't save her now." Vilein's smile was merciless. "She's mine. Untouched, ready for me to mold."

Dominique lifted her head, her eyes glazed with tears. The innocence in the violet leaching away to dark realization.

Rand used all his strength and yanked at the chains. One broke out of the wall. "I'll kill you, Vilein."

Rand woke. Alone in his darkened bedroom.

He sat up, sweat cooling on his skin. He pushed the sheets away and dropped his head into his hands. He hadn't had a nightmare for months.

God. He scraped his hands over his stubble-roughened cheeks. Seeing the strong, courageous Dominique so helpless, so beaten…it tore him to pieces.

His heart continued to hammer a relentless beat in his chest. He needed to see her. To make sure she was all right.

He dragged on his jeans and didn't bother with a shirt. Pausing outside her room, he told himself to turn around. Instead he pushed open the door.

The bed was empty. The sheets a snarled disarray.

Where the hell was she? Rand moved through the house, his nerves tingling. Had she left? Had Vilein taken her?

Earlier, when they'd spoken of his father, Rand knew he'd hurt her. She was nothing like the monsters he executed. Nothing like Zahn. But Rand had used her heritage as a wedge to keep his distance.

She wasn't in the kitchen or the living room. Then he noticed the sliding door to the deck was ajar. Hands coiled into fists, he stepped outside.

And saw her.

She was every man's fantasy of light and dark, strength and femininity, innocence and seduction. His fantasy come to life.

Her skin was porcelain pale, her hair the darkest shade of night. Her body was long, lithe and made to wrap around a man. Yet the beautiful face in profile showed no knowledge of the picture she made. Or the longings she stirred.

But the lines around her mouth spoke of the horror of lingering nightmares.

He moved closer, drawn, unable to stop the need to touch her. To comfort.

She leaned against the railing, wearing one of his shirts. The length of long, smooth leg it displayed had Rand's blood pumping thickly in his veins.

When he was a foot away, she turned. "Rand, I'm so sorry."

He stilled. "Why?"

A warm desert breeze ruffled her hair. "My nightmare leaked into your sleep. I never meant to project it…" She brushed a strand of hair back behind her ear, her eyes miserable. "I forced you to relive your father's death."

Rand brushed a hand over her shoulder. "I've had the

nightmare before. What was worse was seeing what you went through with that bastard Vilein."

Fighting to keep his hand gentle, Rand cupped her smooth cheek. What he really wanted was the bastard chained up so he could show him what it felt like to be helpless.

She pressed her cheek to his palm. "I'm safe for now."

For now. The words echoed through him. Because he wouldn't help her—take her into his arms and make her his.

Rand pulled her closer, felt her cheek press against his bare chest. Fire ignited, hot and strong. His blood went from warm to boiling.

His hunger was fierce, but the need to protect burned white-hot as well.

She moved her head, her lips brushing over his nipple. Flames licked down his body, pooling in his groin. When her teeth grazed his skin, he groaned.

She stilled. "Rand?"

In just a few hours he'd gone from never fraternizing with the creatures he hunted to needing one of them more than he needed to breathe.

Somehow, in one night, Dominique had shattered a lifetime of preconceptions.

He slid his hands down her sides, shaping her curves. "I want to make love to you, Dominique."

Chapter Six

Rand watched Dominique pull away, her hands pressing to his chest.

She sank her teeth into her bottom lip. "You want to make love to me because of the nightmare? To save me from Vilein?"

Rand saw a hint of fang and for the first time in his existence, he was turned on by it. "No. This has nothing to do with him."

Her dawning smile was radiant. "Good."

He wanted Dominique for Dominique. Because she was everything he'd never known he wanted. Everything he'd thought he couldn't have in the darkness of his life.

He let his hands slide behind her, cupped her bottom and lifted her onto the railing.

"God, you are so beautiful." He brushed her hair back from her magnificent face.

Her hands slid up to his shoulders, ran over his skin. "Show me what it's like." She leaned forward and nipped his bottom lip. "And don't think just because I haven't done this before that I'm going to be all wide eyes and breathy sighs." She sank into a deep kiss, tongue sliding into his mouth to tangle with his. She pulled back, amethyst eyes glittering. "Because I'm going to give as good as I get."

Rand laughed. She was perfect.

She stilled, a smile curving her lips. She ran a finger over the corner of his mouth. "You should laugh more often."

When her hands ran down his chest, tracing over his stomach, he sucked in a breath. Laughter was the last thing on his mind. Desire, swift and urgent, roared through him.

Nudging her thighs apart, he stepped between them. They were face-to-face and he wondered if he'd ever get tired of looking at her.

He undid the first button of her shirt. Her bared collar-bone drew his attention and he ran a thumb along it. Another button and the top curve of her breasts came into view. Ravenous for her, he finished unbuttoning the shirt in quick, desperate moves.

The shirt slid off her shoulders, catching on her elbows. His hands moved up her ribs, under her breasts, and he cupped them, weighing them in his palms. She murmured and arched her back.

"Beautiful." He lowered his head to one taut peak. He tugged at her nipple, catching it between his teeth.

"Rand." Her hands pulled at his hair. "More."

He switched to the other breast, never once taking his lips off her skin. She tasted like she smelled—fresh and sexy. He laved his tongue over her and used his mouth and teeth until she was writhing.

When he felt fingers at the waistband of his jeans, flicking open the top button and working down his zipper, he tensed. Air hissed through his teeth.

"I want to touch you," she murmured. Long, slim fingers freed him and wrapped around his hard length.

He groaned against her shoulder. "Touch me. Whatever you want, take it."

Her hands slid down him, then back up. Torture.

"Big, like the rest of you." There was a smile in her words.

He growled and pressed his face against her neck. Her pulse beat against his lips and he licked her skin there. Her tormenting fingers skimmed the head of his erection.

"I want to taste you." She shifted to slide off the railing, but he stopped her.

"Sweetheart, you go anywhere near me with that mouth of yours and I'm not going to last." He slid his hands to either side of her head, held her gaze to his. "I want to be inside you. I want to slide inside your snug warmth and make you come."

Her eyes darkened and she licked her lips. "Show me." She lifted her knees to wedge against his hips, her ankles crossing behind his back.

The night breeze rushed over them. It did little to cool the fire in Rand. He burned for this woman. She drove away the darkness, the death, the blood. She made him yearn for more than he had.

He ran eager hands down her body, caressing and teasing. When his hand dipped between her thighs, past dark curls, he found her wet and wanting.

"*Oui*. Now." Her hands found his erection again and guided him to her.

"Dominique." He leaned down and kissed her.

She returned the hot kiss, pulled back. "I want to watch you join us."

Her words made his body harden more. He was at the breaking point.

He pushed her hands away, nudged her legs wider open and cupped his erection in one hand. Her gaze was glued to him, a flush riding her cheekbones.

When he stroked himself, he heard her excited sigh. When he moved forward and pressed the head of his erection to her soft folds, a small cry broke from her lips.

"Watch," he groaned. Then he pushed inside her.

Her back arched. Her hands scrambled at his shoulders, nails raking over his skin. "Yes, Rand."

She was tight, wet. A deep groan wrenched from him. He met her thin barrier and ruthlessly pushed past it. She cried out again, but pleasure underscored the sound.

With a final thrust he was seated in her, deep as he could go. Her gaze met his, her lips trembling.

Damn, if he'd hurt her… "Are you okay?"

"Yes. Show me." She pressed her lips to his.

Kissing her, feeling himself drown in her, he pulled

back, then thrust forward. He gripped her hips, pinned her as he buried himself inside her. Hard, fast, deep.

He needed to imprint his claim on her. Let her know this was more than saving her.

Let her know she was saving him as well.

Lightning whipped through Dominique. She felt the smooth wood beneath her bare backside and the hot male powering into her.

She was full, stretched, and it felt so good. Rand's hands dug into her hips, possessive. Heat lashed at her senses, sizzling her nerves. Her husky cries echoed into the night.

This was better than anything she'd imagined. Heat ran though her veins, so much better than the chill of rigid control.

His hands stroked lower, his thumb touching where he thrust into her body. Then he nudged at the small nub nestled there.

She let out a long cry. Her eyes closed.

"Look at me, Dominique."

Helpless to do anything but obey, she opened her eyes.

The green of his eyes had changed, deepened. The intimacy of watching each other was shocking.

Heat raced over her skin, leaving her anxious for something else. Something she didn't understand. She'd come to this man to lose her virginity, but she feared she was losing so much more to him in the process.

He kissed her again. This time she sensed something

else in it. Like an elusive taste of a long-forgotten delicacy. Tenderness. Care.

Heat rose up around her, wrapping them in a tight embrace. As her skin heated, she realized her energy was melding with his.

The skin stretched taut over his cheekbones, his thrusts turned frantic. She sensed his control at the edge. In response, her own body tightened, coiling tighter and tighter.

His clever fingers stroked her. She twisted, unsure if she wanted to flee that intense touch or if she wanted more.

"Touch me." His tone was guttural.

She knew what he wanted. Her hands slid along his shoulders to his throat.

When she pressed her thumbs to the corded muscles of his neck, his body spasmed, thrusting deeper inside her. "Rand!"

He left one hand between her legs, working her. Not once did he slow his urgent plunges into her. His other hand slid up her cheek. Then his finger brushed over her brow.

Molten heat exploded. Her energy rushed into him, and in turn, his flooded into her body.

Mon Dieu. Along with his energy, she felt his emotions. Scalding, they seared through her.

She felt the loneliness and hurt of his past. The driving urge for revenge. The thick guilt that he couldn't save his father.

But she also felt what layered over it. The bright, confusing emotions Rand felt for *her.* And there was no mistaking the desire.

Dominique couldn't hold on any longer. When the escalating feelings inside her ripped upward, tearing her apart, she threw her head back and screamed.

She heard Rand's wild groan, felt the warm spill of his release.

Her hands dug into his shoulders, holding him to her. She surrendered to him, helpless against the sensations rocketing through her, as hot and wild as the man in her arms.

She had no idea how long she stayed like that, the echo of pleasure still humming through her. Wondering if her bones had turned to liquid, she blinked her eyes open. She was still sitting on the railing, her face buried against Rand's throat.

One of his hands was smoothing up and down her back. His fingers running over the bumps of her spine. She smiled. She loved his touch.

She could easily love him.

That thought evaporated her smile. Beneath her lips she felt the surge of his pulse. The blood in his veins called to her. She hadn't fed for many hours and now her hunger was growing. His blood beckoned her like the darkest drug to an addict.

He had never let a vampire bite him. That told her all she needed to know of what he thought about feeding.

And he'd never want to keep a vampire around forever. Her chest constricted.

A big hand smoothed her hair back. "I'd heard tantric sex was mind-blowing. But it was better than I imagined."

Dominique forced a smile. She wouldn't let her thoughts interfere just yet. "It was amazing."

"You don't have anything to compare it to."

She punched his shoulder. "I know good when I feel it."

He smiled. The first genuine smile she'd seen from him. She felt a pinch of pleasure in her heart. One smile and one rusty laugh. Not that she was counting.

"It was better than good." His green eyes swirled with something she couldn't name. "Try soul-destroying."

Heat flushed her cheeks. A part of was thrilled it'd been good for him. A thumb flicked over her lips. Her breathing sped up.

"It was perfect." He dragged his thumb over her mouth again. He parted her lips, stroked down one of her fangs. "You touch something in me and I don't know if that's good or bad."

She gasped. Was he admitting he felt something for her? "Rand?"

His hand pressed to the nape of her neck and brought her mouth back to his. This kiss was deeper, longer, and seeped inside her. Her fingers gripped his muscled biceps, to hold herself upright. She felt something shift inside her and it left her dizzy.

When he lifted his head, they were both breathing heavily. Whatever had been in his eyes before was gone. Hidden.

"You should take a shower."

She raised an eyebrow. *No way.* She wasn't going to let him retreat. She slid off the railing, scooped up the shirt she'd borrowed and slipped it on. Sauntering naked to the door, she looked back over one shoulder. "Why don't you join me?"

His hot gaze slid down her body and back up again. "That sounds like a brilliant idea. But I need to grab something to eat first. You've worn me out."

Her stomach somersaulted. He was pulling back. Behind him, dawn was lighting the eastern horizon, outlining his silhouette.

Dieu, he was gorgeous. She wanted more from this man than the moment they'd shared.

She wanted things she'd never thought would be hers.

But she wouldn't push him. "Don't be long."

In the big bathroom, Dominique turned the shower to scorching hot. As steam billowed in the room, she stared at herself in the mirror.

She was no longer the pure ajna her parents had promised to Vilein. But more than that, her short time with Rand had changed her.

She didn't want to be a part of the coldblooded court. She wanted heat, laughter and love. While she loved her parents, they would always be cool and reserved. She wanted what Rand had given her a taste of tonight. She wanted to help a lonely man realize he could have more.

Pressing a palm to her eyes, she tried to fight back the feelings multiplying inside her. Surely she couldn't be stupid enough to fall in love with The Darkness?

What did she know of love? Not much, but she was certain you couldn't fall in love in one night. She dropped her hand to her chest and rubbed her heart. A hot shower should help.

A tremor went through her body. Frowning, she lifted her hand, saw it shaking.

Dark compulsion flooded through her limbs. Her foot scraped over the floor in a reluctant step. *Non!* She recognized the sinister command overtaking her—Vilein.

She tried to fight it. Threw all the power she possessed into it. But dragging steps took her into the hall, toward the back door. Away from Rand.

She wanted to scream but the compulsion left her silent.

Her screams echoed only in her head. Where no one could hear them.

Chapter Seven

Rand stared at the breaking dawn. He pressed his palms against the glass and fought down the swirling mass of emotion inside him.

She wasn't for him. He glanced at the spot where he'd just taken Dominique. *God.* He'd just made love to her— her first time—outside on a railing. His hands curled into fists. She deserved silk sheets, candlelight and pretty words.

He forced his hands to uncurl and studied his rough palms. She deserved better.

More than a burned-out vampire hunter.

Rand glanced over at the photo on the shelf. *Don't let this job take you over, son. The best way for a hunter to stay sane is the right woman. Love balances everything.*

He remembered the day his father had said those words.

Only days before his death. A forgotten memory Rand had buried.

Why had he let himself forget? His father had trained him to kill rogue vampires, but he'd also stressed the importance of balance.

Rand had been so busy avenging his father, he'd let some of the most important lessons fade to the back of his mind.

What would Brody Wilder have thought of Dominique Valois?

Rand smiled. He'd bet his dad would've thought she was gorgeous and too damned good for Rand.

He reached out with his senses. Even being in a different room was too far away from her. He sensed her unique energy.

When a shaft of pure fear speared through him it took him a moment to realize it wasn't his fear he was feeling, but hers.

He exploded into action, running down the hall, into the bathroom. Steam billowed.

Dominique wasn't there.

He followed her energy signature to the back door. It was open. *Damn*. He grabbed a titanium stake off the wall in his den and raced outside.

A trail of footsteps led into the desert. Dominique's small, bare feet had made one set of marks. Beside them were a larger set with the slick tread of expensive men's shoes.

Rage fired through Rand, but he fought to stay controlled. Dominique needed him.

He stalked over a rise and saw them.

Vilein had a handful of Dominique's dark hair and was savagely yanking her along with him. The little idiot was fighting back, twisting and trying to kick at her captor.

The vampire must've sensed Rand. He spun and thrust Dominique to the ground. She fell on her knees, her face stark white.

"She stinks of you, hunter." Vilein's voice was ice cold.

"Let her go."

"She's mine." The ajna ran a hand down her cheek. She thrust her head away from him, but he caught her chin. "I was to be the first to have her."

"You don't deserve her."

"And you do, Darkness?" Vilein shook his head. "She is royalty and yet you sullied her with your hunter hands. Hands that have killed so many of her kind."

Rand swallowed. His gaze caught her pleading violet eyes.

"Get out of here, Rand."

God, she was worried for him? He didn't deserve her, but she certainly deserved more than this torturing bastard.

He focused on Vilein. "I said let her go."

The vampire shrugged. "She's tainted goods now. But she'll be entertainment for my friends. And her back will still welcome my whip."

Molten heat exploded through Rand. He wouldn't let this perverted creature lay a hand on her again. He lunged forward, leading with his stake.

Vilein's blow sent Rand flying through the air ten feet.

He hit the sand with enough force to drive the air from his lungs.

Spitting the blood from his mouth, he rose. He couldn't beat this vampire with strength alone.

He looked again at the woman—the vampire—on her knees. In that one clear moment, he knew he'd give his life to protect her. Using all his speed, he attacked Vilein. The powerful kick knocked the vampire back a step. As long as Rand didn't let Vilein land a direct blow, he had a chance.

He ducked a fist, jammed his own into Vilein's side. The vampire grunted. Twirling, Rand attacked with kicks and strikes, avoiding the ajna's own swings.

The vampire was powerful, but he hadn't spent years honing his combat skills like Rand had. The trick with vampires was to use their own energy against them. Brute force wasn't what would win the fight.

Suddenly Dominique moved forward, preparing to attack.

"No, Dominique," Rand called out.

Vilein moved so fast he blurred. He backhanded her across the face and she went down hard in the sand.

Rand gritted his teeth, his muscles bunching. Without thought, he launched himself, desperate to make the ajna pay for every wound he'd inflicted on her.

Vilein took advantage of Rand's wild charge and thrust a fist against his chest. He felt ribs crack. The force of the blow sent him to his knees, fire tearing through him.

He fought to block the pain. Dominique's life depended

on him. He got one foot under himself and pressed a palm to the sand. He forced himself upright.

"You want more, vishuddha?" Vilein shook his head and held up a palm.

Rand's body froze. The vampire's mental command held him in place. Stronger than any chains.

Blood pounded through him. He watched Vilein stalk over to Dominique. *God, no.* He fought against the mental hold, frantic to break free.

Vilein yanked her against him, one hand tangled in her hair. "I might sample her right here." His other hand slid down to cup her breast. She struggled, but he controlled her. "And there isn't a single thing you can do to stop me, hunter."

This was worse than watching his father die. Helplessness twined around Rand like ropes. His stomach revolted. He poured all his energy into breaking Vilein's thrall.

But it wasn't enough.

Vilein slashed a hand down and tore Dominique's shirt open, baring her breasts. She turned her head, tried to bite him, but he shook her like a doll.

His dark gaze collided with Rand's. "You can't save her."

Just like he hadn't been able to save his father. Rand broke enough of Vilein's control to rub his fingers together. He wouldn't fail again. He wouldn't watch another person he cared about die because he was helpless.

He looked at Dominique. Her lips were bloody but as they stared at each other, the energy between them tightened. Pulling tight like a connection that would never let go.

Knowing moving through him. "Dominique, I don't know how, but I'm falling in love with you."

Her violet eyes widened. Vilein's laughter filled the air, but Rand stayed focused on her.

A smile edged her lips and he watched the fear in her eyes give way to fire. The need to survive.

At Vilein's feet, Rand saw the early morning light glint off something metallic. His stake.

He looked back at Dominique. She nodded.

A wild rush of energy poured into him. Through the growing link between them, she fed him her energy.

It roared through him like the charge of a powerful animal. It shattered Vilein's thrall and left Rand bursting with power.

He rolled, coming to a stop at Vilein's feet. Rand grabbed the stake and lunged upward.

The vampire was quick. He let go of Dominique and sprang away. Rand tackled him to the ground.

They struggled against one another. With Dominique's energy combined with his, Rand was an equal match for the ajna. He rolled on top, lifted the stake.

Vilein's hands gripped Rand's forearms. They strained together, Rand trying to force the stake down.

Then slim hands covered his. He lifted his gaze and saw Dominique beside him.

"Together," she said.

Both of them lunged down with the stake, their combined strength behind the strike.

The stake speared between Vilein's eyes. He died without making a sound. His dark eyes, drained of all energy, stayed open.

"It's over." Dominique swayed, staring at her tormentor.

"You're safe now." Rand's mouth dried up. She was free. To do whatever she wanted. To leave.

"Safe." She said the word like it was foreign to her. Then her legs went out from under her. Rand reached out to catch her.

Thank God she was okay. He scooped her into his arms and headed back to the house.

"The body—"

He lengthened his stride. "I don't give a crap about the body."

His arms trembled. All he felt was the desperate need to be with this woman. To show her he belonged to her as much as she belonged to him.

Her fingers toyed with his hair. "Rand, are you all right?"

"Just be quiet." He moved inside and headed straight for his bedroom.

The morning light was reaching out over his bed. He laid Dominique down in his sheets and pushed her back. Her black hair spilled across his pillows. Her alabaster skin was pale against the blue linen.

Finally. Where he wanted her.

She watched him as he stripped the torn shirt off her.

Bruises stained her skin. "Jesus, sweetheart." He ran a gentle finger over one on her shoulder.

"I'm fine."

"He hurt you." Rand pressed a kiss to one bruise, then another.

"You, too." Her fingers brushed an ugly knot on his ribs.

He didn't care. Already felt his body healing. "I'll run you a bath, or a shower." He needed to make it better, to wipe away the ugly memories. "I'll make tea. You can drink fluids, right?"

"Rand, stop." She cupped his cheeks. "What I need is you."

He stilled.

"Are you really falling in love with me?" Her voice was quiet, her gaze never leaving him.

"Yes." He slid his hands across her belly and watched her shiver. "You're everything I thought I'd never have." He cupped her face with shaking hands and leaned down to press small kisses across her cheeks.

Pulling back, he looked at her exquisite features and saw everything he needed right there. His balance. His light. His love.

With his heart pounding, he summoned his courage. "Think you might want to hang around for me to fall the rest of the way?"

Something sparked in her eyes.

Afraid of her answer, Rand continued. "I can't give you a château, or things you're probably used to—"

"I've developed a fondness for the desert and I don't

need a château." She pulled him to her and when he covered her body with his, she wrapped her legs around him. "I bet they even need lawyers here in Las Vegas. And since I'm falling in love with you, too, it sounds like a wonderful idea."

Feeling burst through him. Desperate for her, he rose and shucked his jeans. He tugged her to the edge of the bed.

She wrapped around him, fit against him like she'd been designed for him. He eased inside her, joining them.

The tight clasp of her body had the blood in his veins boiling. He tried to be gentle, but her nails scratching along his back and her undulating hips urged him to move faster, harder.

Mindless to anything but her and the heat between them, he plunged into her. He gripped her thighs, tilted her hips so he could go deeper.

She moaned, hands gripping the covers. Rand felt his energy moving out to seek hers. He felt the shimmer of her power against his skin. But it was weak.

He kept moving into her with slow, easy thrusts and studied her. Her face was paler than usual. Maybe the aftereffects of the fight with Vilein?

But as Rand opened his senses more, he heard the erratic beat of her heart. She needed to feed.

He pulled back, sat on the bed and pulled her to him. She let out a protest, but as he settled her on top of him, both of them facing each other, she smiled at the new position.

When she sank down, taking him inside her, deeper than she had before, they both groaned.

"You feel so good, Rand."

"So do you, sweetheart." He cupped the back of her head and pressed her lips to his throat, his stomach tensing. "Now, feed."

"What?" She froze, then her lips moved against his throat. She trembled, her tongue fluttering over his pulse. She pulled back. "Are you sure?"

He brushed the hair off her face. "Yes."

She leaned down and Rand kept his fingers against her chakra. Her fangs scraped his jugular and his body jerked. With a moan, she bit down, fangs sinking deep.

His hips lunged up, thrusting into her. They were joined by body, blood and energy.

She sucked at him and an inferno of sensation and energy ripped through him. It burst from his chakra, through his body, down his limbs.

He thrust into her again and she met him with a hard downward plunge of her body. They both erupted at the same moment. She screamed and he followed her over, emptying himself inside her.

Afterward, Rand laid back, pulled her tight against him and yanked a sheet over them. It didn't matter that the sunlight was invading the room, or that the world would be waking up to start the day. All that mattered was their little world, right here.

The world they'd make together.

Dominique snuggled against him with a sigh. Her breath blew against his neck. "I'm hoping you have plenty more to show me, Wilder."

He smiled. He was no longer alone. "I'll do my best to make you happy, sweetheart."

In the dark of the night, a vampire had snuck through the defenses of the biggest, baddest vampire hunter in the business. Without a single regret, he'd taken a vampire to his bed, let her feed from him and taken her into his heart.

A vampire—his Dominique—had brought light to The Darkness.

* * * * *

A sneaky peek at next month...

NOCTURNE™

BEYOND DARKNESS...BEYOND DESIRE

My wish list for next month's titles...

In stores from 18th October 2013:

❏ The Keepers: Christmas in Salem —
Heather Graham, Deborah LeBlanc,
Kathleen Pickering & Beth Ciotta

❏ Siren's Secret — Debbie Herbert

In stores from 1st November 2013:

❏ Twilight Hunter — Kait Ballenger

Available at WHSmith, Tesco, Asda, Eason, Amazon and Apple

Just can't wait?

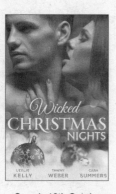

Join the Mills & Boon Book Club

Want to read more **Nocturne**™ books?
We're offering you **1** more absolutely **FREE!**

We'll also treat you to these fabulous extras:

- 🌹 **Exclusive offers and much more!**
- 🌹 **FREE home delivery**
- 🌹 **FREE books and gifts with our special rewards scheme**

Get your free books now!

**visit www.millsandboon.co.uk/bookclub
or call Customer Relations on 020 8288 2888**

FREE BOOK OFFER TERMS & CONDITIONS
Accepting your free books places you under no obligation to buy anything and you may cancel at any time. If we do not hear from you we will send you 2 stories a month which you may purchase or return to us—the choice is yours. Offer valid in the UK only and is not available to current Mills & Boon subscribers to this series. We reserve the right to refuse an application and applicants must be aged 18 years or over. Only one application per household. Terms and prices are subject to change without notice. As a result of this application you may receive further offers from other carefully selected companies. If you do not wish to share in this opportunity please write to the Data Manager at PO BOX 676, Richmond, TW9 1WU.

SUBS/ONLINE/T1

The World of Mills & Boon®

There's a Mills & Boon® series that's perfect for you. We publish ten series and, with new titles every month, you never have to wait long for your favourite to come along.

Blaze.
Scorching hot, sexy reads
4 new stories every month

By Request
Relive the romance with the best of the best
9 new stories every month

Cherish™
Romance to melt the heart every time
12 new stories every month

Desire™
Passionate and dramatic love stories
8 new stories every month